ACROSS THE RED SKY

SILICON VALLEY MURDER BOOK 2

VICTORIA KAZARIAN

FOG HOLLOW BOOKS

Second edition, published June 2024

Fog Hollow Books

To my mother, Sue Powell Vierk,
storyteller and video game player.
You are missed.

edrych i finw

When the dark plumaged birds go flying, flying
Quiet lies the earth
Wrapt in her mournful shadow
Her sightless eyes turned to the red sky
And the restlessly seeking birds.

Katherine Mansfield

ONE

Saturday

ON THE COOL, damp path that morning, Detective Daniela Grasso felt as she always did near the end of a run. Fierce.

Her feet pounded the trail in a rhythm, gravity gently nudging her back as she headed downhill. It was a nice reward for forcing herself up the switchbacks thirty minutes ago.

She ran at Rancho San Antonio Open Space Preserve five days out of the week, before showering and going into the station. She knew the trail well, anticipating every protruding tree root in her way, every blind curve. She leaped over a puddle that remained from last week's rain. It reflected a fiery glint from today's red and orange sunrise.

Today's sky looked unreal. Over-the-top, like a background in one of her post-apocalyptic video games.

As she eased into the end of her run, her thoughts returned to the case she'd wrapped up yesterday, an elder abuse investigation. An adult son had pushed his eighty-two-year old father, who'd fallen out of a patio chair onto concrete and sustained a broken leg and wrist. It was the first case she'd led on her own as a new detective for the Monte Verde Police Department. She taken the job last year, against the objections of her family.

She heard footsteps on the trail above, and her heart pounded. It spurred a competitiveness she'd learned growing up with two older brothers. *C'mon, Dani. Get your ass moving. What the fuck's your problem?* She instinctively sped up.

In a blur of blue spandex and a swinging blonde ponytail, a woman passed her. No warning. No calling out *on your left.* The woman was tall and, unlike her, had the build of a runner--long legs and a streamlined torso. Her long stride propelled her past Grasso, then she effortlessly maneuvered around a clump of senior hikers who had their poles out, making their way cautiously down the hill.

A few minutes later, Grasso reached the parking lot, already full. Cars lined up at the entrance, watching hikers returning to the lot, waiting for their car lights to go on.

By now, the sun had edged higher in the sky, and it was warming up. Feeling the uncomfortable dampness of her sweat, Grasso slipped her arms out of her hoodie and tied it around her waist. She paced around the trailhead to cool off, then headed toward the stretching bars.

She lifted her leg to the bar and pressed back on her left leg. The stretch felt so good, she could practically hear her muscles cry out their thanks.

She felt proud of her work on the elder abuse case. It took a lot of persuasion from both her and the social worker to get the old man to realize what had happened was a crime and that, yes, she was arresting his son—his own flesh and blood. *Your son assaulted you, Mr. Niemeyer.* But with persistence— she'd handled it. For her six months of field training, Detective James Ruiz had closely supervised her work. He hadn't looked over her shoulder on this one.

As much as she liked her mentor, she was happy to have

some distance from Ruiz. Back in January, he'd witnessed the brutal shooting of elderly Karl Schuler on an expressway in San Jose. Though San Jose Homicide handled the case, the murder and investigation seemed to have taken a toll on Ruiz.

He kept to himself now, usually eating at his desk. She'd asked him yesterday if he wanted to walk down to Garcia's for lunch–his favorite burrito spot in downtown Monte Verde. I mean, who would turn down Garcia's? He shook his head and hunkered down over his yogurt, crackers and carrot sticks.

She and Ruiz had developed a working friendship over the past year, but she didn't think he'd share his thoughts with her. That was fine. It was his business. But she hoped things improved. Facing the Ruiz scowl in the morning at the station was like facing a pissed-off bear. He was a big guy. He took up space, physically and emotionally.

As she stretched, she saw the woman runner from the trail, looking down at her phone as she paced in front of the restroom. She'd seen her here before. But she also recognized her from somewhere else.

The woman slid her phone into a pocket in her running pants then headed her way, toward the stretching bars.

Had she come into the station? Grasso studied her as she took her place at the bar next to her and began stretching. No, she would have remembered her. The woman had an air of authority. The calm expectation that everyone around her would do exactly what she wanted them to do.

"That sunrise this morning." Grasso smiled over at the woman.

"Out of this world, wasn't it? You get out here early, you see what no one else sees."

The woman turned in her direction as she stretched her leg out across the bar, and Grasso noticed dark circles under her eyes. She looked in her 40s. What her grandfather would call a handsome woman. Her features were angular, almost sharp. With hollowed-out cheeks, either from genetics or from too much exercise and not enough food.

Grasso stood in front of the bar and did squats till her thigh muscles complained and she had to back off. On the plus side, she felt the endorphins taking effect. She felt a surge of energy and optimism even though she'd have to go through the transcript of Shawn Niemeyer's bullshit testimony this morning. The lift was better than anything she'd get from her cup of coffee at the station.

"Don't know what I'd do if I couldn't get a run in before work." Grasso pressed against the bar, pushing her left leg out behind her and feeling the pull in her calf muscles. "It prepares me. Maybe more mentally than physically."

"Right?" The woman nodded across the bar, a fellow believer in the church of the morning run. There was a drivenness about the woman, as if she were powered by some inner electricity. Her words shot out like well-aimed arrows.

Grasso wanted her confidence. She was determined to do well at her job. Because of her name and family—and the fact that she was the youngest detective on the force, she knew a few people who'd like to see her fail.

The woman's lips twitched. "I have a meeting this weekend with my execs. By then, the endorphins will be flowing. I'll be warrior woman. Don't fuck with me, boys."

Grasso laughed at the woman's girl boss tone and continued stretching her right leg, which seemed comically short compared to this woman's.

"I know what you mean." Grasso smiled at her. "You got this."

The woman's phone pinged with a text. She pulled it out of her pocket and scrolled through a message.

She shook her head slowly. Without taking her eyes off the phone, she opened a sleek lightweight water bottle and took a gulp.

"So it begins." She sighed. For a moment, Grasso saw a trace of sadness in her face that didn't seem to fit. "Now you have a good one."

Grasso watched the woman put away her phone, then walk with purpose toward her Tesla in the parking lot.

Cars rounded the corner, watching her like vultures, waiting to take her spot.

***

"Can we go already?"

Monte Verde Detective James Ruiz strapped his helmet on and settled himself onto the seat of the old 10-speed and looked behind him. Jacky was on his bike, impatient to get this ride started.

It was May. The weather had been overcast lately, but the sky today was a clear, bright blue. Kids were outside in the warm weather on their skateboards and bikes, looking forward to being released from their classrooms next month.

Ruiz hadn't ridden a bike in twenty years, but when Jacky asked if they could ride in the park, he'd said yes, as long as he could find a bike. Jacky had spotted the old 1970s 10-speed at a garage sale two weeks ago. As a kid growing up on San Jose's east side, Ruiz had learned to repair bikes. It was the only way he'd have something to ride.

He'd worked with Jacky this week to clean out the 10-speed's rusty gear assembly, re-string the brakes, and put on new tires.

He'd been looking forward to this. After three hard months, Ruiz wanted to get outside, too. Outrun his feelings. Feel the fresh air on his face.

Back in January, he found out about the affair his wife

Reyna had with Mario Flores, the San Jose homicide detective assigned to the Schuler case. After Reyna's admission that she didn't love him—that she'd never loved him—he lived in a holding pattern.

He lived life in short sprints. Today he woke up, and he still had a home with his wife and kid. Today was a good day. He wasn't living in a divorced dad's apartment like a few cops he knew—including Frank Ladera of MVPD. Divorce was a fact of life among cops; the job was demanding. Regular exposure to the worst in people changed you.

He loved his job, he always had. Right now, it kept his mind off the end game: what would happen when Reyna left. When they had to sit down and dismantle their life together. Work out custody arrangements.

"Let's go," Ruiz called back to his son. "Stay in the bike lane until we get to the park."

Ruiz took off, wobbling first on tires that seemed too thin to support his weight, then stabilizing as his body remembered it knew how to do this. He weighed fifty more pounds than when he'd ridden last. He sped up. The muscles in his thighs and calves felt the unexpected exertion and seemed to welcome it. He glanced back and saw Jacky following him, pedaling effortlessly.

They turned into the parking lot for Santa Clara's Central Park, then found the bike path through the park. They circled the pond, where a group of scruffy ducks floated, and a young family with a double stroller stopped to watch them.

He looked behind him to see Jacky, his cheeks glowing, grinning as they rode.

"We're by my school. Can we go see it?"

"Follow me. Stay close." Ruiz guessed the path that would take them to the school, which was near the north entrance to the park. They headed north, then turned onto the loop the school was on. It looked desolate on Sunday, but that was good for this first bike ride. Excited to be on his school playground, not even on a school day, Jacky circled the blacktop on his bike, then tried to pull a wheelie. He didn't get off the ground.

"Nice try," Ruiz called to his son. He watched the boy beam with excitement, happy to be moving. Back in January, a bullet had nearly taken Jacky's life, a few streets away on Benton, as they drove home from school. Yet another reason it had been a shitty year.

Jacky returned from a circuit around the blacktop and pulled his bike up in front of Ruiz. As he took off his helmet, he looked longingly over at the basketball court. "I wish we had a ball."

The kid puttered around the blacktop and finally spotted a dirty, deflated soccer ball at the edge of the grassy field. He threw his bike down and went off to get it. He ran back triumphantly.

"I found one. Let's shoot baskets."

Ruiz laughed at him. He admired the boy's enthusiasm. He leaned his bike against a bench and waited as Jacky scrambled to throw the ball.

When Ruiz caught it, the sagging bag of vinyl felt pretty pathetic. It wasn't going to bounce, but that didn't seem to bother Jacky. Funny what kids could do with nothing. He remembered what that was like growing up—playing with castoff toys and sports equipment. There would be no dribbling in this game. Ruiz ran to the court and tossed it in the basket. It dropped like a rock to the blacktop.

"To me! To me!" Jacky called, jumping up and down. Ruiz picked up the ball and threw it to him. The boy dropped the ball and flapped his hand in pain.

"That hurt!"

"What did you expect?" Ruiz snorted and ran to the ball, picked it up, and ran to make another basket – which at his height, on an elementary school playground, was easy.

Jacky, recovered, ran over to him, and started blocking

him. He flailed his scrawny arms in front of him like a cartoon character, while Ruiz calmly switched the deflated ball from hand to hand over the boy's head.

"That's not fair!" Jacky screamed, then dissolved into a fit of giggles when Ruiz put the deflated ball on his head as a hat.

Finally, Ruiz bobbled the ball on purpose. Jacky caught it on the way down, then ran toward the basket and tossed it in.

"Two points, people!" The boy did an exaggerated victory dance under the basket, bobbing his head and holding up his hands. "Two points!"

"Okay, Steph Curry." Ruiz swept past him and picked the ball off the asphalt with one hand, then ran around to toss it in the basket. It hit the rim and tumbled to the ground.

Jacky caught it on the way down and clutched it, running around with it in crazy circles trying to avoid him. Ruiz chased him at first, then stepped back, sweaty and exhausted. His side hurt, and he stopped to catch his breath.

Jacky flung the ball up and it stuck – wedged against the backboard at the top of the basket. He stood underneath the basket, staring at the ball, his mouth open in awe.

"What the f—"

"Game over." Ruiz called out before Jacky could finish saying a word he'd regret. The boy groaned and walked reluctantly back to his bike.

The boy strapped on his helmet and stood his bike up. The look on his face was serious.

"That was fun. Can we do it again sometime?"

Ruiz laughed as he straddled his bike. Hard to predict what the boy would like. He'd coached Jacky's soccer teams for two years and Jacky showed little interest in the sport, except that it let him hang out with his friends. But he couldn't get enough of playing basketball for a half hour with a deflated soccer ball.

"Sure, *mijo*. We will."

As they rode back, Ruiz felt the wind on his face and a new freedom pumping through his body. It felt good to be outside, away from the tension hanging in the air at home. Maybe there was no tension on Reyna's part, but he'd felt it. She looked at him tiredly, as if it wore her down just to be around him. As if she couldn't wait to make a break for it. In January, he'd found out about Reyna's affair with Detective Mario Flores of San Jose Homicide. As far as he knew, from a little personal detective work he'd done on his own, Flores had kept his word and hadn't contacted Reyna.

It had been four months since he'd confronted Reyna about the affair. He wondered why she was still here.

Then it came to him--the question he should be asking himself.

Why was *he* still there?

TWO

Sunday

GRASSO WOKE with a sour taste in her mouth.

She rolled over and looked at the clock. 8:35.

Yesterday had been the end of her week, and she'd stayed up till 3 a.m. playing on the PlayStation, driven to get to the next level on last month's purchase, the fantasy role playing game *Gates of the Scarlet Dawn*.

She threw her head back against the pillow and looked up at the skylight in the vaulted ceiling of her Cupertino condo. She felt the delicious relief of knowing she had nowhere to go today.

After midnight, she finally got to the final boss of the game. She got the shit kicked out of her the first time, but the second time she had help from another online player. They worked together to defeat the Gorgon King, closing in on him from two sides in the canyon, and she felt exhilaration rush through her as she wounded it with fire arrows and saw her unseen helper finish the monster off. *Victory!*

There was nothing like the thrill of completing the game's

final quest. She'd been looking forward to this for the past week.

Her mind racing, she went to bed and lay there for an hour before she fell asleep, reliving the steps in the quest line, imagining how she could have improved her approach.

Grasso would never tell him, but while she and Ruiz were making the rounds for a case in Monte Verde last week, she'd been secretly planning her strategy for defeating the gorgon.

She'd have a hard time explaining to other people--especially Ruiz--how a game on a screen made her feel. Ruiz wasn't even a boomer. He wasn't forty yet, but he thought video games, even social media, were time-sucking distractions. Jacky, his nine-year-old son, played games. He was a good at it, too. Grasso had gotten some strategy tips on a game from him on her last visit to the Ruiz house.

Why wasn't real life as satisfying as a game?

She wished being a detective in the quiet South Bay Area suburb of Monte Verde came with some of the feel of a video game. That when she finished off a case, she'd receive experience points.

When she entered the house to fill out a report, she'd be able to smash some planter boxes or one of Monte Verde's stately streetside mailboxes and find gold coins. Or pick up health elixir or arrows hidden in the Japanese stone temple ornaments in some of the residents' carefully landscaped Zen gardens.

She loved her job, but it was usually tedious, detailed work. The gratification definitely wasn't instant.

Her parents wouldn't understand, so she never talked about this part of her life. Even to her older brothers, who still played games themselves. She'd grown up playing their console games and, every once in a while, played with Alex and Anthony online.

It had been hard enough to tell her parents she wanted to go to the academy. Her parents had plotted a timeline for her life. They were not happy with her choice of job. They would *really* not be happy if they knew she was spending her off time with a game console instead of a potential mate. And of course, that potential mate had to be a husband, not a wife.

As the sun poured down from the skylight more insistently, Grasso rubbed her eyes and rolled out of bed. She stumbled into the kitchen to make coffee.

Through the floor-length windows in the living room, she saw the hills that formed the western side of the valley, green and shrouded in thick fog—spilling down over the town she worked in. The circular Monte Verde PD seal on the patrol cars showed a small, wooded slope topped with an ice cream swirl of white fog - with the perky slogan, *Service and Safety.*

The condo was sparkling clean today, counters and appliances wiped down till they shone, the faint scent of lemon in the air. The floors were swept and mopped. The cleaners, paid for by her mother, came every week – cleaning the bedrooms, removing old takeout containers from the fridge, whisking away all the debris left from dinners and snacks eaten in front of her game system at night. At times she felt like an adolescent. Her mother was still cleaning up after her, even though she was 24 years old.

She couldn't tell Jimmy Ruiz she had a house cleaner. For one thing, his mother had worked as one. She'd be lumped in with the rich, pampered women his mother had scrubbed and cleaned for.

Grasso had put up with a lot of teasing about her family and the chain of stores her Italian-immigrant grandfather had founded almost fifty years ago. Grasso's Fine Foods had become an institution in the valley, the place to buy fresh produce, high-quality meats, and European breads made onsite in the store bakeries.

The name was recognized everywhere, and she couldn't get away from it. But that wasn't the problem.

The day she'd taken her place in the academy, she had done the unthinkable.

And most of her family wasn't speaking to her now.

When she finished her criminal justice degree at San Jose State, her parents and brothers assumed that she'd taken a small detour to follow her personal interests.

She'd heard them at family get-togethers, speaking just loud enough for her to hear:

Dani's been obsessed with strange things since she was a kid. She's always been different from the rest of us.

She's gotten to study this police stuff for four years. Let's hope it's out of her system.

Then when she firmly announced her decision to go to the academy:

Who knows? Maybe she can do something with store security.

Within a week of graduation from San Jose State last May, she was invited by her grandfather, 84-year-old Giovanni Grasso, to tour his flagship store in San Jose, eat an Italian dinner in his office suite, and have The Talk.

Afterward, her life would follow the path her brothers had taken: She'd be assigned to work in one of the five South Bay stores, to begin her training.

But it was at that point that Dani Grasso, who had worked hard all her life to please her family and stay off the radar, stood up and said no.

She sat down with her *unnon* and told him she didn't want to work at his stores. She was not interested in taking a management job with the chain, as her father, her aunt, and Alex and Anthony had done.

She'd accepted a place at the academy, and as far as she was concerned, family tradition could go to hell.

She didn't tell Giovanni Grasso that, of course.

She sat in a quilted red velvet chair in her grandfather's

office and listened to the softly accented voice of her short, stocky grandfather, his hair carefully dyed, probably darker than its original color.

Giovanni Grasso talked about how he'd saved his money from selling produce on the streets of Naples, so he could come to America. To fulfill his dreams of starting a business in his adopted country.

She took a deep breath as all the *spaghetti alle vongole* formed a heavy lump in the pit of her stomach.

It was time.

She'd rehearsed it. Written it out and practiced it every day on her run, so that when it came time, she wouldn't get flustered and chicken out.

"*Unnon,*" she started in, her throat constricting, "I appreciate what you have done with the stores and what a great accomplishment that was, coming to this country and building your business from the ground up. I'm thankful that the stores have benefited our family so much."

Her grandfather was listening, nodding. She sucked in her breath. *I'm really doing this.*

"But I've been training for a different career. Something I've wanted since I was thirteen. I want to be a detective. A police detective."

The old man's smile faded, and his jet-black moustache turned down at the corners.

On his face, a look of confusion: Had he heard her correctly? Then a look of sadness, his face slowly turned red. He tapped his fingers on the table. He looked at his watch, as if he suddenly had somewhere else to be. His face radiated anger.

She had spit in the face of the family patriarch.

"Daniela, you are telling me you will not work in the store."

"I am." She swallowed hard. She felt nauseous, bile climbing in her throat.

"You will change your mind." He leveled his dark eyes at her, his jaw set like stone.

She met his eyes, and realized to her surprise, she was not as fazed by his anger as she'd expected. "This is what I want to do. I've studied it in school. And in a few more months, it will be my job."

"You are my only granddaughter. I had hopes for you, Daniela." His face contorted, as if he was trying not to cry. "You have hurt me terribly with this."

On her side, she had no excuse. She had known since she was in kindergarten what she'd be expected to do with her life. It was an unwritten family rule that everyone just knew. She'd even worked two summers in the Saratoga store when she was in high school, bagging groceries, then working as a checker.

The family had all fallen in line. Alex and Anthony had accepted their positions at the store once they graduated from college–both of them, it seemed, happy to do what they'd always known they would do.

She remembered a party thrown by her grandfather the weekend before Anthony started work.

Her very drunk brother had hugged her, telling her he couldn't wait to see her here in five years. Maybe it was her imagination, but there was sadness in his eyes. The look of someone trapped.

In the back of her mind, she'd known even then. This decision would change things. Her relationship with her family would not be the same.

Three weeks later, after a hard day of physical training at the academy, she sat eating takeout food at her kitchen counter when she received a call.

The display read G GRASSO - PRIVATE. She felt like throwing up her dinner. She remembered his face, red with anger, when she'd told him she wasn't going to work for him.

He was calling to yell at her. Make it official that she was no longer part of the family.

Her body pumped out a round of sweat. It was coming and she waited for it to hit her.

"Tell me how you are, Daniela. How is the academy?"

He talked in a friendly way, asking her questions and keeping conversation light. He would switch over to anger soon. She could expect it.

She quickly tried to swallow her last bite of food, so she wouldn't answer him with her mouth full. She began choking and took a drink of water. She set her fork down, and her hands began shaking.

"It's g-good, *Unnon*. A lot of hard work."

"I want you to know that I am sad that you won't be working for the store. Very sad. I did not expect this."

No words came to her. She had no defense. Her face felt hot.

"Daniela, I have thought about your decision all month." His voice seemed to soften. "You are different. I have always known that. Life will be harder for you. You will be following the path I've walked my entire life."

She was finding it hard to follow his words. So, he *wasn't* angry? This was the last thing she'd expected after their disastrous meeting over lunch. Her father had stopped speaking to her as soon as she'd told him about her conversation with her grandfather. Her mother had called her all that week, crying, to get her to reconsider.

Her thoughts went to Mr. Niemeyer in Monte Verde. The way her family was acting, telling Giovanni Grasso she wouldn't work for him was the equivalent of her assaulting him and throwing him out of his chair.

What did he mean, she was "different?" Maybe she was. She didn't seem to fit with her family, as far as her interests or appearance. Like her grandfather, she was short and dark, not light-skinned and blonde like her mother and brothers.

"My words are for you only." There was a sharpness in his accented voice. A warning. His authority crackled over the phone. "You must promise me you will not let anyone know we spoke about this."

Can this be happening?

Relief surged through her. She thought she might wet her pants. The words came out of her in a cracked whisper. "Don't worry, *Unonn.* I promise."

After the phone call, she wasn't sure what was said, only what she'd agreed to. She remembered the fear she'd felt during The Talk. Of this man she loved but had been carefully taught to fear. This couldn't be real.

Giovanni Grasso, who ruled the family with an iron fist, had given her a pass. It made her head spin. It did not make any sense.

Even then, she was aware enough to wonder: What would this cost her?

THREE

Sunday afternoon

ROSALIND MABREY CROSSED her arms and waited for her VP, Kevin Dredger, to finish his presentation at the impromptu Sunday afternoon meeting of execs at Infinitas.

It would not sway her–her decision was made. But she kept listening, tried to keep the smile carefully formed on her lips from fading, as Kevin clicked through slide after slide.

"This is what we can expect in terms of profit, from year one of the acquisition to year five." He looked around the room expectantly, as the men watched him, their eyes widening, many of them nodding. "As you can see, the acquisition will add to our capabilities significantly. We expect the merging of operations to be complete by the end of next year."

"There are redundancies with this acquisition, Kevin. Why don't you tell us about the level of downsizing this would involve?" Rosalind knew the layoffs would be significant, with some operations shifting to the acquired company's headquarters in Texas, which she was not comfortable with.

She'd started Infinitas twenty years ago, here in Palo Alto, not long after her graduation from Stanford. She'd learned her job as CEO as the company had grown.

This would be letting go of control, on a whole new level.

"We'll be eliminating 600 positions on the West coast. But we expect a reduction in labor costs, due to lower wages and cost of living in Texas. We'll also shift some of our software engineering to Shanghai, which will cut costs by 30 percent."

Again, heads nodded around the room. Rosalind felt the balance in the room shift. She looked at Tom Weber and Blake Hennessey, both of them VPs. Tom was a founding member of Infinitas, and Blake had been VP of Marketing for almost ten years. Both were looking away from her awkwardly.

"This will have a significant impact on the company, Kevin. If we decide an acquisition is the direction we want to go in, let's find a better prospect. Prismatic's product line doesn't give our customers any special benefits. And we're risking losing control by focusing so much of our operations in Texas."

She could sense the flow of power in the room–from herself to Kevin. Around the table, managers began looking at Kevin expectantly.

Tom Weber looked across the table at her, his blue eyes sympathetic. He spoke in a low voice—at a slower pace, in the comforting twang of a fellow Midwesterner. He spoke as if he wanted to reach her and not the rest of the attendees.

"Rosalind, I have the same concern about layoffs. But the fact is, we do need to look at cutting costs over the next five years. With the cut in costs, we'll be able to invest in updating our product offerings. We've got a lot more competition now. I know you've said this yourself. If we don't acquire Prismatic, we need to think of other possibilities."

Blake Hennessey, to her left, was silent as he jotted on a notepad. He wrote LANGDON and embellished it with wavy lines and a star. It wasn't that she hadn't considered Philip Langdon's startup in Vegas as a possible acquisition, but there was a downside. Langdon had been a founding member of Infinitas. He hadn't left on good terms. Yes, Langdon, with his ambition and personality, was another risk entirely. He'd be looking out for himself and his own bottom line first.

Rosalind felt forced to choose between the lesser of two evils. Why did this choice even need to be made? Why now?

She resented Kevin's pressure tactics and didn't think his idea made sense for Infinitas. Over the past year, Kevin's opposition to her leadership had ratcheted up.

She nodded at Hennessey to acknowledge his note and spoke under her breath. "We'll talk later."

She looked up to see Kevin looking at her with contempt, no doubt empowered by the support he'd gathered this morning. He could glare all he wanted. Infinitas was her company. She was CEO and had managed to keep it competitive in the field of productivity software. She'd survived threat after threat to her leadership and wasn't about to give up now.

Rosalind stood up, raising herself to her full height of six feet. "We'll talk again tomorrow afternoon. You know my concerns. This acquisition threatens Infinitas and what we've built here. It's a foolish risk. I'm shocked that so many of you can't see that."

Her face must have shown her anger, because as she spoke, managers looked up from their handouts, eyes wide. A few looked scared.

Well, good. They should be.

This was serious—a threat to the company. And to the company culture, she'd carefully built over the past twenty years.

Everyone on the management team but her seemed in favor of it.

She shut the door to her office and sank into her chair, then spun it around to look out the window. Arastradero Road wound across the foreground, bounded by trees on the hillside.

Unlike the people she dealt with every day, nature had a permanence. Despite the company's in-fighting, schemes, and product launches, the eucalyptus trees outside her window continued swaying with the wind, releasing their menthol scent. Hawks circled the hills looking for small prey. And the fog continued to creep over the hills in the late afternoon-- uncomfortably damp in the winter, a sweet cool relief in the summer.

This place and her home in the hills of nearby Monte Verde had become her refuge. Years ago, in another life, she'd grown up in a small, flat town in Ohio, surrounded by farms. Humid summers. The smell of cow manure. Slow, lazy days. She couldn't imagine living there now.

There was a tap on the side door from her assistant's office. Amber Kennedy popped her head in. She'd been in the meeting and she, too, looked a little scared of her. Her big green eyes seemed unnaturally wide.

"Kevin wants five minutes with you. What should I tell him?"

"I'll talk to him tomorrow." His opinion hadn't changed. Hers certainly hadn't. What was the point? She needed a break from him. Kevin might still genuinely care about the company, but his and her outlooks had diverged over the past few years.

Differing views weren't necessarily a bad thing; Rosalind disliked sycophants. She'd hired, and fired, a few. Her attorney father had taught her to surround herself with good counsel even when it wasn't in agreement with her views-- she'd come to value that over the years. A team of rivals. As Abraham Lincoln had surrounded himself with those who had previously opposed him. She owed the success of the company to her ability to listen to the honest and differing opinions of her VPs and managers.

This situation, however, was different. Without consulting her, Kevin Dredger had researched and committed himself to a plan of action that was in direct opposition to her ideas and to common sense.

Now he was openly recruiting management to his side. There was a difference between suggesting a plan to cut costs and outright mutiny.

Rosalind saw Hennessey's smooth, balloon-like face through the window panel next to her office door and heard the tap.

She waved for him to come in. If he'd had inspiration about Langdon during the meeting, she wanted to hear it.

"I don't know if you heard. Langdon wants to be acquired. It might be a year on the horizon, but Philip Langdon publicly committed to it in an interview this week." Hennessey spilled out the words with obvious delight.

Of course, Hennessey would be excited. As one of the four founding members of Infinitas, Philip Langdon had headed up marketing and had mentored Hennessey himself.

Rosalind sighed, smiling ruefully. "Philip is full of himself. He's always wanted to be king. But his company's offerings do complement ours."

"Langdon Software Solutions seems to be doing well. Their latest spreadsheet with database capabilities is all over the tech news right now."

Rosalind felt her heart speed up. She wasn't going to jump right into this opportunity because of Kevin's pressure, but she wanted to meet with Philip soon to examine the possibilities for herself.

A half-hour ago, she was boxed in, outnumbered in a

meeting in which she felt obsolete. Irrelevant. She hadn't felt that way in a long time, and it was unsettling.

Now Langdon Software Solutions looked like a possibility on the horizon. But she didn't want to jump into anything.

First, she'd have to figure out how to work with her ex-husband.

FOUR

Tuesday

"PHILIP LANGDON CALLED. His flight's delayed. He should get into SFO by 10:40. He'll be here to meet with you by noon."

Amber placed a thick envelope on her desk. "Kevin left this. A report from the CFO at Prismatic. He wanted you to have it before the meeting."

Rosalind groaned and leaned back in her chair. "Tell him I'm rescheduling our afternoon meeting. I need to do some research first."

She turned and looked outside the window, where clouds were beginning to gather over the valley. "Tell Hennessey I want to see him soon—at 9:30."

Amber nodded. "Got it. By the way, Philip Langdon said he was bringing someone with him."

"Did he say who?" Typical Philip behavior. Keep her in the dark so he could have the upper hand in their talk.

Had she forgotten? This is how the man operated in business and in his personal life. He hadn't changed. The position she and Infinitas were in right now was handcrafted for Philip. It's almost as if he'd set it up. He could sweep in and appear to bring the answers–the rescuer. Then she and the company would become ensnared in his plan to save the day–for a price.

He'd done this to her twenty years ago. She'd fallen for it, thinking this man shared her vision for Infinitas and for their future together.

Twenty years as CEO had taught her a lot. She'd be on her guard and would flip the scenario and maintain control. Langdon Software Solutions could be a good partner – but Philip would bring them only what they needed, and she'd make sure to keep him in check.

Amber was still talking, and Rosalind just realized it.

"--didn't say, but it sounded like a financial consultant. Some woman he'd been working with. Her name's Katherine Stromberg. Langdon's assistant said she's a business consultant. She's been working with him for the past year, talking about new directions for the company and the possibility of selling."

This could be a good thing, Rosalind thought. A third party to balance Philip out—someone who'd focus on actual information not marketing bullshit. She'd prefer not to deal with Philip alone.

"Good work, Amber." She nodded at her assistant, who'd proved her weight in gold over the past five years.

As Amber left, Rosalind spun her chair around to the window. She could see planes in the distance, heading toward SFO. She felt a knot in her stomach as she glanced at her watch.

Hennessey came in while Rosalind was sitting at the conference table in her office, reading through the report from Prismatic that Kevin had dropped off.

Infinitas's VP of marketing took a seat across from her. Hennessey had the smooth-faced, gullible look of a college frat boy, but he'd been with Infinitas for seventeen years, since his college internship here.

"Kevin's proposal does look good in one way, Rosalind. I can't deny it'll help us cut costs in the short-term. But moving that much of our software engineering to China? Not sure about that."

Rosalind handed him the printout, and he began going through it. She wanted to ask him about Kevin and what had happened in the meeting yesterday, but she was afraid to show her insecurity. It was close to the surface right now.

Hennessey pushed the printout back to her.

"Infinitas's strength is in product development—in the experience of our technical staff. Prismatic isn't in the same league. In my opinion, we will outgrow them."

Rosalind drew in a big breath. "Why does Kevin want it so much?"

Hennessey studied her face in a way that made her uncomfortable. As if he knew something she didn't. Hennessey was a loyal, longtime employee. She hoped he'd be honest with her.

"Kevin's been here since the beginning," he started in. "I think this is his last shot at doing something big at Infinitas. He's willing to take a risk to make a deal he can brag about when he goes somewhere else. He sees this acquisition as his last chance. All he can see is that you're the one standing in his way. You're the obstacle."

This shouldn't have been a surprise to Rosalind, but she widened her eyes and let out a choked laugh.

"*I'm* the one in his way." She sat back in her chair and shook her head. "If he isn't happy with the situation, I'll make sure he's free to work somewhere else."

Rosalind was not one to make decisions rashly. But she'd given Kevin time and too much autonomy. She'd assumed that as one of the company's founders, he'd come around to what was best for Infinitas. She had to stop this.

"I appreciate your honesty, Blake. I've got a meeting with Philip Langdon at noon."

Hennessey smiled a little too cheerfully. "I wish you luck, Rosalind."

She watched him leave, then turned to the window.

Over the trees, a hawk circled the sky, then swooped down to hunt its prey.

Philip arrived alone, an expensive Italian leather messenger bag slung across his chest.

He wore tailored khaki pants and a red and blue striped button-down shirt with a '60s mod look, open to one button. Silicon Valley semi-casual, with a flash of style that said, *Sure, I'm a capitalist, but I'm one of the cool ones.*

If it was possible, he looked better than he did when they'd been together. His pretty-boy looks had been softened by just the right amount of lines around his eyes and mouth and a slight receding hairline. He was nailing the hot dad look.

"Roz, it's great to see you." He approached her for a hug, which she granted, then carefully backed off at about four seconds.

"Strange to see this huge building. This is how far we've come from those days."

Why was he using *we?*

A shiver ran through Rosalind. She kept a neutral smile on her face as she led him to the conference table, where Amber had set up coffee cups and a carafe, and a fruit and vegetable plate.

"Still living healthy." He nodded, a smile on his lips. He looked her up and down as he took the seat across from her. "It shows."

"Phil, I have no intention of talking business until you stop acting like a smarmy, inappropriate ass."

His mouth gaped open. He was caught off guard by her response.

She was relieved to see he was still the sleaze ball he'd been years ago. It would make working with him easier. No chance of complicated feelings on her part.

Philip turned to look at the framed photos of Infinitas's history on the wall.

He let out a laugh when he came to one of the early photos. She and Philip, both barely grownups, smiling from behind bulky, beige computers in a tiny room stacked with cardboard boxes.

"I was just thinking the other day about that first year. Remember in the beginning when we were still at the building in downtown Mountain View? You, me, Tom and Kev in that office next to the Italian restaurant. The smell of the garlic was so strong, Kev started to cry. We just assumed he was having problems with his girlfriend."

Rosalind leaned against the table and her lips twisted into a smile, despite herself. "He wondered why we kept asking if he was okay."

"Remember when Tom accidentally hired those gang members to work in the mailroom?" Rosalind kept her lips pressed together, unwilling to give him the satisfaction of a smile. "How is our friend Tom these days, by the way?"

She'd been tricked into a moment of intimacy. She reflexively crossed her arms.

"Admit it. You haven't kept in touch with anybody, have you, Phil?"

"You'd be surprised." He raised an eyebrow and gave her what she recognized as his *I-know-more-than-you* look. "I have my sources."

"You've come here to talk to me about Langdon Software Solutions. My assistant told me you brought someone with you. I'd like to meet her."

"Katherine will be up soon. She's taking a call downstairs.

She's been working the past few months to find a suitable match for us as we consider selling. It made sense to have her here."

"As I said on the phone, this is an exploratory meeting, Phil. I'm looking at our options. I'm curious to see what you can offer."

"We can give you more than Prismatic can." He raised an eyebrow, barely able to contain his disgust at the prospect. He smiled warmly. "And, of course, on your terms, Roz. You won't need to compromise."

He'd talked to someone at Infinitas. But who? She wondered how much else he knew about Infinitas's current situation. They weren't in a bad position, but she knew growth was needed. Kevin had forced her hand.

Rosalind decided to force Philip's.

"What exactly *are* my terms, Philip?"

Philip smiled cheerily. "Well, I know you don't want to give up any control." He picked a baby carrot off the tray and popped it into his mouth with a loud crunch. "You're a classic entrepreneur CEO after 20 years and want to keep your hands firmly on the steering wheel. Understandable. It's worked pretty well for you so far. The idea of giving up control to someone you don't know in Austin is intolerable to you."

The heat rose in Rosalind's face, and she wondered why she'd invited him here.

"Of course, it is," she said calmly. "Especially when there's no need for it."

Philip Langdon smiled, that confident smile that had impressed her twenty years ago when they were both young and just out of college. It wasn't going to work now. He'd been smart and good-looking then; she had, too. Both of them graduates of Stanford, with bright futures ahead of them. Lots of opportunities.

He'd written the marketing plan and most of the business

plan with her. He'd become head of marketing. Then in a decision that had been more closely related to working side by side, day and night, at a startup, they'd gotten married.

"What if your staff thinks there *is* a need? What if the people you've surrounded yourself with have a different idea of where the company should go? What if it turns out that the people you trust—" He leaned forward, cocking his head slightly. "--can't be trusted as much as you think?"

This was heavy-handed, even for Phil.

"It's not going to work on me, Phil." Rosalind shook her head. "Ditch the fear tactics. I asked you here to see if we could work together. I'm looking for a company that can add value for our customers. If you're not interested in providing that, let me know."

"I'm here because I care about you, Rosy." His voice dropped in volume, and the cocky smile faded from his face. "Seriously, I've kept in touch with my old contacts here at Infinitas. You think everything is fine. The fact is, it's not."

Oh, dear God. He'd pulled out his old nickname for her, which she hated. It reduced her to a girl in a gingham crop top and cutoffs, shucking corn. Was this a new tactic he was trying? Only he could protect poor lil Rosy Mabrey from her mutinous management team.

"Phil, if you're going to pull this shit on me–someone who knows you and your past–I don't want to work with you."

Her raised voice still hung in the air when Amber came into the room, followed by a well-dressed young woman carrying a briefcase. She looked to be in her thirties. By her attire and makeup, Rosalind could tell she wasn't from the laidback Bay Area. Los Angeles. Vegas, maybe.

"Katherine Stromberg is here." Amber announced, then turned to the woman and nodded. "Let me know if I can get you anything else."

Katherine took a seat on the same side of the table as Philip, which Rosalind thought was odd. Maybe she was paranoid after Kevin's meeting on Sunday. She didn't feel like facing another wall of opposition.

"It's good to meet you, Rosalind," Katherine said demurely before she sat down next to Philip. "Philip says wonderful things about you."

"Is that right?" Rosalind raised an eyebrow at Philip, amused. She observed the proximity of Katherine to Philip and wondered if they were more than business associates.

"Philip says the company wouldn't have gotten funded without you. And your decisions over the years have kept Infinitas on a stable growth track. You've avoided the mistakes of the competition." Katherine cast a quick check-in look at Philip; it lasted a fraction of a second, but Rosalind noted it. "That's why we're here today."

Philip's lips were tight, and his face was serious now. "We were a team, Rosy. Remember? The business plan. We did that ourselves. We launched this company. And that's why I'm asking you now. Let's work together again. Work with someone you can trust. Back in the old days, you knew the people who worked for you. Now the company's grown, and that's not the case. I don't think you know all that's going on at Infinitas."

A look of concern crossed his face, a wrinkling of that neatly tanned brow. "Sometimes the CEO is the last to know."

Rosalind sat back in her chair and looked at the two of them. It all came together now: Philip's scare tactics. His familiar gaslighting. Katherine Stromberg's glances to Philip for confirmation. This young woman wasn't the balancing third party that Rosalind had hoped for. But this was Philip. What had she expected?

"Unfortunately, this isn't going to work out. I have no intention of acquiring Langdon Software Systems." Rosalind stood up and nodded at the man she'd been married to for three years. The man that she'd been crazy enough to imagine having a child with at one point in her life.

"Show Mr. Langdon and Ms. Stromberg out, will you Amber?" She called to her assistant, who hurried in, a look of surprise on her face.

"Katherine, it was good to meet you." Rosalind then wearily turned to her ex-husband. "Philip, best of luck with your plans to sell."

"Oh, Rosy." Philip stood up, a sad look on his face. He went around the table to Rosalind and touched her shoulder. "Listen to me. I'm only trying to help you. I don't think you understand—"

"Mr. Langdon, Ms. Mabrey said the meeting is over. I'm going to have to ask you and Ms. Stromberg to leave now," Amber said sternly as she opened the door and gestured to the hall.

"In fact, I'll walk you both down to the front desk myself."

FIVE

AT 3:30, Kevin Dredger walked into her office.

The same as he'd done for the past twenty years.

It should have been casual. A meeting between two colleagues who'd gotten together regularly for updates, planning sessions, and brainstorming. Fire-fighting sessions when problems cropped up.

"Have a seat, Kevin."

Unsmiling, he sat down at the conference table, a folder in his hand. He helped himself to a cup of coffee from the carafe, took a sip, and waited till Rosalind took her seat across from him. There was an air of contempt in his actions, as if he didn't want to be there, and was hoping to make a quick exit with what he came to get.

"I've gone over your plan." She took her reading glasses off and leveled her eyes at him. "And I've talked to the board members. Kevin, we're not going to acquire Prismatic."

Kevin's face turned red. "You're refusing to even consider it. You were never open to the idea."

"I understand some of your concerns. I get it; we need to cut costs. But this isn't the right company or the right time." She folded her hands and leaned back. "I've seen this coming for a while, Kevin. I should have talked to you sooner. You're making deals behind my back. You haven't been upfront with me. You've made decisions that suit your agenda better than the company's."

Kevin's eyes widened. His hands dropped to his sides.

"You'll receive a compensation package, of course."

Amber brought in a folder and placed it on the table in front of her. Rosalind opened it and pushed a stack of papers across to Kevin.

"Here are the details of the package human resources drew up this morning. You've worked here since the beginning, so you'll receive more than what's fair for your time here. You're free to work for another company, as long as you abide by the agreements you've signed."

Kevin's eyes burned with anger, and his neck turned red around the collar of his shirt. He glanced at the agreement but didn't pick up a pen to sign it. He pushed it back at her.

"You think you'll get rid of me so easily? You have no idea of the power I hold here. And you forgot what we talked about in the desert twenty years ago. Don't you remember? You *can't* terminate me."

He poked at the paper with a big finger. "And this? This is a fucking insult, for all the time I've spent here. I've given my life for Infinitas. In the beginning, I was here 24/7 to keep things going. There were years when Angie didn't see me for six months, while I traveled for the company."

He stood up, looking disoriented as if her words had knocked out his underpinnings and he couldn't remember where he was.

The rage in his voice scared Rosalind, but she hadn't expected Kevin to take it well. She waited for it to die down, for him to come back to his senses. It might not happen today, but she felt it would eventually. In her time as a CEO, she'd seen this response before, and it no longer unsettled her. She had gotten used to making hard decisions. The terms of his severance were fair. With this package and his money from the IPO five years ago, he could easily retire. Or move on somewhere else.

"I'm sorry you feel this way, but my decision is final. It's clear we're no longer on the same team." She nodded firmly. "I wish you the best, Kevin."

"You godammed bitch."

Kevin slammed his coffee cup down on the table. Shards of stoneware flew across the table, as coffee spattered Rosalind's face and streamed down the edges of the table. "You know you can't do this."

He stood up and kicked an antique Chinese cabinet of hers, bashing in its lacquered doors.

Amber came back in, fear in her eyes.

"I just called security."

Rosalind nodded, as she calmly wiped coffee off her face and hair.

"Thank you, Amber."

Two security guards arrived and escorted Kevin out. Kevin's indignant complaints rang in the hallway as his escorts took him away.

Keep your fucking hands off of me

I started this company.

I've been here for twenty years.

She'd kept her composure while it was happening and fifteen minutes later received a message from security that Kevin had left the premises.

Rosalind's hands were shaking as she went into her office and swiveled in her seat to take a look at the hillside. Geese flew in a perfect V formation, in the direction of the bay, as the sun began to dim in late afternoon.

She'd read how birds keep their formation. The flock, moving together to maintain order, readjusts almost instantaneously as needed to keep together. The birds draft behind the birds in front of them to conserve energy. The head bird could fall back when tired, to be replaced by a bird who'd been conserving energy and waiting for the moment to switch in.

Rosalind found it fascinating. No human organization could function with such precision. Human beings had egos. Agendas.

There were times when she felt tired. Like that head bird, who needed to be replaced. It wasn't like she hadn't thought about stepping down. Maybe when Laurelwood Foundation's nature center in Monte Verde was up and running. More and more, her thoughts, her dreams, were about Laurelwood. A place for teaching children and adults in the valley how to value nature and take care of it. Maybe that was a better use of her skills.

She remembered her last walk through the construction site up in the Monte Verde hills. The foundations had been poured, and she stood on the slab that would be the education center, looking out at the oak and laurel trees surrounding the clearing.

Maybe soon it would be time for her to fall back. To let someone else take the lead.

"Are you okay?" Amber stood in the doorway to Rosalind's office, her voice full of concern.

"I'm fine, thanks." Rosalind let out a low sigh and spun from her window back to her desk. "He always had a temper. I knew that. I wasn't on the receiving end of it till this year."

Amber's face looked pale. "Is he having some kind of a mental health issue?"

"He's frustrated. With me, with the company." Rosalind flexed her hands, willing the shaking to go away. "It was time for Kevin to leave Infinitas. It was unrealistic to expect that we'd all be here forever. Kevin may be upset now, but he'll find a new opportunity. He'll see it was for the best. He's a smart man."

"You're not afraid he'll—try to get back at you somehow?" Amber's face showed genuine fear, but Rosalind wrote it off. Amber didn't know Kevin like she did. She hadn't known him for twenty-three years. Hadn't grown up with him, from college days through the years of building the company. In college, he'd get tense about his engineering projects, especially if he waited to the last minute. His anger and frustration built up quickly. Just as quickly, it released, and he was fine and asking why everyone was giving him funny looks.

"Why did he keep saying you had no right to do this? To terminate him?"

"Years ago, when we were at our first big show in Vegas." Rosalind pressed her lips together. "Twenty years ago. We wrote a company charter. We were all drunk. We decreed that none of us could ever be fired. That's what he was referring to." She smiled softly as she remembered the solemnity of the ceremony the four of them held in the desert one night outside Vegas. "I can't believe he's pinning his hopes on that."

"I'll ask security to make sure he doesn't come on-site unless he's escorted," Amber said firmly, as more color returned to her face.

"Excellent idea." Rosalind brushed her hair off her shoulder and began reviewing a speech she was scheduled to give at the Commonwealth Club in the city on Friday. "Thank you, Amber."

The year 2000 had been a strange one.

It was the end of a millennium. Rosalind remembered driving through San Jose and seeing a billboard proclaiming in red, fire-tipped capital letters that January 1 would be the end of the world. Repent because Jesus was returning in a blaze of fire, with vengeance.

As a side note, computers would go haywire due to the

Y2K bug. Planes would fall from the sky. Banks would shut down.

Because of a software issue with rolling over to the digits required for the year 2000, there was the fear that computers, now something everyone was dependent on, would suddenly stop working.

Her father, an intelligent man, had called and asked her if he should be worried about Y2K.

"You and your friends know about these things, hon." He called her that week she and Philip were writing the Infinitas business plan. "Should I be worried? Take my money out of the bank? Should I stock up on groceries down at Kroger's?"

January 2000 came and went, and people breathed a sigh of relief. They'd dodged disaster. The US had established a commission to deal with the Y2K issue and make software fixes to accommodate the rollover to the year 2000. But even for countries who'd done nothing, there were few glitches. Rosalind could have predicted it.

No banks shut down.

No planes fell out of the sky.

That would not happen until September of the following year.

By the time the year 2000 had been rung in, she, Philip, Tom, and Kevin had worked nearly 24/7 to prepare a business plan and raise funding for the new company. Philip had come up with the name Infinitas. Their product would provide limitless opportunities for businesses to improve their productivity.

After testing and innumerable bug fixes, the product was released in September.

When they flew off to Las Vegas for the show in November, the presidential election had just happened. When they returned, there was still no president. Bush and Gore were locked in an unprecedented virtual tie. The four principals of Infinitas had arguments over drinks, evenly split as to who should win.

As for herself, she hoped for Gore, because he seemed the only one who understood the threat of global warming.

It would be a month before the Supreme Court would choose the winner.

The year had lurched along uncertainly. They weren't sure Infinitas would be funded. Tech companies, especially internet-based businesses, were failing at an alarming rate, and investors were more skeptical now. Funding a high-tech company wasn't considered a slam dunk decision as it had a year or two ago, in the dot com boom.

She'd hooked up with Philip back when they were writing the business plan. He'd written most of it, though she'd had to scrutinize everything. Philip wanted to tell a good story and sometimes made up features that weren't in the product. Features either impossible or much harder to implement than Philip thought.

Babe, you know we need this. How hard would it be for Kevin to put it in?

Before they finished the plan, they were sleeping together. Philip began staying at her apartment in Palo Alto. They lived in a haze of sixteen-hour days and mutual infatuation. Her defenses had been worn down, she rationalized to herself years later. Otherwise, she wouldn't have made the decision to be with this man. With the long hours and stress, she was too tired to fight her attraction. And Philip's brazen confidence.

Vegas that year had been a crazy blur of activity—handshakes, and introductions. Food she was served but never got to finish. Too many rounds of drinks for her to keep up with. It was a lot like her and Philip's wedding that next summer.

Infinitas released their product the month before, so they were getting a lot of attention. Before she arrived in town, she had a full schedule of meetings with CEOs and tech publications. After that, parties to attend.

As an introvert, she hated it. If she could talk about the product–the technical specs and how it would integrate with customers' office systems–she was fine. If she had to go to corporate suites and parties and make small talk, she was lost. That's where Philip came in. He went everywhere with her. She talked knowledgeably about the technical side; he explained how the product gave customers exactly what they were looking for. He schmoozed the hell out of everyone they met.

She and Philip were opposites. Together they made an attractive, but somewhat conflicted, whole. It was exhilarating.

It was Thursday, their last night in Vegas. They were all exhausted. Kevin had partied every night, and tonight he looked sad and in need of a shave, his eyes bloodshot, his clothes rumpled and smelling of sweat. Tom had a pale, wistful look He was obsessed, apparently, by a girl with bright blue hair at the booth opposite them.

She and Philip made the rounds talking to possible partners, hardware companies, and anyone Philip identified as good connections to make. When they weren't at meetings and parties, they were back in their room making love. At first, she'd tried to keep their relationship secret, but Tom and Kevin had figured it out. She could tell by the looks they gave each other. By the end of the show, she'd stopped hiding it.

The evening of the show's last day, the four of them started drinking at the hotel bar.

Philip's arm was around her. He leaned across her to the other two. "Let's go out to the desert tonight. Let's bury a time capsule."

Tom laughed, but excitement glowed in his eyes. "What the fuck? That's so random, Langdon." He was intrigued.

"What? Just drive out to the desert?" Kevin looked scared. Sweat beaded on his forehead.

"I've still got the rental car." Philip held up the keys. "It's our last night in Vegas. We blew everyone away this week. Let's drive out into the desert and bury a fucking time capsule. To remember what we did this week."

When the three of them looked back at him with skepticism, Philip set his third margarita down and turned to them with a serious look.

"Now, guys. Listen to me." "This is really *important*."

Rosalind leaned her elbow on the bar, exhausted from talking to people all day. Philip was looking very attractive to her right now. After her second gin and tonic, the idea sounded pretty good. She nodded.

"Let's do it."

They giggled all the way to the parking garage, taking the steps two at a time like kids. Tom had only had half a beer, so he got behind the wheel. They pulled out of the garage and onto the Strip, then headed out of town on State Road 160.

They drove for about half an hour till the glow of the city faded behind them. Shadows of rock formations loomed ahead. They were out among sage brush and a few alien-looking Joshua Trees, their fisted limbs punching up into the night, caught in the sweep of the Chrysler's headlights.

The night was black and clear. A thick carpet of stars gleamed above. Rosalind had never seen so many stars, not even in the cornfields of her rural hometown.

Kevin looked terrified. "Wh-where are you taking us?

Tom pulled off the highway at a gap in the barbed wire fence, which looked like a dirt road.

"No, Tom. Go farther down." Philip called out from the back seat, as if Tom were his personal chauffeur. "Pull up down there, by that rock."

Tom parked and left the headlights on, and they wandered out onto the dirt to scope out a spot. Philip found a twisted stick of dried wood. He walked around brandishing it as if it was his sword and he were a pirate walking the deck of his ship.

Everything was oddly silent.

They could not hear their own footsteps. Or breathing. The black night sucked out all sound. Rosalind shivered. The night had gotten cold, and the air felt dry and hard. Goose-bumps covered her arms.

"I've got a Big Gulp cup. Think this would work?" Tom brought out a large plastic cup with a lid and a straw, big enough to be a bucket. The rest of the group, still drunk, nodded admiringly. Yes, a perfect choice.

Philip and Kevin smashed beer bottles against a rock, making shovels. It took a while to get the right edge for digging, but then there was no lack of empty beer bottles in the car. The two set about digging a hole big enough for the massive cup.

"All right. Everyone needs to put in something," Philip announced.

They dug through pockets, and Tom ran back to the car, his skinny legs pumping.

"Ladies and gentlemen, the Infinitas Key Chain." He stepped in front of the car and held it up in the headlights. The aluminum tchotchke gleamed like an artifact of precious metal.

"Here's Bill Gates' business card." Philip held up the card. "Apparently, he loves us."

"I've got condoms." Kevin pulled a pack out of his pocket. "And a card from the Chicken Ranch."

"That's disgusting, Kevin." Tom rolled his eyes.

"That's right, kid. You wouldn't know what these are for, would you, Tom?" Kevin laughed as he stood with his legs apart and let the roll of condoms unfurl.

"People, c'mon." Rosalind said sternly as she struggled, while still tipsy, to keep her balance on the uneven ground.

"What we need is a company charter. To say who we are. Infinitas. Now and for infinity."

She had a flyer of features on the Infinitas system in her purse. She clicked on the flashlight on her keychain, flipped the flyer over on the hood of the car, and began writing on the back.

The Infinitas Charter. November 16, 2000.

We are The Fantastic Four. We are Infinitas.

Then, inspired to include an homage to their alma mater, she wrote GO CARDINAL.

Through the haze of drinking and the years since passed, Rosalind couldn't remember now exactly what she'd written. She remembered saying something like this: *Every one of us is free to leave Infinitas, if we so choose. But no one can be fired.*

Infinitas is forever. We are forever.

Philip and Kevin scraped and dug at the dry ground a bit more till the hole was deep enough for the bucket-like cup. Then Philip put in the business card. Kevin dropped in the condoms, and Tom tossed in the key chain.

Rosalind stood in front of the hole. Philip stood behind her, his head resting on her shoulder, arms wrapped around her waist, as she read the charter out loud to them all.

By the time she finished, Tom and Kevin were crying. Philip took the charter from her and rolled it into a narrow tube. He slid it into the cup. Tom snapped the lid on, and Kevin pushed the pile of dirt in over the hole.

Tom stamped on it till the dirt was tamped down. They all stood in silence around the mound.

"Infinitas is forever." Tom looked down at the spot soberly.

"Long live Infinitas." Kevin and Philip said together, goofy looks on their faces. Kevin and Tom raised their hands in a Vulcan live-long-and-prosper salute.

"This was a good idea." Rosalind remembered saying as she craned her neck up at Philip behind her.

After the ceremony, she returned to her practical self as she saw the headlights still shining on the group.

"Let's get the hell out of here before we run the car battery down. The last thing we need is to get stranded out here."

She looked at them as they stood blearily in the head-lights, just now starting to sober up. That picture of them was preserved in her mind. Excited by their success. Smart but still naïve. Still good friends.

"We've got a company to run tomorrow, guys."

SIX

Wednesday
7 a.m.

THE MORNING SKY was pink and new.

Dani Grasso headed downhill on the trail at Rancho. She'd only found clean running shorts, not leggings, in her drawer this morning. As a result, her exposed legs were stinging as her breath came out in clouds in the crisp morning cold.

She'd need to be showered and ready to roll at the station at 8, so she was here a little earlier than usual. Runners were sparse on the trail. Today she'd forgotten to charge her earbuds, so she went without music. She wasn't happy about it, but she was pleasantly surprised at what she could hear without them.

Rabbits scuffling in the grass, birds making their morning calls in the trees, and the soft brush of a deer in the bushes. She swore she'd heard footsteps on the path behind her, but when she turned around, she saw nothing.

As she got closer to the bottom, a couple of turkeys waddled across the trail. They were odd-looking animals, bobbing their heads and making their way unhurriedly, no matter who was coming. They sounded like they were having a heated conversation. Maybe a domestic dispute.

She waited for them to pass, jogging in place so she didn't lose her rhythm. When they finally moved to the other side, she continued down the trail.

Though her thoughts kept pinging back to the campaign she played on the PlayStation last night, she was looking forward to this morning. She'd meet with Ruiz and Sergeant Doug Schallert to get any new assignments. She was also starting up a community service project in the elementary schools.

Right after she'd started with MVPD, Ruiz brought her in on the one he'd done, and she'd loved working with the kids. This year she was planning it herself and had an idea for turning the presentation into a kind of game. Ruiz seemed completely puzzled by her approach, but she assured him: *Dude, trust me. The students will get it.*

Gravity was carrying her downhill now, her favorite part of the run. It was the closest thing she could imagine to flying.

Her feet fell into a rhythm almost effortlessly, and her breath was regular. It had been a while since the rains, and the ground felt firm beneath her feet.

As she rounded the last ridge before the big downhill stretch, she had the odd feeling that someone was watching her. Her senses tingled, warning her to stay on the alert. She looked around her as she sped up. She scanned the woods on either side of the trail. Suddenly she heard a gurgling sound. Like somebody with a bad cold trying to take a breath.

The bushes? She looked to either side. It was a guttural sound, like an animal.

She looked up the hill she'd just run down. Nothing. She'd been up here when a deer was hiding in the bushes near the trail and had this feeling before.

Take a deep breath, Dani.

As she continued down the hill, she heard a clump and

crackling. Something heavy thumping through dry leaves and underbrush. She stopped, even though her body was screaming to keep moving. *Get away.*

As she descended to the switchback below, she saw something in her periphery.

A flash of color that shouldn't be there. Her senses shrieked: *wrong!* She kept running till she came to the area.

She looked up on the hillside above but saw only clumps of ferns and roots, growing sideways out of the bank. Nothing on the trail. She stood and looked down the hill, full of greying, fallen branches and clumps of red and green poison oak.

There she saw it. A shock of bright blond hair. A body in a grey and blue running suit and bright blue running shoes, nestled facedown against a fallen log.

With a sick feeling in her stomach, Dani knew. This was the woman she'd seen at the stretching bar. She could tell by the shoes and hair. Edging sideways down the hillside, she reached the woman. At first, she thought the woman had a bad fall off the trail.

When she gently turned the woman face up, she saw a deep, wide gash across her neck. No blood was coming out. She felt the woman's arm. No pulse. The woman's hair and jacket were soggy, saturated with warm blood.

Grasso felt the urge to do something, but CPR didn't make sense at this point.

Hoping she had reception on the trail, she called 911. A wave of intense nausea surged up from her stomach. She walked a few feet away and vomited.

She was washing her mouth out with water from her Hydro Flask, when she heard a cacophony of sirens from the parking lot below. Soon a truck pulled up the dirt trail with an officer and two EMTs, who jumped out and quickly made their way down the hillside to the woman.

Dani watched as they began their assessment. It didn't take long.

The EMTs set up the stretcher, then lifted the woman's body onto it to bring it up to the trail.

The young patrol officer, whom she now saw was from MVPD, approached her with a nod and a friendly *hey*. He was maybe thirty and had short blond hair and a mustache. She'd seen him around the station but couldn't remember his name.

"Dani Grasso, right?" He'd been around longer than she had. She was one of the newer hires. "You work with Jimmy Ruiz. I'm Ryan Dawson." He watched her, as if he knew what she was thinking. "There was nothing you could have done. Her carotid artery was cut. After a run like that, her heart would be pumping out blood fast. She had maybe five to ten seconds."

Soon a trail cart pulled up, and two officers got out and started securing the site.

"We've closed the park," one of the officers reported. "We've started a search of the trails. Everyone's being funneled down to the parking lot."

The two officers were stringing up tape around the area where the woman had lain.

Grasso's arms and legs felt shaky and rubbery, and now her hands, arms, and face were itching. Those bright red and orange leaves. Poison oak. She hadn't thought to avoid it in her rush to get to the woman.

"I talked to her just a few days ago. By the stretching bars. She's a regular here." She blurted the words out quickly and shakily. Her head throbbed, and she felt dizzy.

She felt ashamed of her reaction. What kind of a cop was she if she couldn't handle seeing a dead body? She wasn't about to tell this young male cop she was feeling dizzy. She stood up straight and kept her feet planted on the trail.

"She seemed familiar to me. Like I'd met her before."

"She's Rosalind Mabrey." Dawson looked at the body on

the stretcher as the EMTs prepared to head down the trail. "CEO at a tech company up in Palo Alto. She lived in the Monte Verde hills. You probably saw her around town."

"She ran the same trail, around the same time in the morning. We talked a few days ago." It felt odd to have known this woman—or at least to have seen her and chatted with her. Now she was dead. Dani thought about the feeling she'd gotten—of being watched. "When I was running this morning, I got a feeling there was someone just off the trail."

"You hear a scream? Any other noise?" Dawson asked.

"A gurgling noise. I thought it was an animal. Those turkeys gobbling." She looked up suddenly. "Then a loud thump. At one point, I did feel like I was hearing footsteps. I'm here early today since I have to be at the station at 8. There aren't that many people here at this time. I dismissed it."

Officer Dawson tapped some notes onto a tablet. "In your conversations with Ms. Mabrey, did she say anything about feeling afraid of anyone?"

Dani shook her head—then thought about it. "She did say something about a tough meeting coming up at work. She was joking about the endorphins from her run helping her get through a meeting full of guys. I thought she was kidding."

Dawson's eyes connected with hers, and he lowered his voice. "How are you feeling, Dani? Looks like you hurled down there."

She was ready to feel offended; the last thing she wanted was to appear weak. But the look on his face was friendly and matter-of-fact.

"It was—a shock when I saw her body. All the blood."

"I saw my first body in a bad collision on Foothill two years ago." A shadow passed over his face. "I know it's rough."

The two officers who had set up the crime scene were now talking to another runner who'd come down from the trail above, directing him back to an adjoining trail to avoid the area.

An hour and a half later, after a hot shower and a change into work wear, Grasso was at the station. She picked up a breakfast burrito at Garcia's on her way in. Even though she hadn't been hungry, it tasted good—a comforting combination of cheese, potato and sausage. That and a tall glass of cold water took care of her dizziness.

She ate it in her cubicle, and it wasn't long before Ruiz came in. He seemed more upbeat than he'd been lately. He nodded, then pulled up a chair and sat down a ways from her desk, and worked on his tablet for a few minutes, giving her some space.

She crumbled up the foil wrapper, wiped her fingers off with a moist towelette, and finished off the water. It was 9:30 a.m., but she felt like it was 4:30 in the afternoon. Hard to believe it was the same day as her discovery off the trail a couple of hours ago.

"I heard about your run." He looked up from his tablet, a smile of sympathy, or maybe amusement, on his face. "Poison oak? You're going to be itching for a while."

Dani looked down at her hands, which she'd scrubbed so hard after this morning's run, she felt like Lady Macbeth. They itched like crazy. Also her face and her legs. There was a very itchy red patch on her wrist. She hadn't gotten poison oak since Girl Scout camp ten years ago.

"So you knew the woman?"

"Not really. She ran the same trail I do. We talked when I saw her last."

Ruiz maintained good eye contact and listened quietly, which made it easier to calm down and share her feelings. "It was a shocker when I saw the body there. At first, it was hard to realize what I was seeing. I'm okay now. I wish I'd heard or seen something that helped. I wish I could have—well, I wish

I could have saved her. She was beyond saving when I got there."

"Today at our meeting with Schallert, I was going to give you the car theft downtown. But we'll work this together."

"You're serious?"

With his drooping eyes and deadpan look, Ruiz wasn't kidding. He pulled out his notepad and nodded.

"When you're ready, let's talk about logistics and what we know so far."

SEVEN

.

Wednesday
10 a.m.

AFTER RUIZ LEFT, Grasso sat quietly for a moment, sipping another cup of coffee.

She hoped it would give her some focus and blur the images of Rosalind Mabrey's body still on replay in her mind. With all the upscale coffee shops in town, the coffee of Monte Verde's finest was not typical cop coffee: earthy rich organic French roast, with a variety of dairy and non-dairy milks on hand. There wasn't much incentive to go out.

This was really happening.

She'd be working her first murder case, something she hadn't expected to come her way for years. Something her twelve-year-old self had dreamed of. Monte Verde wasn't exactly a hotbed of murder; there'd been a deadly home invasion a few years ago, then one or twice a year, the occasional suspicious death of a spouse or elderly person. She wanted to be excited.

She'd feel better about taking on the case if it hadn't been someone she'd met, even admired.

At noon, she and Ruiz met with Ryan Dawson, who updated them on the search. The CSI team Monte Verde shared with other departments in the area was going over the scene and a large section of the trail. The search would continue, but no weapon had been found in the park so far and the trails had been cleared of anyone who'd been in the preserve at the time.

"You remember that car that drove onto the trail and hit a hiker a couple of years ago?" Ryan asked as they sat in the squad room.

Grasso nodded and looked down at the notes and reminders she was accumulating on her tablet.

"That was tragic, of course." Ryan leaned back in his chair and grabbed his coffee cup. "But before that, nothing. Rancho San Antonio is a safe place. Families bring their toddlers to see the animals at Deer Hollow Farm. Seniors hike in groups. People run before and after work."

"Rosalind Mabrey ran at Rancho regularly. Usually the same days as me. This could be more than a random incident. Someone knew Rosalind would be there at that time—and that there wouldn't be many witnesses."

"You could be right, Dani. But it's also possible someone wandered into the park and had a violent episode."

"She could have been in the wrong place at the wrong time." Ruiz nodded. "But we still have a lot to learn about Ms. Mabrey."

In the next half hour, Grasso had the number to call Rosalind Mabrey's next of kin, her father Gordon Mabrey, who lived in Greenly, Ohio.

And she'd made an appointment to talk to Rosalind's personal assistant at Infinitas, Amber Kennedy.

Infinitas's headquarters was in a wooded, hillside area of Palo

Alto, off the Page Mill exit of Highway 280. Nearby was the Arastradero Open Space Preserve.

Rosalind Mabrey liked nature enough to surround herself with it, both during her runs and her workday.

Grasso hadn't been in any high-tech headquarters before, but this place didn't look like her idea of a high-tech company. The two-story complex was weathered wood, not concrete, and featured large picture windows that gave the building's occupants views out on the lush, wooded areas around it. The grassy, landscaped front lawn had a large pond with a natural rock waterfall.

The visitor lobby was decorated in greys and browns. Entire walls were covered in patches of living ferns, moss and lichen. The lobby itself seemed as if it had been set up to nurture plants more than humans.

Again, this was not anything like Dani had imagined when she heard this was a software company. She'd pictured tiny fabric-covered cubicles with lots of nerdy guys drinking Mountain Dew, eyes glued to their screens, programming.

The receptionist looked up as she came in, and Dani saw her eyes were red.

"May I help you?"

"Detective Dani Grasso, Monte Verde PD. I'm here to see Amber Kennedy."

"Of course. I'll let her know. She'll be down soon."

The receptionist blotted her red nose with a tissue. "You'll have to pardon us, detective. We just heard the news about Rosalind."

Within a couple of minutes, a young woman a few years older than her emerged through the double doors into the lobby. As if trying to blend in with the company's earthy décor, the woman wore a tan and brown suit, with a leaf-patterned scarf. Her red hair contrasted with her very pale face. Her eyes were also bloodshot.

"Detective Grasso? I'm Amber, Rosalind's assistant. Let's

go into a conference room. I'd rather do that than have us go upstairs to the office. You'll understand why."

Grasso followed the woman down another corridor, to a door labeled Laurel Conference Room. Amber looked down either side of the hall, then took out a key and opened the door.

Was this secrecy necessary? Dani had zero experience with high-tech companies. The closest she'd come to living the high-tech life was trying to install a better video card in her computer so she could play the newer video games that required more processing power.

"I'm glad you're here, Detective Grasso." Amber sat at one end of the wooden table and gestured to her to take a seat.

"I need to ask you a few questions about Rosalind, Ms. Kennedy." Dani opened her tablet. Instinct told her that she needed to let Amber talk.

"Ms. Kennedy—is there anything you'd like to tell me about what was going on with your boss?"

Amber Kennedy took a breath. She continued with a catch in her throat.

"Yesterday afternoon, our VP Kevin Dredger came in to talk to Rosalind." Amber was finally able to talk calmly. She blotted her eyes with a tissue. "They were not getting along. They hadn't been for a while. Kevin was trying to push an acquisition with a company in Texas. Rosalind didn't like the idea. Kevin refused to back down. This was not the first time that Kevin had gone up against Rosalind. She'd been keeping Human Resources and board members in the loop, and they agreed if he didn't agree to make a change, it was best to terminate his employment with Infinitas. So she did. He was let go yesterday afternoon."

"What was his reaction?"

"Kevin told her she couldn't let him go—that he'd given his life for the company for the past twenty years. Then he slammed a mug down on the table, shattering it and splashing Rosalind. He called her a—" Amber took a deep breath—"a goddamned bitch and left, breaking a piece of antique furniture on his way out."

"What did Rosalind do?"

"She told me to call security. They escorted him out of the building."

"Has anyone seen him since he left?" They needed to talk to Kevin Dredger—and bring him in for questioning.

Amber shook her head. "I was keeping my eyes open this morning. I came in early. I was afraid for Rosalind. Kevin's assistant said she didn't hear anything from him after yesterday afternoon. But then we heard the news about Rosalind. It's been hard to focus on anything else."

"Excuse me, Ms. Kennedy. I've got to make a call."

Dani stood up and walked to the other side of the room. She called Ruiz and asked him to track down Kevin Dredger and bring him in for questioning. She'd be there as soon as she could.

Kevin Dredger could be a man angry that he didn't get his way.

Or a murderer.

EIGHT

Wednesday
11:30 a.m.

KEVIN DREDGER SAT in the reception area, looking pale and sweaty in his thin jacket as he scrolled through messages on his phone. His hair was scruffy, and he had stubble on his chin. His shoes were wet and covered with flecks of grass.

Ruiz watched the man for a while, as he pretended to read something on the reception desk.

Kevin Dredger had the look of a man whose wife had kicked him out of the house, and who'd had to sleep on a friend's uncomfortable couch—or lawn—for the night. He had a strange smell on him. It reminded Ruiz of a farm.

"Mr. Dredger." He nodded as the man looked up. "Come with me." There was a look of fear in the man's eyes as he stood up and came to the alarmed door.

Ruiz buzzed them in and walked behind him to the questioning room.

Ruiz motioned to a seat--a chair he knew had one shortened leg. Anyone sitting in the chair would constantly rock, unable to keep the chair firm and in place. It was infuriating to sit in, and a good place for someone who was being questioned for the possible murder of their boss.

Grasso would be here soon, but he planned to keep the man a little bit on edge until she got there. It was something he was good at.

"Coffee? Water?" Ruiz gave the man a pleasant smile. "Detective Grasso will join us soon."

Dredger looked up startled, caught off guard by the offer.

"Water, please."

Ruiz buzzed the receptionist, who brought in a glass of water for Dredger and coffee with his standard cream and three packets of sugar for himself.

Ruiz pressed to start recording, then sat down opposite Dredger and began drinking his coffee.

"I'll start us off by getting some information from you. Full name?"

"Kevin Douglas Dredger." The man said sullenly.

"Employer?"

Dredger hesitated. "Infinitas in Palo Alto."

"Profession?"

Another hesitation, with a look of distaste on his face. "Vice president, software engineering."

At this point, Grasso rushed into the room. She pulled out a chair on Dredger's side of the table.

"Sorry. Traffic was bad." Grasso looked at Ruiz then set her tablet on the table and took the seat next to Dredger.

Jesus, Grasso. Don't apologize for coming in late. Show him you're in charge.

Soon Grasso calmed down and settled in. She gave Dredger a long hard look. She could handle this after all.

"Mr. Dredger, where were you this morning at 7 a.m.?"

"*You're* questioning me?" Dredger looked at Grasso then back at Ruiz. "Is it Bring Your Daughter to Work Day?"

"Answer the question, Mr. Dredger," Grasso said firmly.

Dredger blinked nervously.

"I was in Portola Valley. At my mother's house. I-I spent the night there."

"We will have to verify that. Did you leave the house at any time between 6 a.m. and 8 a.m. this morning?"

Dredger's eyes narrowed. "I did."

"And where did you go?"

The man hesitated. He rubbed his eyes. He shifted in the chair, which wobbled. He readjusted himself in the chair, and it still wobbled.

"I went into Infinitas to get a few things from my office before anyone else was in." His eyes moved from Grasso to Ruiz, a look of fear on his face. "I had to go through company security. They recorded my entry and exit time."

Grasso jotted something down in a notebook. "When did you go in, and when did you leave?"

"I went in at 6:15 and left by 6:45," the man said, robotically.

Ruiz knew this would have given Dredger enough time to drive south, against traffic, to Rancho San Antonio. He could have been there by 7 a.m. He would have had plenty of time to kill Rosalind Mabrey.

"Tell Mr. Dredger." Grasso sat back in her seat, maintaining eye contact with the man. "Why did you need to go into your office so early?"

"Rosalind Mabrey told me yesterday afternoon that my job was terminated at Infinitas." Dredger said the words carefully, almost robotically. "I still had clients and suppliers to speak to. I needed to get the paperwork on their accounts so I could wrap up my work with them."

"Tell me about your last meeting with Ms. Mabrey, yesterday afternoon."

The man rubbed his eyes again and shifted his weight in the chair, which caused it to rock again. "Do you have a different chair, detective?" He looked past Grasso and directly at Ruiz. "This chair isn't working for me."

"We don't," Grasso shot back. "Now, answer the question, Mr. Dredger. Tell me about your meeting with Ms. Mabrey yesterday afternoon."

He cleared his throat. "We had been discussing acquiring a company in Texas. I'd been talking to the company for several months. The Infinitas management team and I agreed that the acquisition was a good idea. Rosalind did not. She called me in yesterday to tell me she didn't support the acquisition and if I continued to support it, I would be terminated."

"And how did you respond to this?"

"I told her she couldn't get rid of me. It wasn't in her power to do so."

"Did you threaten Ms. Mabrey?" Ruiz asked.

"I did not."

"Did you strike her or damage property in her office?"

Kevin Dredger turned red. "I set down my mug too hard. It shattered. Then I ran into a cabinet on the way out—I guess I might have damaged it. But I didn't strike Rosalind or hit her in any way."

Grasso connected with Ruiz's eyes across the table.

"Can you tell me why Rosalind and her personal assistant would have called security that afternoon?" Grasso asked.

"Rosalind was trying to discredit me because of our disagreement. She was deliberately trying to make me look bad."

"Amber Kennedy said that she and Rosalind were scared during the meeting in Rosalind's office." Grasso leaned in toward the man. "They were afraid of you."

Dredger wasn't backing down. "They both had a complete overreaction to what I was saying."

"Mr. Dredger. I want you to think about this carefully. Be honest with us. It sounds like you cared for your job and for Infinitas. Hearing that you were being terminated after twenty years of hard work must have been quite a shock. Anyone would be angry." Grasso raised her eyebrows sympathetically.

This only seemed to make Dredger lash out more.

"She didn't understand. She had no idea how much I did for the company." Dredger's eyes burned in his face. Ruiz wondered how much was anger toward Rosalind Mabrey, and how much was anger at himself for making poor choices. "I gave up years of my life. Time with my wife, my kids."

"It sounds like you sacrificed a lot for the company, Mr. Dredger."

Ruiz watched with interest as Grasso took on the role of sympathetic listener. Good move.

Grasso moved in closer to Dredger and paused. "Kevin, I have to ask you. Did you kill Rosalind Mabrey?"

Dredger blinked and his eyes watered. Ruiz saw the man slowly entering that time during questioning where he could break and confess—or double down and deny everything. It was hard to tell which. He looked close to either outcome.

Dredger shook his head as tears ran down his face. He buried his head in his folded arms on the table.

After a few minutes, Ruiz looked at Grasso, who nodded. He had a feeling this was all they'd get today. It was time to verify facts and interview other players at Infinitas--and anyone else who'd spoken with Rosalind Mabrey recently.

He wasn't sure what to make of Kevin's tears in the interview today. They could be tears of self-pity. The man could be feeling persecuted at work by Rosalind and now by the police.

Or maybe he was genuinely grieving that his boss was dead. Whichever it was, Kevin Dredger wasn't off the hook.

Grasso went back to her cubicle and began making calls. She

wanted to verify Kevin's time at work this morning with Infinitas security.

They verified that the man had checked in with security at 6:16 and had left at 6:40. This scenario could have had him at Rancho by 7, which means he could have slashed Rosalind's throat on the trail sometime between 7:15 and 7:30 a.m.

Dredger had given her the phone number and address of his mother in Portola Valley. They decided Ruiz would go out and talk to her. Ruiz was a good choice to talk to an older woman. He was polite, a good listener. Not a young noob like she was.

Meanwhile, Grasso would work with the names Amber Kennedy had given—Tom Weber, one of the original employees of Infinitas, and Charlotte Baldwin, who was working with Rosalind on a philanthropic project--to build a nature retreat center in the Monte Verde hills.

Amber had also mentioned Philip Langdon--who had met with Rosalind yesterday morning about being acquired by Infinitas.

According to Amber, Langdon's meeting with Rosalind hadn't gone well either. He'd left, preparing to fly back to Vegas in the morning.

She'd caught Langdon on the phone, right before he left his hotel room in Palo Alto for the airport.

"Mr. Langdon, this is Detective Daniela Grasso, Monte Verde Police Department. We'd like to ask you some questions about your whereabouts early this morning."

"I don't understand." Langdon sounded genuinely confused. "Why? What's the problem?"

"Rosalind Mabrey, Infinitas CEO, was killed this morning, and we're questioning anyone she spoke to recently. Is it true that you met with her yesterday?"

First, there was quiet. Then she heard a guttural noise. "Oh, dear God. She's dead? Rosy is dead. How? What happened?"

"Can you come by the station in Monte Verde today, Mr. Langdon?"

"Of course, detective. Let me reschedule my flight home and get back to you."

Tom Weber, who lived in the Monte Verde hills, offered to drop by the station. Then Philip Langdon called back that he'd rescheduled his flight and would be coming in at 2 pm—in an hour.

Today felt like a blur to Dani Grasso. She was energized and exhausted at the same time. The coffee she kept downing kept her body moving, while her brain sputtered raggedly, warning her it would need a break soon. The itching from the poison oak had spread to her hands and neck. Her skin was on fire.

It was the longest day she'd ever lived.

After seeing Rosalind's body on the trail, she'd been plunged into her first murder case—feeling unprepared and inadequate. She felt no joy that her career opportunity came at the expense of a smart, capable woman who had been murdered then rolled off the trail into a thicket of poison oak.

The more she thought about the loss of this woman, the angrier it made her feel.

NINE

AT 12:45, the receptionist buzzed her that Tom Weber was here.

Tom Weber was Infinitas's VP of operations. He was dressed simply, in a jacket and jeans. The light scarf around his neck made him look European.

She took him back to the interrogation room and motioned him to take a seat across from her. Maybe it was too early to judge at this point, but she didn't feel the need to make him sit in Ruiz's special interrogation chair.

Sternly, Grasso chided herself. Anyone and *everyone* was a suspect in this case so far. Though some signs pointed to Kevin Dredger, she had just started this process.

"Thank you for coming in, Mr. Weber."

Tom Weber's blue eyes looked pained. He shook his head. "I'm in shock. This gives me something to do, after what happened to her. I feel useless. It makes me feel better to do something to help."

Grasso could relate to that.

"I need to ask you where you were this morning between 7 and 8 a.m."

He flinched at first, then nodded. "I was at home. I live just down the road from Rosalind's house. The tenants in the house on my property can vouch for me. I had to meet at 8 with roofers working on their unit. I didn't go into work till 8:30."

"How long have you worked with Ms. Mabrey, Mr. Weber?"

Weber's face tightened and he looked down. "I was one of Infinitas's original employees. I graduated from Stanford with Rosalind. The Fantastic Four, they called us--Kevin, Philip, Rosalind, and I."

"You were good friends."

Weber's lips twitched. "That ended eventually. But we worked well together back then. I liked to remember us as the Fantastic Four. We each had something we were good at. When we were working together, Infinitas did well. Especially at the beginning."

With the comic book reference, Dani felt more comfortable with Tom Weber. He was speaking her language. Nerd.

"I'm VP of operations. My job is to keep it all running. Make sure we're able to keep producing product, hiring, and paying people. I've got a gift for fighting fires." He frowned as if that last part wasn't one of his favorite aspects of the job.

"Rosalind was good at planning and securing financing. Her superpower was keeping calm. She impressed the venture capitalists. Kevin pulled together the tech team and designed and coded most of first product himself."

"Langdon. What did he do? Amber told me he was married to Rosalind."

Tom Weber's face turned dark. "Yeah, she was. For about three years. Philip was our bullshitter in chief. Wrote our marketing plan and worked on the business plan, which got us all that funding."

Dani wondered what happened. Was it one thing that happened? Or just the passage of time. Twenty years was a long time to work together. People change. Maybe it was inevitable that the relationships that had built and powered the company had fallen apart.

Dani wanted to find out more about Philip Langdon. Weber's face made it clear how he felt about the man.

"Do you know what Langdon's relationship was with Rosalind more recently?"

Weber shrugged. "After the divorce, it was awkward. Langdon couldn't really stay. He left and eventually started his own company-- about twelve years ago. I haven't seen the numbers, but from what I read in the industry pubs it's doing well. Rosalind was exploring working with him again—at least, acquiring his company. After all they went through with their divorce, I was surprised she'd consider it. It seemed more because she wanted an alternative to Kevin Dredger's choice of an acquisition—a company called Prismatic."

"Amber Kennedy told me about this earlier today. Can you explain the disagreement between Kevin and Rosalind?"

"I'll try." Weber cleared his throat. He looked a little uneasy. "Rosalind has—*had*—a few control issues. From the start, she was a great entrepreneur. Not that she wasn't still. But we've grown. Kevin was pushing her to acquire a company in Texas. He thought acquiring Prismatic would help us cut costs, so we could invest more in our product. Rosalind didn't think it was worth the downsides. Kevin wouldn't stop pushing."

Grasso breathed an internal sigh of relief that she didn't work for a corporation. Or a chain of grocery stores. Company politics sounded like kids fighting each other on the playground.

"How would you describe Kevin's feelings about Rosalind this past week?"

Weber looked uneasy. "You don't think Kevin killed her, do you?"

"I'm not saying anything. I'm asking you, Mr. Weber. How did Kevin feel about her—given their disagreement?"

Weber shifted in his seat and looked down at his hands. She wondered if he felt like he was ratting on his fellow employee.

"I don't know if I can answer that, Detective Grasso. Kevin and Rosalind hadn't been getting along for a while now, but I can't imagine him killing her."

"Mr. Weber, did you know that she terminated his employment at Infinitas last night?"

Weber nodded, looking uncomfortable.

"Human Resources is part of what I oversee. I had to approve it." He flexed his hands and swallowed. "That was hard for me. But I went over this with Rosalind. I understood why she did it, and I supported the decision."

"I wanted to ask you about something Kevin said." Grasso looked down at her scrawled notes for the day. "When Rosalind told him he was being let go, he said, 'She can't do that to me. She doesn't have the power.' Do you know what that means?"

Weber sat still for a moment. A weak smile washed over his face. "Yeah. I think so."

Dani waited. He seemed to be collecting his thoughts.

"Twenty years ago, after we launched our product, the four of us went to Vegas. It was Comdex, a big computer show back then. The four of us were young. Maybe you can understand this, since you're young." He had a wry smile on his face. "One night, Roz, Kev, Philip and I drove out into the desert. We'd just started a company together, and we were getting lots of love at the show.

"We drank a lot that last night, and I drove everyone out to the desert in the rental car. Philip told us we needed to bury a time capsule. We were very proud of ourselves—and we'd been drinking. We found a spot on a dirt road running through the brush a half-hour outside town, near the mountains. Rosalind wrote an Infinitas company charter on the back of a product flyer. We made up a mission statement—I can't remember what it said—probably something cheesy about excellence and empowering. We called ourselves The Fantastic Four and signed our names.

"We wrote in the charter that the four of us would stay together forever. We were free to leave the company, but none of us could ever be fired. No matter what. If we wanted to work for Infinitas for the rest of our lives, we could."

Grasso was fascinated by the story. "Dredger thought this was a legal document?"

"Rosalind said that night that we would have one drawn up when we got back, to make the promise official." Tom leaned one elbow on the table and turned his blue eyes on Grasso. "But Rosalind, like the rest of us that night, was— sorry for the language--buzzed as fuck."

"Do you think she ever had one drawn up?"

"If she didn't remember with Kevin last night, she probably didn't do it. Rosalind wouldn't forget something like that. Everything felt unreal that week. Our success at the show, the crazy things all of us did to let off steam. The four of us had worked like dogs to get the company started."

Tom seemed focused on something in the distance, as if a video of memories was playing in his head.

"That week in Vegas, when things were finally going our way, the four of us—well, we got a little out of control."

Ruiz checked the address Kevin Dredger had given him, then rounded the circular driveway, pulling up at the front of a two-story wooden house.

The house seemed huge to him. Who needed that much room? A row of four windows peered out from the top story, and the bottom story was fronted by a long, fenced-in deck with wooden porch swings on either end.

In the corral next to the house, horses huddled near a fence as if they were having a conversation. They swayed, tails swishing. Ruiz watched them, mesmerized by these exotic animals. He was a city kid. The closest he'd gotten to horses was a field trip with a youth program in middle school, where they'd ridden a group of tired, very old horses down a series of trails on a blazing hot day in Gilroy.

This ranch was another of those places that was in Silicon Valley yet felt far away from it. Unlike any place Ruiz had lived in the valley. The wooded area of Portola Valley looked posh, but rural—rambling roads, large, sprawling houses with a few acres, trees everywhere.

He pulled at the brass door knocker—another odd thing. Was it a decoration or was he supposed to use it? He covered all bases and pressed the doorbell, too.

A small, white-haired woman in a puffy jacket, jeans, and boots answered the door. From the stern look on her face, she made it a point to deal with intruders personally. She looked up at him up suspiciously. He gave her a friendly smile, which he hoped would win her over and make her cooperative.

"I believe you talked to Detective Grasso on the phone, Mrs. Dredger. I'm Detective James Ruiz, Monte Verde Police Department."

She released a heavy sigh and reluctantly held the door open for him. "Come on in, officer."

Mrs. Dredger hobbled down the hall, with a gait that showed she was dealing with an injury or the effects of arthritis. He followed her into a side room, full of antiques: a fancy upholstered sofa with wooden carved legs, an oval wooden table with frilly decoration around it, and two large chairs upholstered in red and brown. A grandfather clock dominated the room, with a brass pendulum that swung back and forth.

Nothing in this house looked new. It all felt old and fragile. If he sat on it wrong, he'd break it. He felt like he'd gone back in time a century or two.

Mrs. Dredger, on the other hand, did not look fragile. The woman looked tough and wiry, with skin as leathery as a pork chop. He wouldn't be surprised if she maintained the house and small ranch on her own.

As he sat down, he launched into his business.

"I'm here to ask you a few questions about your son, Kevin. He says he stayed here last night?"

Mrs. Dredger frowned. "He showed up at 8 pm and told me he was staying the night. Gave me no advance notice. Didn't come to help with anything around the place. Just needed a place to stay."

"Did he say why?"

"Of course not." Mrs. Dredger snorted. "Usually when he comes here, it's because he's had a fight with Angie. His wife."

Instead, this time, Kevin Dredger had had a fight with his boss. From what he'd seen of her, Mrs. Dredger didn't seem like a very warm place to run for comfort.

"Mrs. Dredger, what time did he leave here this morning?"

"Maybe 6 a.m. The sun wasn't up yet. I'd just put the coffee on, and I was headed out to the horses. I saw him throw some things in his car, then drive off. He didn't bother to say goodbye."

"Did he come back here at any point today?"

"He didn't." Having vented a bit, she looked at him, studying his face. "Why are you here? What's going on?"

"I'm asking questions regarding an incident in Monte Verde this morning, Mrs. Dredger."

"Kevin had his troubles with Angie a few years back."

Mrs. Dredger frowned and looked past him to the hallway. "But he went to that program. He said it helped him."

Red flags lit up across Ruiz's brain.

"What program was that, Mrs. Dredger?"

"Some class for managing your anger." Mrs. Dredger pulled in her lower lip. She looked like she immediately regretted bringing it up.

"No one else lives here?" He wondered if any other residents could vouch for Dredger's presence here.

"Just me and the animals. My husband Sam died two years ago."

"Notice anything missing after he left?"

"Not that I've seen, officer." The woman's eyes narrowed. "Why? What did he do? Is Kevin going to be arrested for something?"

"He came down to the station voluntarily to answer some questions. I'm trying to verify his whereabouts early this morning." He nodded and stood up. "I appreciate your help, Mrs. Dredger."

The tough lady escorted him to the door, following close behind him, as if she were afraid he'd change his mind about leaving.

With more questions about Kevin Dredger than he came with, Ruiz gave a nod to the horses as he passed the corral on his way to the car.

TEN

Wednesday
afternoon

ON HEARING he'd been assigned to Lloyd Jesperson's team for the near future, San Jose Homicide Detective Mario Flores had resigned himself to his punishment.

He didn't blame Sergeant Buckley. He had been right. He had been distracted while working the Schuler homicide case back in January. He'd only realized the extent of it when he'd closed the case, after an intense hostage situation up on Mt. Umunhum. Jimmy Ruiz had sat him down and told him to stay the hell away from his wife, Reyna. No contact. No texts. No stalking.

Ruiz had found out about the affair.

Flores suspected that Mandy Dirkson had told him. If she'd done that, she'd probably told his sergeant, Buckley, too, angry at his inattention to the Schuler case that she'd worked so hard on.

So Mario Flores, the bright young star of San Jose Homicide fell spectacularly. Fell not into disgrace as much as into anonymity.

The phrase Buckley used in his meeting with him was "inconsistent performance." Lloyd Jesperson, a plodding and passive-aggressive veteran of the department, was now in charge of his team—and his future.

The truth was, he had been falling for a while.

If he chose to stay in the valley, he'd live with his failures and the likelihood that he would never be that rising star again. He'd thought about leaving everything behind, moving on to some other city. But he was self-aware enough to know that he would be bringing his worst baggage with him—himself.

Reyna Ruiz still lit up a small, dark closet in his mind. He saw her fine-boned face, her tight little body, honed by work-outs. And that mischievous smile she'd had when they were together. But he no longer had that driving need to acquire her and wondered how it had possessed him so strongly, at a time when he'd needed the energy and focus for his job.

He'd gone down to visit his father in Orange County after the Schuler case. To understand why he'd done what he'd done, he wanted to talk to his father to see how Anthony Flores had become the man he was. Why he'd carried on multiple affairs while married to his mother. He'd hated that his father had done these things. Now he'd proven he was no better than his father.

Their talk hadn't gone well. Anthony Flores wasn't inter-ested in talking about why he did anything. He wanted to drink with his son, introduce him to his friends as his famous police detective son, and impress him by showing him his new boat and boathouse at Huntington Beach.

Flores had left with one thought – wherever he went in his life from this time forward, he would be nothing like his father.

Flores thought about Jimmy Ruiz. He was the anti-Anthony Flores. A good and honest man. A man of integrity. A good father.

He imagined himself sometimes, talking to Ruiz, as they used to when they met up at Someplace Bar and Grill.

He imagined everything being reset as if that week with Reyna had never happened.

ELEVEN

November 16, 2000
Nevada State Road 160
Outside of Las Vegas

We, the founders of the company Infinitas, formed March 24, 2000, do solemnly swear the following:

WE WILL HONOR *innovation and creativity in all we do.*

Whatever we see as our very best, we will push past that to do better.

We will leverage each of our skills and experience so that the whole is greater than the sum of our parts.

We will value our friendship above any work goals.

Membership in this group is for a lifetime; every one of us has the right to leave Infinitas at any time, but none of us can be fired or let go.

WE ARE INFINITAS
INFINITAS IS FOREVER
Go Cardinal!

Signed,
The Fantastic Four:
Kevin Douglas Dredger
Philip Avery Langdon
Rosalind Erin Mabrey
Thomas Nathaniel Weber

Kevin dug the hole at first, scraping with frustration at the dry ground with every tool on his Swiss Army knife. Philip finished his Corona, then wrapped a t-shirt around it and rapped the bottle against a rock.

He then handed a scoop-shaped bottle fragment to Kevin, who took it with a grunt and went back to digging.

"We're missing the last of the post-show parties." Tom leaned against the rental car and watched the others silhouetted in the glow from the headlights. He'd finally met up with the girl in the booth across the aisle. They'd spent the night in her room at the MGM. They'd said goodbye this morning, hurrying to get to their booths. He was a little terrified, stymied as to what he should do next. Should he call her?

"Who cares about parties?" Kevin sat back on his heels to take a break from digging. "We're nerds. At least Tom and I are."

Tom shrugged in distracted agreement. "I guess."

Rosalind looked up at the sky. "The booth was packed today. Everyone wanted a demo. All the magazines. Microsoft came by. Guess what? Bill Gates wants to be our friend."

After the Big Gulp cup was lowered into the hold and filled with its treasures, Tom put the lid on and pushed the dirt back into the hole. He stomped on the hole to pack it in.

They all stood up and looked down at the unremarkable spot on the ground, covered with the tread of Tom's shoes, their mark on the desert.

Kevin stared at the spot. "Someday we'll come back with our kids and dig it up."

There in the still, dry cold, they stood. Tom still remembered the ring of young, smooth faces with puffy eyes, tired from working the booth all week and drinking each night afterward.

"This is a historic night," Rosalind proclaimed like a queen. They turned to her with that level of respect. She was pretty, she was smart. Tom had fallen a little in love with her over the past year. If she'd told him to dance naked with the Stanford Tree, he'd have done it.

And though they claimed to be equal members in this enterprise, she was and would always be their leader.

"A new era." Rosalind smiled softly in the ethereal glow of the headlights, and all Tom could think of was Galadriel in Lord of the Rings. "We'll always remember this. Our beginning. And as Infinitas, there will be no end."

After Tom Weber left the station, Grasso poured herself another cup of coffee, then topped it off with a packet of sugar for the extra boost. She had twenty minutes before Philip Langdon came in.

She did a quick assessment so far. Rosalind Mabrey had fired Kevin Dredger yesterday afternoon, and the man had shown signs of violence and had to be escorted from the building by security. He'd spent the night at his mother's in Portola Valley, had gone into work early, with more than enough time to head down highway 280 to Rancho San Antonio for Rosalind's death at 7:15-7:30 a.m.

Tom Weber had been at home till 8:30 am, by his own admission. Though she'd verify this with the tenants on his property and the roofers. He seemed to have no grudge against Rosalind, but she was interested in the story he told.

There was a history to Rosalind and the other members of the "Fantastic Four."

There was Philip Langdon. He'd been married to Rosalind, and it hadn't gone well. But yesterday, they'd met to discuss working together again.

How had that meeting gone? Maybe Amber Kennedy would know.

As Grasso prepared questions for her meeting with Langdon, Ruiz came in. He poked his head over the cubicle wall.

"Got a minute?"

"About ten. How'd it go?"

"Mrs. Dredger was helpful. Kevin was there when he said he was—left at 6 a.m. to go into Infinitas. Didn't come back to her place. Didn't take anything with him. But she let slip that Kevin had to take anger management classes because of some problems with his wife."

Grasso wrote this down in her notes. "Seems in character from what we know. You in on the meeting with Philip Langdon? Turns out he was married to Rosalind Mabrey for three years. Ended on bad terms."

"Sure, why not. See you in just a few."

Grasso grabbed her mug of sugary coffee. She snagged a couple of old-timey Lorna Doon cookies from Frank Ladera's desk on her way to the interview room. They'd been her grandmother's favorite. Either they still made the cookies, or they'd been on Frank's desk that long.

She'd be in trouble when she hit her sugar crash in an hour or two, but for now, she had the energy to keep going through one more interview.

TWELVE

Wednesday
2 p.m.

THE FIRST THING Grasso noticed about Philip Langdon was that he did not look well.

His eyes were bloodshot, and his skin was pale and waxy. He was dressed in work attire, with a navy-blue suit and a brightly colored button-down shirt that seemed to be chosen to highlight the color of his blue-grey eyes. A smell of floral aftershave began to disperse through the room. Behind the man, Ruiz got a whiff and raised his eyebrows.

Ruiz brought him in and let him choose his seat. Maybe he took pity on Langdon because of his sad face. The man chose to sit across the table from Grasso.

"Good afternoon, Mr. Langdon." Grasso nodded. "This has been a hard day, I'm sure."

Langdon's eyes teared up. "Thank you for calling me and telling me about Rosy this morning, Detective Grasso."

"I need to know your whereabouts this morning between 7 and 8 a.m., Mr. Langdon."

"I was still at my hotel in Palo Alto, preparing to leave for the airport. Katherine Stromberg, my consultant, was with me."

"You didn't leave the hotel at any time before 8 that morning?"

"Katherine and I slept in." Langdon rubbed his eyes. "We didn't even wake up till 7:30."

"Just to clarify, were you sleeping together?" Ruiz spoke up from the end of the table. She was glad he'd asked. She'd need to talk to the woman to validate his whereabouts at that time.

"She was in the adjoining hotel room." Langdon said, indignantly. If this was true, Langdon could have easily slipped out without her knowing. "We were up till 1 a.m. working on a presentation for a new prospective buyer."

"I'll need Katherine's contact information so I can verify these details, Mr. Langdon."

The man's waxy complexion reddened. He spat out the words with exaggerated enunciation. "Are you accusing me of murdering Roz? If you knew me, you'd know I'm the last person who would do that. There were plenty of people at Infinitas you should be talking to."

Ruiz raised an eyebrow and looked down at his notes.

"Mr. Langdon, you were married to Ms. Mabrey. When was that?"

"We married the year after we started Infinitas. We were married for three years. It was my fault we divorced, not Rosalind's. I was an asshole." He frowned, then his voice took on a self-effacing tone. "It started out great. Then I got jealous of the attention she was getting. We saw each other at work and seeing her in that role made me angry. Needless to say, it wasn't good for the relationship."

An interesting admission. Grasso studied the man's face. Was his remorse real?

"How would you describe your relationship with Ms. Mabrey recently?"

Langdon threw one hand up in the air. He shook his head. "As good as could be expected, I guess. We hadn't talked much in the past fifteen years. When we did, our conversations were about business."

"You met with her yesterday. Tell us about your meeting." Ruiz's voice turned calm, almost soothing, as if he were calming his son who'd woken up after a nightmare.

Philip Langdon closed his eyes and took in a deep breath.

"Ros called me the day before. Her management team was pressuring her to make a deal she didn't like. She called me because she was interested in what we could offer. I tried to warn her that her management team had been trying to steer her in a wrong direction."

"How did she react to what you had to say?" Langdon reminded her of a salesman. Someone used to putting a spin on things, to cast himself in a good light. To move good things closer within his reach. She wondered if he couldn't stop himself from doing it.

"She accused me of trying to manipulate her," Langdon bit his lip and looked down. "I think she was still carrying a grudge from our marriage. She discounted everything I had to say. She refused to continue with the meeting and asked Katherine and me to leave."

Grasso found it hard to figure Langdon out. He seemed like a manipulator, and he could have been trying to gaslight Rosalind Mabrey into making a deal with his company. Yet the guy admitted he'd been an ass while they were married. Was that to make himself look better now that he could be considered a murder suspect?

Maybe he had been genuinely afraid for his ex-wife, trying to warn her that her executives could not be trusted. Maybe there really was something going on behind Rosalind Mabrey's back at Infinitas.

Ruiz leaned forward in his seat. "Mr. Langdon, you said a little bit ago that there are plenty of people we should be talking to—people who could have murdered Ms. Mabrey. You want to explain that?"

Langdon seemed to sink down into his seat. "I just meant —there are a lot of people at Infinitas who thought Ros was obsolete. That she needed to give up control. They thought she was standing in the way of their success. And the company's success. I've talked to them. People I knew from my years at Infinitas. And suddenly—" He sat back in his seat and threw up a hand dramatically, "—she's not an obstacle to them anymore."

"If you know of anyone who made threats on her life, you need to give us names and details, Mr. Langdon." Grasso was getting frustrated with the man. She had to be careful not to let her anger interfere with her questioning. "When you drop hints without giving us any information, it looks like you're trying to distract attention from yourself as a suspect."

Ruiz flashed a smile at her, which she read as *good job, kid.*

"I would need to have my lawyer present in order to give you more details." Langdon said self-importantly, as he looked from Grasso to Ruiz. It sounded like Langdon didn't have any real information as to threats on Rosalind Mabrey's life.

By the time Langdon left, Grasso was exhausted. She and Ruiz met to discuss the day's developments. There was an autopsy scheduled for tomorrow, which could provide more info on the murder method, since the murder weapon hadn't been found yet.

She and Ruiz then took a crime tech with them to search Rosalind Mabrey's office at Infinitas, then her home in the Monte Verde hills. A large study and much of the downstairs at Mabrey's home was devoted to her Laurelwood Foundation and the retreat center under construction.

Grasso left the station with a tablet full of notes and a list of people to call. What she really wanted to do was blow off steam by playing a game. Nothing relaxed her as much.

She wanted to fight bosses on a screen because she knew how to defeat them. She knew the tools at her disposal. If her character was killed in a fight, she could always respawn—come back to life ready to fight again. Good as new. No harm done.

Here she was overwhelmed with the gravity of life. And real death. A cast of characters tied together in the past. She didn't know them well enough to tell who was lying and who was telling the truth.

She'd always wanted to do this job. Someone commissioned to find the truth. Fight for justice. But now the demands of the job—and what she'd seen on the trail this morning—weighed heavy on her. She felt young, younger than these people around her. Ruiz with his grumpiness that she was beginning to think might be related to his marriage. Then the men at Infinitas with their grudges and their twisted love-hate relationships with Rosalind Mabrey.

She needed something to take her mind to another place. A magical world.

What she *knew* she needed was a good, long night's sleep.

But the game would have to come first.

THIRTEEN

Wednesday
5:30 p.m.

BY THE TIME he got home to Santa Clara that evening, Ruiz was energized.

It was the first time he'd felt so good about work in months. Between them, he and Grasso had handled the interviews and searches in a short period of time, trying to take advantage of that first 12-hour window after the murder. Grasso handled the interviews like a pro.

For the first time in four months, he hadn't been mulling over what was going on with Reyna all day. He did his job. And he loved it.

Reyna had picked up Jacky from the afterschool program, and when Ruiz came in, the boy pounced on him.

"Dad, Colin's having his birthday at the miniature golf place on El Camino. And he asked if me and some of our friends could spend the night. Can I?"

Nine seemed young for a slumber party.

"Your mom and I will talk about it, *mijo*."

Jacky gave him a skeptical look. Then he sighed heavily.

"It takes forever for you guys to talk about things. Can you guys decide tonight?"

Sorry, kid. That's what happens when your parents have stopped talking to each other.

"You'll get an answer. Is your homework done?"

"Of *course*." Jacky's look could have melted a block of ice.

Ruiz gave him a high five.

Kids seemed to have a short-term memory when it came to their performance at doing what they're supposed to do. Jacky forgot to finish his homework twice just last week. But he'd remembered it every day so far this week, so—*how dare you accuse me of not doing my homework.*

Ruiz took off his shoes and left them on a mat in the foyer. They were a no-shoes household, something he hadn't grown up with. He'd adapted to Reyna's family tradition, and their hardwood floors looked better for it.

He hung up his coat in the closet. He was, he knew, delaying going into the kitchen where Reyna was cooking something that smelled like pork *sisig*, a dish her mom made. It tasted good, but he didn't like to think too much about the ingredients, which included pig ears. She remembered it from her childhood, and he imagined she was cooking it to make herself feel better. She often did this with Filipino dishes.

He walked into the kitchen, grabbed a beer from the fridge, and took the mail out of the basket. He put bills in a pile and began going through them.

Fuck. Insurance didn't cover all of Jacky's dental filling earlier this month. The money would have to come from somewhere. They'd put off the work on the Range Rover for another month or two.

He watched her stand over the stove, this woman he'd delighted in and feared. She had been quiet these past four months. Ashamed she had been caught having an affair. Or sad it was over. Maybe she felt trapped. She'd made her feelings about him clear when he'd confronted her about the affair.

He wanted to say something. Something to connect with her. Something that would reach her.

She was three feet away from him now, but it felt like miles away. Any illusion he'd had that she belonged to him was gone. They were living in the same house. Roommates of the worst kind, coming and going. Rarely talking.

"Dinner smells good."

She turned around and looked at him, startled. She brushed her crow-black hair off her forehead with the back of her hand and looked down at the stove. "It'll be ready at 6."

"Jacky asked if he could go to the slumber party after Colin's birthday party next week."

"I have no problem with it." Reyna washed her hands in the sink and wiped them with a towel. "Colin's family is great with Jacky. The two of them are always together."

"He's only *nine*." Ruiz reached under the sink to pull the edges of the trash bag up, to take the trash out. "He's never spent a night away from us—except for your parents' house. What if he wakes up and gets scared? What if he wets the bed like he does at his *lola's*?"

"He'll be fine." She opened the rice cooker and started filling a bowl with steaming rice. "You say I'm too soft with him. You treat him like a baby."

"He's just turned nine years old, Reyna. Let's wait till he turns ten at least. He'll have lots of time for this later."

She threw the oven mitt down on the counter and turned around to face him, her eyes wide.

"Why are you making a big deal out of this, Jimmy? I know the family. Just because you haven't taken the time to get to know who your son is hanging out with—"

"I *know* Jacky. I've coached his soccer team for three years. I work on projects with him and make sure he does his homework. We go on bike rides together. I know my kid."

"He's not just *your* kid."

She might as well have thrown the hot pan of pork at him. It hit him hard. Jacky was the link between them. Jacky was their bond. Maybe their only bond right now.

Whether they stayed together and somehow got through this hell–or whether they went their separate ways and began sharing custody. Jacky's life would be affected by whatever decision they made.

They'd have to learn to deal with that.

That night, Grasso treated herself to a deep-dish pizza delivery. The Meat Lover. Sausage, pepperoni, linguica and ham. When she opened the box, the aroma was amazing. She deserved it after today.

She ate it slowly. She disciplined herself to only eat two pieces. The worst feeling was carting that thick, heavily laden pizza around in her stomach on her run in the morning.

Tonight she'd play a new game, *Souls of Arendor*. She bought it a few months ago but hadn't had a chance to get into it. Tonight, she'd indulge herself. At least create her character then head out on a small quest.

As she put her character out in her first quest, a feeling of utter release washed over her. She was in a new land but a familiar situation. Immersed.

She read reviews on the Polygon gaming site about how challenging the game was, but she was ready. She'd played a half a dozen other games like it. She let herself explore along the way, getting the layout of the area, figuring out how to get to the tools and weapons she'd need.

About midnight, she laid down her controller and shut down the game console. She felt unwound, satisfied, and tired. She'd go to sleep quickly tonight.

It was a good thing.

For all she knew, they could be solving the case tomorrow.

FOURTEEN

Thursday
morning

IT TOOK Reyna Ruiz a couple of tries to get the Range Rover started.

With a sigh of relief, she backed out of her spot at the gym and headed for work.

She'd showered at the gym rather than going home, even though she hated being in the locker room with everyone else, making pleasant conversation while naked.

She also got a little judgmental about how the stalls and locker room at the gym were cleaned.

But today, she didn't want to go back home and shower. She didn't want to see Jimmy. See that look on his face again. Hurt. Fear. The only alternative—and not a very comfortable one—was to go to the dental office early.

It had taken her a while, but she could finally admit it. Back in January, she blew it.

She'd fallen for Mario Flores and messed up *The Plan*. What The Plan should have been: tell Jimmy the truth then find a man she was attracted to, someone who could give her the life she'd dreamed of.

When Mario had come along, in the early hours of New Year's Day on the expressway, she'd been feeling especially trapped.

She'd let her desires get the best of her with Flores. They had been seen together and somebody told Jimmy.

Jimmy was hurt. He probably thought she didn't care about him. That wasn't exactly true. He was a good man. A great father. He'd rescued her from a bad situation when Mateo was arrested for dealing drugs. Taken her home and let her have his bed while he slept on the couch. He'd helped her financially until she could graduate from the dental assistant program.

She owed him. So when Jimmy had asked her to marry him ten years ago, what the hell was she supposed to say?

She knew what she'd done. Her treatment of him had been thankless. Selfish.

Her coworkers knew her story and hated her for what she'd done; she hadn't told them, but when it came to gossip, most of her coworkers were shameless and they seemed to have eyes everywhere.

Did they think she was so cold? So horrible as to do this to a good man?

She wished she could tell them—she was in a loveless marriage. On her side at least. She'd had no desire to hurt this man. She had no desire to hurt her son, who loved his father very much, probably more than he loved her.

She'd made a mistake. Could none of her coworkers relate to that? Could none of them forgive?

Now where was she? Living with a man she didn't love, who knew exactly what she'd done.

And she was working with a group of women who stopped talking abruptly whenever she entered the room.

Reyna Ruiz unlocked the door of the empty dental office and went to the back room to drink her coffee and read magazines, alone.

———

Even though she was tired, Dani Grasso forced herself to get up while it was still dark. 6 a.m.

The only thing that would center her mind on all she had to do today was running. She needed the smell of the laurels and fir trees, the rhythm of her feet on the cool ground, and the invigorating push up the hill in the morning air.

Even if it meant returning to the scene of the murder.

Maybe she wanted to go back to prove something to herself. That she was a detective, and she could handle what she'd seen just fine.

The park had closed and been evacuated yesterday for a comprehensive crime scene search. It reopened this morning. Retracing the route that she and Rosalind Mabrey took yesterday might show her what entry and escape points the killer might have had onto the trail.

The usually crowded parking lot by the restrooms was nearly empty. News of the murder had kept most of the devoted hikers and runners away, even with the reopening.

The day was going to be another bright, brisk one. The sun burst defiantly over the bank of pink clouds above the hills. The ground released the scents of laurel, grass, and earth. There was a slap of challenge in the air that she loved on cold mornings like this, the lure of the fresh, green hills and all the secrets they'd kept through the night.

The familiar trail zigzagged up into the forest, like a finger crooked at her. *Follow me.*

The memory of seeing Rosalind's body returned to her again and again. She still dealt with the flashbacks—the horror of realizing that the form in the poison oak was a body.

And when she'd drawn near, the mass of her blood-soaked blond hair and the gash across her throat.

What feeling—what reason—could have driven someone to do this?

If it was for an emotional reason, done in the heat of the moment, she could understand—maybe one of the people she'd talked to yesterday had loved Rosalind Mabrey and been rejected. Maybe one of them felt they'd been cut out of the company unfairly after years of dedicated service, like Kevin Dredger—one of the original Fantastic Four, who'd been there and heard Rosalind's Infinitas pledge in the desert outside Las Vegas.

What would be more chilling is if Rosalind Mabrey had been killed for a cold, logical reason. Maybe money. Ambition.

Anyone who would slash the woman's throat to bring a quick and sure death for these reasons—they would be a cold and calculated killer. And she wasn't sure she wanted to come face to face with anyone who could do that and have a good night's sleep.

She pushed these thoughts out of her mind as she made her way up the hill. The sun filtered through the trees, casting pinkish-orange shapes on the path. There seemed to be more animals here today. Maybe while the park was closed to humans, they'd felt freer about coming out. The deer were not shy today. One walked slowly and unafraid along the side of the path as she passed.

She'd chosen not to wear earphones today. She wanted to hear everything, just as she had yesterday on the path. Grasso wanted to focus on every detail of her surroundings—everything Rosalind Mabrey had seen yesterday morning on the last run of her life.

Anticipation of the spot where she'd found the body made her legs feel shaky. She wasn't sure she could relive that today. Maybe it was too soon.

When she reached the top, she did some stretches and looked down on the switchbacks before her. There was a small trail branching off from the main trail, which could have allowed someone to escape to the parking lot more quickly.

She slowed her pace on her run down the hill, not wanting to miss anything. When she approached the spot where she'd found Rosalind, nausea and a wave of dizziness hit her. She stopped and paced back and forth, then bent over and kept her head low for a moment, feeling like a wimp for still being affected by what she'd seen yesterday.

Grasso noticed a bouquet of store-bought flowers at the edge of the trail and helium balloons tied to an overhanging branch. If the park had only opened this morning, someone had gotten here very early to leave these memorials.

A couple of hikers were coming up the trail. They stopped, planting their poles in the ground as they surveyed the spot.

A few feet away, Grasso continued pacing and listened to their conversation.

"This is where that woman was killed. Just yesterday."

"They arrest anyone?"

"Sleepytown PD? Of course not. Monte Verde PD isn't used to first-degree murder."

"Sad when a park like this isn't safe anymore. My kids tell me I should move to Idaho. Get away from the crime around here."

Grasso considered revealing herself and speaking up in the department's defense, then decided against it. She turned around and headed back to the trail that branched off, a way up the path. She'd check it out for what it was worth. The killer could have easily made their way down to the parking lot, blending in with other hikers on that wider, busier trail.

Today that trail was desolate, except for a shirtless runner starting out up the hill. The path was well worn, and it seemed unlikely that she could spot any specific tracks. She made her way down it to the bars and did her leg stretches.

It helped to see a possible route the killer had taken. She'd gotten her run in for the day and had perhaps desensitized herself to the scene of the crime by going back to face it.

She'd take that.

FIFTEEN

Thursday
morning

TOM WEBER LAY awake in the early hours of the morning the day after Rosalind's murder. He couldn't stop fiddling with this phone.

He'd pick it up, search his messages, scan the news, then set it down. Every ten minutes. Nothing changed, yet that didn't keep him from repeating the cycle.

Dull grey light seeped in through the crack in the curtains. He turned over on his back and rubbed his eyes. His clock read 6 a.m. It was officially okay to get up now, so he did.

He opened the curtains and looked out over his land—his feudal estate. He even had his serfs—Bart and Carrie Angwin, the couple who lived in the small house an acre downhill and took care of the organic garden plots and kept the bees.

He lived on fifteen acres in the hills above Monte Verde. He'd bought the land with part of the IPO money five years ago. He built a house, then a smaller unit he could rent out. The idea was to get away from Silicon Valley. Put up a barrier between him and the constant call of his responsibilities at Infinitas, so he could knock off at the end of the day and not have to think about them.

It was his beautiful escape from a valley that was his prison and his livelihood.

If he didn't have this lure in place, he would never leave his office at Infinitas. He was always needed for something: a problem with facilities, a human resources issue. Every solution he scrambled to come up with gave him a hit of dopamine. It was like playing a video game only he never seemed to progress to the next level.

Through the past twenty years, his daily addiction had lost him quite a few things. Ties with his family in the Midwest.

Girlfriends, then a wife. Sonia had stayed with him for five years—she'd put up quite a fight but had eventually realized that his love and loyalties would never belong to her. They belonged to Infinitas. And to Rosalind Mabrey.

Now the golden tether was gone. There was no more tension on the rope. It slipped through his hands, and he watched it fall. He felt the slack—nothing now at the other end. He sucked in his breath, and it turned into a garbled cry.

The relief washed over him. Deep, intense relief that Rosalind was gone.

Gone were all her control issues and micromanagement. The late-night calls that he'd taken upon himself to answer and the problems he'd fixed, at her request. Because, he told himself, he was the only one who could help Lady Galadriel.

He stood and stared out at the bleak morning. In the distance, Bart Angwin was walking to the coop to feed the chickens. It made him long for any other kind of job—a job where he grew things, fed animals, or shaped iron over a blacksmith's fire.

Anything but the vague intangibleness of productivity software.

He picked up his phone and reflexively glanced at his messages. He would never again get a call from Rosalind Mabrey.

He didn't know if what he felt now was anguish or guilt.

Or a deep sense of peace.

Pre-caffeinated and showered from her run, Grasso entered her cubicle to find a stack of messages on her keyboard. Before she could start going through them, the receptionist buzzed from the front desk.

"Charlotte Baldwin is here to meet with you."

Grasso was puzzled until she remembered. This was the woman in charge of Laurelwood Foundation, Rosalind Mabrey's nature center in the Monte Verde hills.

Grasso hadn't contacted her yet. Charlotte Baldwin was farther down the list of people to talk to, after the major players at Infinitas. Better maybe that she talk to her now, since she'd come in to the station. It was an item to check off her list, and Baldwin had made it easy for her.

She went out to reception and saw a blonde woman in a jumpsuit and low leather boots sitting in a chair, writing precise lines in what Grasso recognized as a bullet journal. Grasso had started one last year with the best intentions. It had lasted a week.

"Ms. Baldwin? I'm Detective Dani Grasso. Why don't you come back." The woman raised her head, closed the journal, and tucked it into her bag.

As Grasso followed her down the hall, she noticed how much this woman looked like Rosalind–in her style, her hair and skin coloring, and her body shape. Women like this made Grasso feel like she was a completely different species. It reminded her of high school, where similar-looking people gravitated toward each other. Specifically, all the young, skinny blonde women seemed to group together, a club she'd never belong to.

Grasso would end up hanging out with the nerd girls or the game-playing guys. She wasn't sad about it. She felt more comfortable with them anyway.

"Have a seat, Ms. Baldwin." She gestured to the chair across from her. "I didn't know you were coming in, but I'm glad you did. You run Ms. Mabrey's nature project?"

The woman nodded. "The Laurelwood Foundation. Construction started on the project three weeks ago. Rosalind had been lobbying for support from the city council—trying to get the community to understand what Laurelwood is."

Grasso realized she had no idea what Rosalind's foundation was supposed to do. She could tell from Infinitas's lobby and its setting that Rosalind Mabrey loved nature.

"Ms. Baldwin, can you tell me what the purpose of Laurelwood is? Is it a camp?"

Grasso remembered going to her school's outdoor education camp in fifth grade, in the Santa Cruz mountains. It was one of her favorite school memories.

Charlotte Baldwin shook her head. She flipped her hair over her shoulder and reached into her large handbag to bring out a notebook. She pulled out a brochure and laid it on the desk in front of Grasso.

Baldwin unfolded the brochure to show an artist's rendition of a building with large windows, surrounded by smaller buildings that looked like cabins. There were paths leading from the large building out to the surrounding woods and hills.

"Laurelwood will be a place where people can come to learn about the local environment—whether that's appreciating the varieties of trees or birds in our area or learning how we can preserve our natural resources. Visitors will be able to take classes on local wildlife, hike the trails and learn about things like composting and recycling."

"What are the cabins for then?"

"Rosalind wanted to make sure there was a nature retreat for people in the valley who spend too much time indoors on their computers. She wanted to make retreats available for tech workers and families who needed some time in nature."

"And maybe police detectives?" Grasso smiled, unable to take her eyes off the idyllic drawing. She looked up at Charlotte Baldwin. "The project is going ahead, after Rosalind's death?"

"The Laurelwood Foundation board is still committed to it," Baldwin said firmly. Grasso noticed the woman's eyes were red-rimmed. "I'm committed to this. I want to see Rosalind's vision happen."

Grasso wondered why Baldwin was here. Other than the fact that her boss had been killed yesterday.

"Since construction started, we've been getting complaints on the Foundation line." Baldwin pulled out her bullet journal and opened it. "And some threats."

"What are they saying?"

Ms. Baldwin sighed and read from her journal.

"Let's see. Here's a few—

"This project will bring nothing but traffic and trouble to the Foundation's neighbors."

"Shut down construction immediately. The impact of the center on our city needs to be assessed."

Up close, Grasso saw that the woman's makeup made her look older. In reality, she looked close to her own age.

The woman shut the journal and looked up.

"There are people in Monte Verde who don't want outsiders coming into their town."

"Not in my backyard." Grasso nodded.

"Exactly." Charlotte Baldwin tapped well-manicured nails on the table. "I don't know what they expect will happen, but it's been blown out of proportion. Rosalind loved nature and wanted to share that with people in the valley who don't have the time or privilege of enjoying it."

"How much resentment do you think the community has for this project?"

"There were a few nasty confrontations at city council meetings. As you can see, there are some vocal opponents of the project."

Grasso knew which officers she could check with about that and made a note to do it. There had been some meetings where police were called in. Their presence at the back of the room kept things from getting out of control.

"Anybody in particular that stands out?"

Baldwin took out her bullet journal. "A couple of residents who lived near the proposed site. I wrote down their names because I wanted to approach them later and address their concerns. I'll get you their names. They were the loudest."

"Did it seem to you that they were angry at Rosalind Mabrey personally?"

It seemed like a leap for someone angry about a building project to resort to murder. But even in her short time working in Monte Verde, she'd seen this kind of hostility. People in pricey houses defended their territory fiercely.

Baldwin nodded. "She was the one lobbying for support--- and was the most visible. Everyone in Monte Verde knew her. When Roz was challenged, she pushed even harder for what she wanted."

"When can you get us a list of names, Ms. Baldwin?"

"By noon." Baldwin nodded. "I've got the time. Foundation work is on pause with what's just happened."

Grasso had a sudden flashback to the blonde squad in high school—all of them popular, stylish, above reproach. By contrast, Rosalind Mabrey seemed to be unpopular with everyone, with the exception of her personal assistant Amber and this woman.

One life hack Grasso followed was to keep a low profile.

You dodged a lot of shit when your head wasn't constantly popping up in the shooting gallery.

She'd learned from a young age that the Grasso name brought with it unwanted attention. In school, at the academy, and even in online game-playing, she preferred to drift through without drawing attention to herself. Online she chose a masculine name—CoBruh—to make sure she didn't get pegged as a woman. Depending on the game or the forum, being a woman could get you unwanted attention, even hostility.

At the time of her murder, there were a lot of people angry at Rosalind. She was a female CEO, holding onto control of her company, challenged by a male team of executives. She was heading up a project that neighbors viewed as a threat to their safe enclave. Add to that, she was blonde and six feet tall—easily recognized wherever she went.

One thing Rosalind Mabrey hadn't done was keep her head low in the shooting gallery.

SIXTEEN

Thursday
afternoon

GRASSO STAYED LATE that day to update Ruiz on her progress in the interrogation room.

It was one of his grouchy days; he looked like he was ready to punch someone, or that he had a bad case of indigestion. The bags under his eyes were heavier than usual.

In any case, it was clear that she wasn't the cause of his anger. While she wanted to know what was, she didn't have the right to pry.

She told him about Tom Weber's description of the oath the Fantastic Four made in the desert outside of Las Vegas, and Tom's explanation of the working relationships between Rosalind and her executives.

"If there wasn't enough anger against her, Rosalind was building a nature education and retreat center in the Monte Verde hills. It was unpopular with local residents. There were a few screaming matches in city council meetings."

Ruiz's face lit up suddenly. "I did hear about this."

Grasso did a second take and practically growled at him. "Why didn't you tell me?"

"I heard about the meeting, but I didn't know Rosalind was involved." He shrugged.

"I talked to one of the neighbors near the site an hour ago." Grasso had made the call after Charlotte Baldwin left. She felt the man's angry comments still bouncing around in her head.

"A guy named Rick McCabe, who lives off Laurelwood Road. Not sorry that Rosalind was dead. He was hoping that meant the Laurelwood project wouldn't happen."

"Where was this guy yesterday morning at 7?"

"On the runway at Palo Alto airport, ready to fly his private plane to San Luis Obispo for business." Grasso frowned. "All accounted for."

"It'll come down to who had that window of time and the motive."

"Which right now is Kevin Dredger and possibly Philip Langdon."

"What about Tom Weber—"

"Tom's roofer and tenants verified that he was there till 9 a.m." Grasso jumped in, cutting him off. Ruiz did have other cases right now, but she was getting impatient. She'd handled her end of the case in the past twenty-four hours without too much help from him.

"Jimmy, what's going on?" Grasso studied her mentor's face. "I know it's none of my business. But you've been worrying me."

Ruiz rubbed his face and leaned back in his chair, looking relieved that she'd asked, if she was judging correctly.

He looked like he was going to open up. Then he said, gruffly: "Marriage stuff."

She raised her eyebrows, hoping he was going to share more. Not that she considered herself someone who could give a married person advice. If she was in over her head heading up a murder case, she was even more ill-equipped to counsel someone in a relationship. She'd never been in one.

"You wanna tell me anything more than that?"

"Reyna had an affair." He said it quickly and almost under his breath. He lowered his eyes and she saw in one instant a powerful man deflated, like one of those Christmas Santa lawn decorations powered by air, left in a heap the next morning.

This was a disturbing thing: her mentor, a big man, pillar of stability, reduced to a pitiable figure. Something had been upended, gone wrong in the universe for this man to look helpless and lost.

"I'm sorry, Jimmy."

"The affair's over. It's been four months. I don't know if she's going to leave." His lips trembled. The idea of Ruiz losing it in front of her filled her with panic. "Or if I should."

"Do you want to?"

He shook his head. "It's my home."

Grasso had met Reyna Ruiz twice—once when she came by the station with Jacky to drop something off, and once when she'd had dinner with a couple of other officers at the Ruiz house. The woman was beautiful, and Grasso got the impression that was something she'd worked hard on.

Ruiz deferred to his wife, got up to help her in the kitchen and proudly brought up things she'd done in the conversation at the table.

Reyna didn't seem to acknowledge her husband's presence—except when she wanted his help.

Hard to judge a relationship from the outside, though. Grasso knew she was protective of Jimmy. The idea that someone wouldn't appreciate him filled her with anger. He was wise, considerate and had a great sense of humor. She'd come to admire him as a boss and appreciate him as a friend.

"Marriage counseling?"

"I'm up for it. I'm sure she isn't."

"You afraid to ask her?'

He looked down at the table blankly. "It might push her out the door."

"Yeah, but is it worth it to sit and wait?"

"That's what I'm trying to figure out."

Grasso had run out of things to say and looked at her mentor uneasily, trying to process what she'd just heard. Ruiz seemed to take that as his sign to exit.

"I didn't plan on telling anybody. Keep it on the down low." He smiled, but the look in his eyes didn't match the movements of his mouth. "Let's regroup tomorrow. Autopsy results should be in." He looked up at the clock. "I have to pick up Jacky at childcare by 6."

Grasso watched him get up. There wasn't much left of his usual bluster, sarcasm, and grit.

When the door shut behind him, she sent up a little prayer, like a clumsy handfolded paper airplane, that Ruiz could get through this and get back to being himself.

SEVENTEEN

Thursday
6 p.m.

TOM WEBER HAD BEEN TRYING to get hold of
Kevin Dredger for a day and a half. Finally on his drive back
to Monte Verde from Infinitas, he called and heard a live
voice, sullen and tight, through his Audi's Bluetooth system.

"This is Dredger."

"Fuck, Kevin. You want to tell me what's going on? The
police said you threatened Roz. Went ballistic in her office.
Now she's dead."

Tom was having a hard time controlling his voice. One
moment it sounded like he was going to break down in sobs,
the next he was shouting angrily.

"They know nothing, Tom. It's Monte Verde PD. They've
got a girl who looks like a high school freshman on the case."

"You have a lot to explain right now." Hearing his own
voice, Tom sounded like a teacher chaperone at a dance,
warning a student he was about to be suspended.

"Meet me at my mom's off Portola Valley Road. Park on

the road, then come out to the stables and we can talk in private."

"Angie kick you out again? What did you do this time?"

"None of your fucking business, Tom. It has nothing to do with Roz. Meet me at 7:30." The line went dead.

Tom decided to change course and head into Menlo Park. He needed a beer and a sandwich. And a massive amount of fries. Not his typical dinner, but he had no taste for healthy food right now and wanted to be in a place with people who looked like they were having fun. He was dreading being alone with Kevin Dredger.

He wished he had friends he could call up to join him, but those had disappeared over the years, casualties of his work-life imbalance. He bonded more closely to people at Infinitas because that's where he was most of the time. They all had that work-life imbalance thing going for them, too.

He took a seat by himself at the bar and ordered a Belgian pale ale and a Rueben sandwich with fries.

A young woman a few seats down from him smiled and gave him the onceover. She was at least ten years younger than him and pretty. He smiled back, feeling rusty, out of practice. Funny that women found him attractive now at the age of 45. Twenty years ago he would have done anything to get their attention, but most of them wanted nothing to do with him.

Reflexively, he picked up his phone. His habit of constantly checking his phone had gotten worse. He was on a five-minute cycle now.

He had to know any news on the case, had to read any texts coming in. Maybe he'd become addicted to the adrenaline surge he got working for Roz; he was missing it so bad, he was trying to create his own stress.

•   •   •

As the noise level in the restaurant rose around him, he thought about his meeting with Kevin tonight. He feared it, yet he had to talk to him. He knew Kevin had a dark side—rage would come over him and he would lash out.

Angie, whom Kevin had met at Infinitas, was a saint to have lived with him all these years. Judging by the amount of time he'd been spending at his mom's, Kevin wasn't doing well. The signs were there. His frustration with Roz, the backlog of frustration that had finally led to him try to undermine her this past year.

For years, Tom knew, Kevin had thought that someday he'd be head of Infinitas if he just waited it out. He was sure Langdon had had similar thoughts. That Rosalind would step aside to do the philanthropic work she was so interested in. The nature center she'd dreamed of.

That hadn't happened.

Tom downed the last of his ale, and realized that in the past few months, Kevin's anger at Roz had escalated dramatically. She'd become Kevin's nemesis. He'd built her up as the source of all his problems. The one thing that kept him from success and happiness.

Had Kevin decided to remove that obstacle?

It was time to go home. Grasso was sitting at her desk, going over notes from the interviews, when Ryan Dawson came in. He had that *I'm going to linger* look. Which, if she wasn't overwhelmed by her workload and ready to leave for the day, would have been fine. He was a really nice guy. He'd helped her out yesterday at the murder scene.

If he had word of the murder weapon or anything else being found at the scene, she wanted to hear it.

She turned around in her chair.

"Hey. What's up, Ryan?"

"Just thought I'd stop by and see how you're doing after yesterday."

"Doing much better today, thanks." She smiled. "A long shower and a breakfast burrito helped. Still itchy from the poison oak, though."

"I know you wished you could have helped her. I'm not sure she would have been spotted for a while if you hadn't seen her." He smiled shyly. "Sorry about the poison oak."

Grasso could see and accept the fact that Ryan Dawson was a handsome man. Blond hair and blue eyes. Tanned. Athletic. Probably a former Eagle Scout or something.

Any woman would be happy to be the focus of this man's attention. But apparently she wasn't any woman.

"My sister's a sous chef at Le Cochon, down the block from Garcia's. She gave me a coupon for the Sunday special. I wonder if you'd be up for joining me for dinner this weekend."

Oh, dear God.

She'd never been in this position. Possible responses came into her mind, then scattered as she panicked. If it had been clear that they were two bros going to hang out over beers, she would have said yes. But having to dress up and make conversation over champagne in a place like Le Cochon didn't sound like fun to her.

"Ryan, there's so much going on with this case. I'll be working through the weekend. I can't do it."

He looked disappointed, then nodded. "I get that. Hang in there, Dani. You'll do great."

After he walked away, she wondered what the hell her problem was. Did she just turn down a perfect man for a date?

Did she just not have feelings for anyone? Male *or* female? Her parents didn't understand. At her age, her brothers had been married to their high school sweethearts.

Aside from the pressure from her family, she was fine with her life as it was. If she needed any cautionary tales as to what a romantic relationship led to, she could look at Rosalind Mabrey and Philip Langdon.

Or Jimmy and Reyna Ruiz.

Grasso got home and immediately ordered the only thing that would give her solace tonight, after her day.

A pepperoni pizza.

Then she sunk into her gaming chair and googled *Am I gay?*

After reading it, she googled, *Am I asexual?*

She flopped down on her living room sofa and fell asleep for 45 minutes. She woke to her cell phone beeping that her pizza was being delivered downstairs.

She curled up with a weighted blanket and her pizza and watched some Let's Play videos on YouTube. She'd watch other people play games, since she didn't have a lot of energy to play a game herself.

Then her landline rang.

The only people who called on her landline were her parents. They insisted she keep the landline, despite her objection that a cell phone was all anyone needed anymore.

The only other person who called on the landline was Giovanni Grasso.

She picked up the receiver, then heard her grandfather's voice.

"Daniela, I've been reading about the murder case. The CEO lady. Please tell me what's going on."

Grasso told him the basics of the case, what she could reveal right now anyway. She talked about how she'd found the body herself, which he hadn't known about.

She talked about the process of a murder investigation in

general terms since she couldn't share specific details of the case.

Giovanni Grasso asked a lot of questions.

"And all of this—it's something you enjoy?"

"Well, yes—but no. I'm not happy that someone was killed. But I'm excited that I get to find justice for her. It's a lot of work, and most of it's tedious. Not like what you see in cop shows on TV. But I feel honored that I get to do this."

"Happier than you would be at my store." His voice was sad.

That made her smile for the first time today. "Yes, *Unnon.* Thank you for understanding."

"I know what it's like to have a dream. Is your father giving you a bad time?"

"Yes. He has more to complain about now. That I'm not at the store. That he knows I'm probably playing video games when I should be out finding a boyfriend."

"Are you playing video games tonight, Daniela?"

"Well, yes—"

Giovanni laughed. Then he launched into a funny story of how his first friends in America told him they found a woman for him, and he misunderstood and thought they meant they had found a prostitute for him. A good Catholic boy, he was horrified. Then they introduced him to Elena, her grandmother, whom he married within six months.

This sounded like Giovanni Grasso's way of encouraging her that the love of her life was just waiting around the corner. She could take it as more pressure from her family to find a mate. But after her grandfather's support for her new career, she let it go.

Before they ended the call, *Unnon* asked her to check her calendar. The weather was getting warm, and he'd like to have her over for a dinner in his backyard soon.

The call was a nice way to end a hard day.

She turned off the game console, not feeling the urge to play anymore.

She brushed her teeth and went to bed, where she slept soundly.

EIGHTEEN

Thursday
8 p.m.

TOM WEBER PULLED over to the side of the road, about 25 feet from the Dredger ranch in Portola Valley. It was dark and during the drive over from Menlo Park, the air had taken on a bone-chilling cold. He grabbed a jacket from the back seat and slipped it on.

Jesus, Kevin. Why the cloak and dagger?

His feet crunched on the gravel as he made his way down the road and toward the stables. He looked up at the clear black sky, savoring this look at the stars, which were brighter pinpricks out here, with less light pollution than even in the Monte Verde hills where he lived.

He wondered why Kevin had asked that they meet in the stable instead of the house. Gail Dredger had known him for 25 years—it wasn't like he was a stranger or some undesirable from the wrong side of town. He'd been Kevin's roommate in the dorms for two years at Stanford.

He put it down to Kevin's state of mind. He'd let loose on Roz the night before her death and was probably worried he was a suspect in her murder. And since he was staying at his mother's, there was good reason to suspect that he and Angie had fought and that he was told to sleep elsewhere.

There was a dim light coming from the small living quarters next to the horses' pens. As he grew closer, Tom could smell the manure and the hay. It blended with the scent of eucalyptus trees in the cold night air. It was a strangely pleasant smell.

He found the misaligned wooden door to the stable and rapped on it twice.

"Come in, Tom."

Tom entered and saw Kevin sitting on the striped ticking of an old mattress on a metal cot, a glass in his hand.

"You okay, Kev?" Tom took a seat on a battered captain's chair across from the cot. The room was no warmer than it was outdoors. Mouse droppings, like a trail of raisins, were visible underneath the edge of the cot.

"You think…I killed her." Kevin was slurring his speech, and Tom wondered how much he'd drunk since they talked.

"Did you? If you did, you can tell me. You know I'd understand." Tom made his voice soft, friendly. Kevin could have done it in a rage, not in his right mind. He'd just been fired from the only job he'd ever had, post-college. He had troubles at home.

Kevin gave him an unfocused look, which soured into a look of disgust. He looked down at his glass and took a drink.

"I didn't."

"You want to tell me what's going on then? Why did you want to see me?"

"You and me, we are friends. Since the beginning, Tom. You gotta help me."

Tom swallowed. He started to feel nauseous.

"You need to tell me how. How can I help you?"

Kevin raised the glass above his head and downed its contents. He grimaced and swallowed.

"I started getting these calls last summer. Asking for money."

"For what?" Tom shook his head. He'd known Kevin for 25 years, and he wasn't shocked someone was blackmailing him. Maybe a one-night stand—and someone threatened to tell Angie. Financial wrongdoing at Infinitas? As he imagined the possibilities—especially any of them related to Infinitas—his stomach roiled.

Kevin didn't seem to hear him. His wide brown eyes had a haunted look, as if he'd seen a ghost. He spoke slowly, slurring his speech.

"I was stupid. I thought, well--I'll pay them off and they'll go away. But it never ended. Two months later, I got another call, asking for more than I'd paid the first time. 50K, then later 75K. Over the past year, I had to sell off some investments. Each payment was taking chunks of my IPO payout. Angie started asking questions."

"Go to the police, Kev." Tom said, firmly. "Tell them what's been going on. You can't live this way."

Kevin's mouth twisted. Drops of sweat beaded on his forehead.

"If I call the police, I could be in big trouble." His voice faded to a hoarse whisper. "You don't understand. I will lose everything."

Tom leaned toward his friend. "Whoever it is, they're using fear to manipulate you. Let me go with you if that helps."

Thoughts began swirling in his head, memories of conversations, things Kevin had said in meetings.

"Kev, did you push for the Prismatic acquisition because it would benefit you financially?"

Kevin turned pale. He reached for the bottle on the table next to the cot and filled his glass again. He took a big swig and lay back against the peeling wallpaper on the wall behind him.

Tom felt the anger coursing through him as he felt himself in a familiar situation. This was just another day in his life at Infinitas. Bailing someone out. Cleaning up a mess. It had started with that first year at Infinitas. He was sick of doing this for everyone. Tired of taking out other people's trash. Smoothing things over. He'd done this for Rosalind. For Langdon. Now for Kevin.

They always said, *This is the last time. I swear, Tom.*

"Kevin, tell me. Did you push for Prismatic because you'd get money out of it?" Tom heard his voice rising, cut through with anger. "You were playing it, weren't you? You had investments in Prismatic. You'd get a payout if this went through. To make up for what you were paying out. What the fuck, Kevin."

"I needed money. I couldn't keep paying. Everything would be gone." At that, Kevin leaned over on his side and threw up over the mattress ticking. He clutched his stomach and let out a long, slow moan.

Tom was angry, angry on behalf of Infinitas, and at himself —that he'd been fooled by Kevin's carefully prepared pitch for the acquisition. That they'd all been fooled. And that on Rosalind's last days on earth, she had endured outright mutiny from her executives, all because Kevin was being blackmailed.

His friend lay on his side, reeking and sobbing.

"Tell me now. What was it, Kev? What the hell did you do that someone would blackmail you?" His voice sounded like a stranger's, gravelly and harsh. Twenty years of frustration surged through him now.

Kevin's lips began to move as he stared at the ceiling. Despite the disgusting smell, Tom stood up and moved closer to hear.

"We were driving…there was this girl."

What the hell that meant, Tom didn't know. Kevin lay motionless. He'd passed out.

Tom watched him for a moment, making sure his friend's chest rose and fell.

Then--because he was who he was, and that would never change--Tom took the bottle of whisky and poured it outside the door. He took a roll of paper towels, got water from the stable faucet, and wiped down the mattress and Kevin's shirt and face.

Then he shut the stable quarters door and headed out in the dark to his car.

That November in Vegas, they were careless and a little arrogant.

They'd been the darlings of the trade show, in a year when tech businesses were losing their allure for investors. When people found out what year Infinitas had been founded, they were surprised. It was the beginning of the dot com bust. Stories of abundant funding and products that actually delivered something to customers were drying up.

But the four of them were smart. They'd worked hard through school, top of their high school classes, then were thrown into the big pond at Stanford, where they competed against the best from all over the world. There was always a goal ahead to be met. A carrot coaxing them on to the next level.

After they'd started Infinitas, they'd worked hard, obsessively. With the energy of youth that can handle 18-hour days for weeks without crashing. When they weren't working hard, he and Kevin were playing Super Mario on the Nintendo 64 game system set up in the shipping room in Infinitas's first offices.

When they went to Vegas that November, it was a huge release. For three days they gave themselves, for the first time in their lives, permission to be careless. Their hard work had been rewarded by a successful product launch, and they were ready to party. As much as a bunch of hardworking nerds could party.

Tom noticed it with all of them. Rosalind, though she stayed on task and never shirked her duties, was louder and laughed more. Her relationship with Langdon, which she'd kept under wraps from the rest of them, now came out into the open. More PDAs, even at the booth. Flirtatious looks and inside jokes. The two of them snuck off during lunch to their room. Langdon was full of himself during the week in Vegas, maybe because he was banging the CEO.

Kevin hit on any woman who came into the booth, so much so that Roz took him aside and told him she'd send him home if he didn't stop. Late at night, he disappeared, out drinking and Tom knew where, since Kevin had asked him to come along. Kevin had taken an hour car ride out to visit brothels with guys from the booth down the aisle from Infinitas. He showed up at the booth the next morning, clothes rumpled, huge circles under his eyes.

As for himself, Tom had finally gone out with a cute girl with blue hair who gave out brochures at the video card booth. He'd been trying to get up the courage to ask her out. They went drinking and to an arty circus show that he enjoyed, then walked the Strip together, watching people. They ended up in her room, where they fumbled their way through a make-out session. They spent the next night together. Her company left the show early. He promised to call her but never did.

Then that last night the four of them drove out into the desert.

Some moments lived in his mind, perfectly captured.

That night was one of them.

He still remembered the smell of the cold desert night, so dry that he woke up the next morning with chapped lips. The dry ground crunched beneath their feet. The brilliance of the stars, burning like tiny white fires in the black sky. It was dark enough to see them flicker. The new car scent of the rental, nervous sweat from all the guys after a long day at the booth. Roz's perfume. Cheap beer and a bag of off-brand cheese puffs. The headlights lighting up the burial ceremony.

"Did you ever think we'd actually do this and make it work?" Langdon's voice sounded lazy and soft as they looked out at the covered-up hole they'd dug in the sand.

"We did a lot of work to get here. Don't forget that." Rosalind, the realist, spoke up.

"Everyone but Philip, anyway." Kevin threw it out there. All of them, even Langdon laughed. Because that night, they were still friends. They knew each others' foibles and accepted them. They were a team.

Twenty years had gone by, and year by year, things had changed. Their ideals, their friendships. Like a photocopy of a photocopy of that first year, losing clarity and resolution till it was unrecognizable.

They looked at each other with resentment, a residue of frustration built up through working closely with one another day after day.

If there was any miracle in the Infinitas story, Tom thought, it was that they stayed together as long as they did.

NINETEEN

Friday

IT WAS MID-AFTERNOON. Grasso and Ruiz were on their way to Garcia's, missing the noon rush by an hour. It was a clear day, and they both felt like taking the walk.

Their own shadows loomed before them in the early afternoon light, one big, one tiny. Circus clowns paired for comic effect.

"You read the autopsy report." Ruiz said as they turned onto Main Street. A strange topic for anyone but cops to be discussing on their way to lunch. "It confirms that the carotid artery was cut. The killer had to have reached around from behind her."

"The killer would have to be taller than Rosalind, in order to be in that position." Grasso was trying to estimate the heights of the people they'd interviewed. "She was six feet tall."

"If I'm six-three," Ruiz thought out loud. "Without measuring these people, I'd say both Kevin and Philip are over six feet. Tom's a lot shorter."

The other new consideration had been the knife used for

the murder. "There were a set of light marks on the skin, like a dotted line." Ruiz said, as they approached the block where Garcia's was. "From a serrated knife. Like the killer took a swipe but missed the first time."

"The kind of knife used to cut bread or tomatoes." Grasso shuddered. "A strange choice. I wonder if that's what the killer had available that morning."

They were downtown now, passing clothing boutiques, an antique store, a bank. Monte Verde had the cozy feel of a small town today, though it was larger than it seemed, stretching back into the hills that became the Santa Cruz mountains. Large custom houses and estates along narrow, twisting roads that made her stomach queasy as she drove up them.

They were approaching their destination, when Grasso spotted Charlotte Baldwin going out the door of Garcia's with two large to-go bags in her hand.

"Ms. Baldwin. Great minds think alike." Grasso called to the woman, who was wearing a pristine white, ruffled sundress, a brave choice for eating Mexican food.

"I'm working up at Rosalind's home office today." Charlotte Baldwin looked distractedly at her watch. "I'm going through papers with the board members and trying to combine my files with Rosalind's so we're organized. We need to be ready for legal challenges to the project."

Grasso and Ruiz went inside and found a booth. Ruiz held it down, while Grasso ordered for them, since it was her turn.

Garcia's didn't seem to fit in upscale downtown Monte Verde. It was an inexpensive burrito place you'd find in San Francisco's South of Market area or on El Camino in San Jose. It was a converted diner from the 1960s. The windows were so covered with colorful drawings of food and prices it was hard to see in or out. But everyone in town ate at Garcia's, even those who regularly frequented the high-end, Michelin-starred restaurant on the next block.

After 1 pm, you stood a chance of getting a table inside, and that's why they'd waited till now.

Grasso ordered a carne asada burrito for herself and fish tacos for Ruiz.

Then she grabbed the bowl of chips David Garcia set out for her and loaded up a plastic container of spicy red salsa from the salsa bar. When she looked at the small amount of chips in the bowl she'd been given, she commented to David, behind the counter.

"This is it? You know, I've got this guy with me." She waved at Ruiz in the booth.

"Oh, sorry." The man took the bowl back and heaped it high with more tortilla chips. Ruiz, watching on, gave him a thumbs up.

She slid into the seat across from Ruiz. "It's official. They do give us more food when you order."

Ruiz laughed. She noticed he didn't dive into the bowl of chips like he usually did.

"So how are things?"

He held up a wavering hand to indicate so-so.

"I prayed for you this week." She dipped a chip in the salsa and crunched into it.

"Who is it that you Catholics pray to? St. Jude?" He gave her a tired smile.

"The patron saint of lost causes." Grasso nodded. "Jude found my retainer for me in seventh grade. Seriously."

"Lost in the lunchroom, I bet."

"Worse. The girl's bathroom."

"Go on and keep praying then." Ruiz chuckled.

"We're still set to talk with Angie Dredger at 4." Grasso started to reach for another chip, then thought better of it. "Please take the lead when we talk to her. You're way better with women than I am, Jimmy."

"I'll see what she says about Dredger's anger issues. I

want to know his history." Ruiz took a drink from the plastic tumbler of water. "I know how to approach that."

David Garcia brought over their food, and Grasso smiled her thanks at him, then dug into her burrito, which was worth waiting for. Ruiz slowly worked his way through his two small fish tacos in a very unRuiz-like way.

Grasso's phone buzzed. She wiped her hands on her napkin and picked it up to check the text.

"Tom Weber is at the station. Something's happened. He needs to talk to us right away."

Tom Weber sat in his seat at reception, swiping through messages when they came back in, to-go bags in hand.

He was wearing a blue plaid flannel shirt and jeans. He looked pale and hadn't shaved this morning. To her surprise, Grasso found the unshaven lumberjack look appealing.

Ruiz nodded at the receptionist. "Ana, we'll be back in the interview room."

After they'd settled around the table in the interview room. Ruiz pushed the button to record.

Tom Weber looked agitated. He wove his fingers together and looked to Grasso, then to Ruiz. Then his eyes rested on Grasso again.

"I had a strange conversation with Kevin Dredger last night. I thought I should tell you about it." He explained the call he'd received from Kevin, then what had happened when he'd gone to Portola Valley to talk to him, in secret, in the stable quarters—at his request.

"You ask him if he'd killed Rosalind Mabrey?" Ruiz threw it out there, impatience in his voice.

"He said no. But he was drunk. Puking drunk. But he admitted that he was pushing for the acquisition because of the profit he'd make. He was being blackmailed and it was draining his savings."

"Wait a minute. I want to understand this." Grasso asked, trying to put the pieces together. "Kevin Dredger was being blackmailed—by who?"

"He wouldn't say. I'm not sure he knew."

"Do you have any ideas, from what you know of Dredger, who it could be?" Ruiz asked.

Tom Weber shook his head. "I could guess randomly, but that's not going to be helpful. Just because he's the way he is—Kevin pisses people off. When he told me, I wasn't surprised."

"He didn't say why he was being blackmailed?"

"He didn't." Tom looked blankly down at the table. "Before I left, he said something that didn't make a lot of sense. He said, 'the drive' then 'with that girl.' Not long after that, he passed out."

Grasso remembered the story Tom had told of the Fantastic Four, and their burial of a time capsule.

"Did it have to do with the time you guys were at the computer show in Vegas?"

Tom shook his head slowly. "I don't know. Maybe. What worries me most is that being blackmailed caused him to lie and manipulate people at Infinitas. He paid this person off in large amounts. Whatever it was, it was big enough that he was willing to pay a lot of money to keep it secret."

Grasso shot a look at Ruiz, who was keeping his poker face, something she wasn't quite as good at. Her heart was pounding. She was angry at Dredger and wanted to bring him in right now.

If this was going on at Infinitas, it could have led to Rosalind's murder. Roz was against Kevin's plan for the acquisition. He was furious at her and certainly hadn't hidden it. Tom's news gave credence to the idea of Kevin murdering Rosalind. He had time before he showed up at Infinitas. Maybe he took a bread knife from his mother's kitchen.

Dredger was already top of their list. This news high-lighted his name and drew a big red circle around it.

"It was weird enough," Tom said solemnly. "That I wanted to tell you guys. It could be unrelated to Rosalind's death. I thought you should know."

Ruiz walked Weber out to the reception area.

A few minutes later, Ruiz came back in and sat back down at the table. He tapped his fingers on the table in a way that began to annoy her. Then he frowned and wrote some things down on his notepad.

"Why do you think Tom Weber would come in and tell us this?"

Grasso looked up from her notes, surprised by his question. "He thought it had something to do with the murder."

"He knows Kevin Dredger is looking guilty right now. He didn't have to tell us this. But this seals the deal, and Kevin is the number one suspect." He grimaced. "These people *really* don't like each other."

"I think Weber's telling the truth."

Ruiz looked skeptical.

"That doesn't mean he had to tell us. Dredger made a series of bad decisions. But it's possible those don't have anything to do with Rosalind Mabrey's murder."

By 3:45, they were on Highway 85, heading up to Kevin and Angie Dredger's home in Mountain View. Grasso had many questions for Angie Dredger, and for Kevin, if he was there. Which, if he no longer had a job at Infinitas, was a possibility.

Grasso was still thinking over the interview with Tom Weber. She resented Ruiz's hints that Weber could have come into the station to tell his story just to deflect suspicion from himself. Of the three people they'd interviewed of the Fantastic Four, Weber seemed the most believable. He'd been a good source of info on the interactions of the players at

Infinitas. She was inclined to trust Tom--though she wondered why she felt that way so easily.

What did Ruiz see that she didn't?

The Dredger house was a two-story in south Mountain View, on the other side of Highway 85, off El Camino Real. The house was yellow, with white shutters surrounding the windows of the first and second stories. Three white Adirondack chairs stood on the white fenced front porch, surrounded by two potted plants. The house was a cheery contrast to all the info they'd been gathering about Kevin Dredger in the past couple of days.

Angie Dredger greeted them at the door. She was a tiny, plump woman, with a suspicious look on her face, as if she were perpetually preparing herself for bad news. But that made sense given what they'd learned about Kevin Dredger so far.

"The kids are home." She nodded behind her, toward the stairs. "Let's talk on the front porch."

"Is Mr. Dredger here?" Grasso asked, looking past her to the living room.

"He's with his mother at the ranch." She pressed her lips together firmly. "He may not come back."

They settled into the chairs on the front porch, Angie to the far right in the rocking chair, nearest the front door. Ruiz began the questioning.

"Mrs. Dredger, we hear your husband was at his mother's, then drove in to Infinitas to pick up some things on Wednesday morning—the day Rosalind Mabrey was killed. Did you speak with him that day?"

"He called about 11 a.m. to ask if I'd received something in the mail for him. Then he told me Rosalind was dead."

"How did he sound when he mentioned it?"

"I guess you could say he was matter-of-fact about it.

Maybe a little sad. He wasn't fond of her. He hadn't been for a few years."

"When was the last time you saw your husband, Mrs. Dredger?"

Angie Dredger sighed. "Last week. Friday night. He was drinking at home, after work. He'd been drinking pretty heavily all week. I didn't want the kids to see him that way. He got angry at me, again. Nothing violent, just a lot of yelling. Put-downs, trying to blame me for what his life was like now. He didn't used to be this bad, but it got worse this past year. Friday, I told him to pack his things and go to his mother's."

The tone of Angie's voice made Grasso sad. Resignation. An acceptance that this was the way life was going to be.

"Does Kevin have a history of violence? Has he ever hurt you?" Ruiz had a way of bringing these things up in a natural way that was gentle, conversational. He could be gruff in other contexts, but when interviewing women, that went away.

"He pushed me once. Last year. And that was it. I kicked him out and told him if he had any thoughts of staying with me and the kids, he'd have to get counseling. He got counseling for anger management—it helped some, but he found new ways to vent his anger."

"Mrs. Dredger, do you know what happened a year ago that could have caused your husband to change in this way?"

Grasso knew Ruiz was trying to verify Weber's timeline of the blackmailing.

"It did get worse last fall." Angie frowned. "I noticed some strange things going on in our bank accounts at that time. Kevin said he was moving money around, into investments. That's not my area of expertise, so I didn't question it. But then Kevin said we needed to cut back on some things. We were set for a vacation to visit my parents in Maryland for Christmas, but he said we should hold off." She looked out to the street, her hands gripping the arms of the chair. "In retrospect, I'm glad we didn't go."

Grasso knew she shouldn't be feeling it, but this confirmed Tom Weber's story, and she was secretly glad.

She continued, and the chair rocked a little faster. "He didn't talk deeply about things. I wish he had. He began talking more and more about Roz, pinpointing her as the source of his problems. He started talking about how she needed to step aside so they could bring in a new CEO, that she wasn't competent enough to run the company at its current size."

She looked over at them, a worried look on her face.

"It's not looking good for Kev, is it? I don't know what happened. They'd been friends since college." Angie Dredger swallowed. Grasso wondered if Angie believed her husband killed Rosalind.

"Mrs. Dredger, you worked at Infinitas for a while, didn't you?"

Angie looked startled at the question but nodded. "Kevin and I met there. About sixteen years ago. I worked in product marketing. We worked together on a project and hit it off. He was different then."

"Did you work for Philip Langdon?" Grasso asked.

"For a while. He was only there a couple more years, then he left to start his own company. I didn't mind working for him. He didn't micromanage, which I appreciated. He used to say that how we did the work wasn't as important as getting it done so we could stay on plan. He was a long-term goal, big-picture kind of manager."

"What were the relationships between Kevin, Philip, Tom, and Rosalind back then, if you had to say?" Grasso asked. "Did they get along?"

"Kev, Tom, and Roz were on good terms. They worked together well. Kev and Roz were friends back then. She's our oldest child's godmother. Philip was the odd man out after the divorce—I know Kev and Tom resented him for how he treated Roz. He'd been an asshole. It's like kids in middle school, isn't it?" Angie shook her head.

"Does Kevin have a history of violence, other than the time he pushed you?" As he asked, Ruiz's voice sounded different to Grasso. She knew some things about his childhood. He, his mother, and his brother Mateo had lived with physical abuse from his father. If Ruiz had a trigger, that was it.

Angie Dredger was quiet for a while, as she rocked in the chair, staring straight ahead. "There is something you should understand about Kevin. I'm not trying to excuse his actions. He doesn't respond well when he feels trapped. He's like a cornered animal. That's when he lashes out. I'm not sure where that comes from. We were never close to his parents. But I saw it with our youngest, Bradley. He's on the autism spectrum. We were in an IEP meeting at school, and they told us he couldn't have access to services he needed in order to get through second grade. They told us there was no funding. Kevin went ballistic. He knocked over a table—threw a binder. I tried to apologize, intervene with him."

Angie brushed tears away. "He's not malicious. He has a hard time when he's in an impossible situation. Even when it's on behalf of someone else."

Grasso looked at Ruiz and wondered what he was thinking. He was better at hiding his thoughts than she was.

The blackmailer had almost certainly put Dredger in an impossible situation.

But going after Rosalind on a trail he knew she frequented, planning to be there when he knew she would be —that was different than striking out in frustration in a moment of anger. That was premeditated murder.

"Do you think your husband was capable of killing Rosalind Mabrey?" Ruiz asked it gently, thoughtfully.

Angie began crying. "I don't want to think so."

"Mrs. Dredger, I know this is difficult for you." Ruiz almost looked as if he were going to cry. "I'm wondering if you'd be able to verify something for us. You don't have to. But it would be helpful for us to know if these deposits were made to your account."

He handed Angie a slip of paper with the amounts Tom had told them about— financial incentives given to Dredger for pushing through the acquisition.

Angie looked at the amounts and frowned. "I can look for these online. I'll give you a call."

Grasso heard kids talking loudly inside—the beginnings of an argument. Angie glanced over her shoulder toward the front door.

"If you'll excuse me, detectives, I've got to stop World War III."

After they said goodbye and Angie Dredger went back inside, Ruiz and Grasso connected with a look as they got up out of their chairs and headed to the car.

It wasn't looking good for Kevin Dredger.

TWENTY

Friday
7 p.m.

FEELING disgusted at the amount of time she'd spent sitting at work the past few days, Grasso decided to pick up a healthy salad on the way back to Cupertino.

She was aware of her tendency to eat bad food while playing games, and tonight, without a doubt, would be a night for playing games.

She was processing the fact that they might soon be arresting Kevin Dredger for the murder of Rosalind Mabrey.

It would be a relief—putting her first case to rest, within three days of the murder. It was also stress-inducing because an arrest was only the beginning. She and Ruiz would need to put together the case meticulously, documentation and reports, for Kevin Dredger's guilt. For a case that would hold up in court. She'd be counting on help from Ruiz since he'd been through this many times before.

It was like she was in school again, a ten-page research paper for an AP class hanging over her head, due at some point in the future. It had better be damn good.

The pressure only made the prospect of game-playing more appealing.

After devouring her chopped chicken and kale salad, which was so good it made her wonder why she didn't eat healthy food more often, she sat down to start up the PlayStation.

She noticed a few of her gaming friends online, then her brother Anthony's avatar popped up. He was playing a samurai game she'd been into last year. She was surprised to see him online this early. His wife, Lara, usually didn't let him play till the kids were in bed.

She invited Anthony to a voice chat.

"Games at 7:30 p.m. on a school night? Responsible parenting, bro."

"Lara's at a work thing. I'm letting the kids stay up and watch me play." Grasso heard her nephew talking excitedly in the background. Anthony sighed. "Benny says hi, by the way."

Anthony sounded distant. Maybe just tired. Benny's chatter made her realize how much she missed her eight-year-old niece and five-year-old nephew.

"Wanna play something? How about Minecraft? The kids will love it."

"Sure. Let's play in Creative Mode. I guarantee the kids are going to want us to do some crazy things."

Grasso started up the game on her console.

It had been a while since she'd played the game, which was all about exploring and making things in a block-based world. There were much worse things for Anthony's kids to be watching. It wasn't completely non-violent, but when one of the blocky creatures was killed, they vanished in a non-gory puff of smoke. Why not let them watch their dad play something they played, too?

Benny and Liana were sure to give their dad lots of advice. Which would be very entertaining.

Dani and Anthony started stacking blocks, creating their castles. The kids had lots of opinions on how the castles should be built. They wanted moats, with lots of fish in them, so between them, she and Anthony worked out how to do that.

"Now make a dungeon. A dungeon *prison*." Liana commanded from the background.

"Put dad in it!" Benny couldn't say it without convulsing in laughter.

After clearing out dirt and blocks in the area, Dani began building a square underground dungeon.

It had been a while since she and her brother had played a game like this together. It reminded her of her childhood, when she'd been the little sister watching her older brothers play, wanting to do everything they did. Alex and Anthony hadn't always been welcoming to her when she wanted to play. She'd had to put in time on the games, to reach a level where they considered her worthy to play with them.

Once her and Anthony's castles were complete, Benny and Liana told them they needed to use TNT to blow them up. So she and Anthony began blowing their hard-built creations up. Anthony set up a flying TNT duplicator, which repeatedly dropped boxes of TNT on the castles. Grasso loved hearing her niece and nephew laugh. It had been months since she'd seen them.

A few minutes later, Anthony told the kids to go brush their teeth. After the kids called out goodnight, the laughter and commotion coming through the voice chat stopped abruptly. The silence began to feel uneasy.

"The kids enjoyed that, Dani. So did I."

"So much for avoiding violence in front of the children."

"Well, they've seen worse."

"We should play some *Samurai Star*. Maybe this weekend?"

Grasso waited for his response, which came after a long pause.

"Dani, we can't do this anymore. You know why."

"Why can't you understand? I'm not like you. I'd be miserable at the store. This isn't personal."

"What do you mean it isn't personal? It's *family*. You turned your back on all of us."

"And now you're all punishing me."

"Well, you should have thought about that."

She wanted to tell him that *Unonn* was still speaking to her and that he'd accepted her decision not to work for Grasso's Fine Foods. But she'd made a promise. She regretted almost immediately that she'd made it. It had been unfair to her from the start.

She'd kept her relationship with her grandfather, but she'd lost the rest of her family.

As Grasso went back to playing a game on her own, she considered that things hadn't changed that much since she was seven. Her family was still telling her what she could and couldn't do.

Yet another reason to choose games over real life.

In her games, she called the shots.

TWENTY-ONE

Saturday

THE NEXT MORNING, Grasso woke to a call from the judge's office, which cleared the nastiness of last night's chat with her brother out of her head.

Even this early and on a Saturday, the search warrant for Gail Dredger's house and property was approved.

They were set to talk to Kevin Dredger this morning at his mother's. Afterward, she, Ruiz, and a crime scene team would do the search. The goal was to find the serrated knife, the weapon used to kill Rosalind.

When she and Ruiz came to the door, Gail Dredger gave them a cold reception. She must be catching on to the fact that her son was a prime suspect.

Her grey eyes were piercing and her speech clipped and dry. She was dressed for outdoors, in a red sweater, sturdy tan slacks, and brown boots. She was not interested in staying inside while this was happening.

"He's in the parlor," Gail Dredger said, her face tightening as she led them to the room. "I'll be with the horses."

Grasso heard the clump of her boots on the hardwood floor as she headed outside.

Gail Dredger might be protective of her son. She might be afraid that her son was a murderer. Whatever her opinions were, she was keeping them to herself.

Kevin sat in a brown brocade winged chair, the size of which made him look small. He crossed his feet, then uncrossed them again. His eyes searched both of them, trying to figure out where he stood.

"Good morning, Mr. Dredger." Grasso gave him a nod as she took a seat on the sofa opposite him. Ruiz sat on the chair next to Kevin.

"We're here to ask you about your whereabouts and actions on the day of Rosalind Mabrey's murder. And a few other questions."

The man took a deep breath but tried to act casual and at ease, a slight smile on his face. It reminded Grasso of the murderer of the old man in Poe's "The Telltale Heart," acting casual and serving the police tea while the old man's body lay in pieces under the floorboards.

"Certainly. Go ahead and ask me."

"Mr. Dredger, we need you to account for the time after you left Infinitas at 6:45 Wednesday morning. Where did you go?"

"I came back here. To make some calls to customers. I thought I told you this down at the station." He sat still, his hands folded over his knee. Anyone else could have sat in that position and looked relaxed. Dredger looked like a tightly wound spring.

"Your mother told me on Tuesday that you didn't come back till the evening, Mr. Dredger." Ruiz said calmly. "Tell us the truth. Where did you go?"

"Fine. I had a meeting." Dredger blurted out. "I met with my financial advisor. Donald Springer, on First Street. Downtown San Jose. I was making some changes to my investments."

"Thank you." Grasso stepped in. "I'm going to ask you a question, and I want you to tell us the truth. You were trying to convince the executives at Infinitas to back the acquisition of a company called Prismatic. Did you have a financial interest in the acquisition?"

Dredger crossed his feet again. He laughed. "My incentive was for Infinitas to cut costs and become more profitable if that's what you're asking. Who wouldn't want the company they founded to be profitable?"

"Did you receive a deposit in your account from Prismatic in the amount of $25,000 last week? With the promise that you'd receive more if the acquisition was approved?"

Dredger turned red. "That had nothing to do with Rosalind's death. My personal accounts are none of your fucking business. Where did you get this information?"

"We know you've been having financial problems, Mr. Dredger. You would benefit from this acquisition financially. Did Rosalind Mabrey find out about the payoff?"

It happened quickly, but Grasso saw it coming. Dredger stood up and, in a flash, came at her, his fist clenched.

He was a couple of feet from Grasso when she plunged forward, wrapped her arms around his calves, and took him down. There were advantages to being lower to the ground.

Ruiz had his gun out and told the man to roll over, face down. The man lay spread eagle on his mother's antique Persian carpet.

Shaking a bit, Grasso got out the cuffs and stood over him, securing the man's hands behind his back as Dredger threw out every curse word she knew and some she didn't.

She read him his rights, as Ruiz called an MVPD car for backup.

Gail Dredger watched silently from atop a horse in the corral as her son was escorted to the back of the patrol car.

Her face showed no emotion as her scowling son got into the car.

"That could have gone worse." Grasso settled into the passenger seat, happy for Ruiz to drive as she decompressed and tried to calm her racing pulse. "It's not like we weren't warned by his wife."

Ruiz turned onto Foothill Road as they headed back to Monte Verde. "Angie was able to give us the details on the deposit. We'll talk to the financial advisor to verify whether Dredger was meeting with him that morning or not, when he said he was. And maybe we'll find out more about his finances."

Grasso wondered, as they drove, whether Dredger was just being himself. A man under extreme pressure with his finances, reacting just as he was known to in situations like this.

Or if he was feeling trapped because he'd murdered his "obstacle" on a trail two days ago and the police were closing in on the truth.

The afternoon's search didn't give them what they'd hoped to find.

Until mid-afternoon, CSI combed the property's twelve acres, searching the corrals, the barn, stable, and the greenhouse.

There were many knives and sharp tools around the Dredger house and ranch. Ruiz and Grasso searched the kitchen, inspecting every drawer, cupboard, and rack. All were meticulously clean and in their designated spots. According to Gail Dredger, none of them had gone missing.

The musty barn had a tool bench, with a wall of saws above it. Grasso winced at the thought of someone taking a saw to Rosalind Mabrey's neck. None of the tools on the wall had been used for a while, judging by the layer of dust covering them.

The stable's living space was ancient, a low, grey wooden structure that looked like it had been built in the 1930s. It reminded Grasso of the living quarters for the itinerant ranch hands Lennie and George in John Steinbeck's *Of Mice and Men.* Two small rooms had white painted iron cots with old-school striped mattresses.

When they entered the stable bedroom farthest from the main house, it smelled so bad, Grasso started to gag. She stepped out the door and took a deep breath of fresh air outside.

"Must be the room Dredger threw up in," she said when she came back inside.

Ruiz had put a cloth to his mouth, as he opened cupboards and drawers. He pulled out a half-empty bottle of scotch and inspected it with raised eyebrows. He snorted.

"I didn't know Costco had their own brand."

Grasso began pulling out drawers in the small bureau next to the cot. There was a stack of receipts, from a liquor store, Target, and gas stations. A pair of reading glasses.

In the next drawer, she found a leather-bound journal. She pulled it out and began leafing through it.

"Jimmy. Come look at this."

At the back of the journal, there were pages with hand-drawn lines from top to bottom. There were letters at the top of the columns. They looked like acronyms. There were numbers written in the columns, with plus and minus signs.

Jimmy leaned in and ran a finger across the column headings.

"Looks like a ledger to me."

Grasso turned the pages. Stuck to the back inside cover of the book was a yellow post-it note.

Kevin--I don't understand these numbers. What does Angie think of these changes?

Call me. We need to talk.

-D

Ruiz frowned. "I want to know who was getting all Kevin Dredger's money."

There were so many questions about Dredger's actions that had gone unanswered.

"We have him in custody—that's the good news." The smell was getting to Ruiz, and he stepped toward the open door. "But it will be harder to talk to him freely. He'll have an attorney with him."

"He could be released on bail soon, too." Grasso said, with a roll of her eyes. "If anyone wants to post bail for him."

It certainly didn't sound like his mother or wife would be eager to do it.

TWENTY-TWO

Saturday

TOM WANTED TO PLAY HOOKY.

But he had a meeting on-site with his managers to work out Operations priorities for next week, in the light of Rosalind's death.

The outdoors smelled richly of fir trees and fresh-cut grass this morning. He sat in his kitchen drinking an espresso with the back French doors open, looking out onto a clearing in the trees behind his house. It was a beautiful view. He could honestly say he never once took it for granted.

While he looked, a deer came out of the trees and started nibbling on the plants in his backyard. In Monte Verde, especially in the hills, deer were unwelcome pests. They destroyed plants. The Angwins had a hard time keeping them out of the gardens and had devised a natural way to deter them, a smelly mixture involving chili powder and yogurt.

Tom sipped from his tiny cup while he watched the deer make its way tentatively through his yard, nibbling as it went, from the buffet that was his landscaped backyard. It was especially bold to come so near to the house, but it moved so gracefully, he couldn't take his eyes off it. He didn't want it to leave.

Homeowners along the Monte Verde hills resented the animals, but they weren't malicious. They didn't plot and scheme like humans. They didn't hold grudges, blackmail people, or try to cause harm. They were just hungry.

Lightly the animal stepped toward the plants surrounding the deck and began eating. He went to the door and watched the animal as it grazed. For a moment, the deer turned its liquid brown eyes on him and froze in terror. It fled back to the forest on thin, graceful legs.

Tom finished his espresso and thought about calling Langdon. He hadn't gotten to talk to him when he'd stopped in for his short and unsuccessful meeting with Rosalind on Tuesday.

Tom didn't hate the man. To be fair, Langdon was good at what he did. Langdon had played a more important part in Infinitas's initial success than he had.

He heard a knock on the front door. The contractors were here to begin demolition on the downstairs bathroom. He let the men in, and they clumped noisily down the stairs, to make even more noise.

He'd get more peace at Infinitas. And after fielding a series of phone calls this morning, his to-do list had grown.

He'd call Langdon when he got home.

Downtown San Jose wasn't busy at 9 a.m. on a Saturday. Once Ruiz got into town, he parked at a metered spot on First Street and found himself a cup of good, strong coffee. While he stood in front of the coffee shop, he looked over at the Adobe Almaden building a block away, with its series of spinning circles that glowed at the top—called the San Jose Semaphore. Each wheel had four possible settings; together the four wheels transmitted a message in code. Since it was installed, there had been two coded messages—which had been solved by the public. It fascinated Ruiz. If he wasn't busy solving other things, he'd be up for trying to crack the code himself.

He entered the office building, looking for Donald Springer's office. Kevin Dredger's financial advisor must be making a nice profit.

Donald Springer was on the third floor, in a posh office with lots of dark, leather furniture. Springer was the only one in the office and came out of his door to greet him in the waiting room.

"Detective Ruiz." He extended his hand and Ruiz shook it. "I'm glad you called. I've been worried about this situation for a while. Let's go in my office and talk."

Springer's office looked out onto the busy streets below, but its location didn't provide much of a view, other than the windows of the building directly across the street. Unlike San Francisco, San Jose was short on scenic views.

"Kevin Dredger met with you last Wednesday—that's correct?"

Springer leaned back in his seat and looked down at the calendar on his desk.

"Wednesday. 8 a.m. No, wait—it was 8:15 a.m. by the time he got here. We don't normally open the office till 9 a.m., but he requested an early meeting."

Ruiz raised an eyebrow. Kevin Dredger said he'd met with Springer at 7 a.m. He claimed he'd gone directly from Infinitas to his advisor meeting.

"Mr. Dredger said he met with you at 7 a.m."

"He was off by an hour. At 7 a.m., I was home in my shower." Springer smirked.

Another piece of information that made things look bad for Kevin Dredger. But Ruiz had a few more things to ask Springer.

"When we searched Dredger's mother's house—where

he's staying—we found a notebook with some figures in it. And a note from you."

Ruiz had taken a photo of the ledger and the post-it note. He passed his phone over to Springer.

Springer's face turned dark. "I was concerned about his financial decisions. I was ready to call his wife. Kevin was making strange moves with his funds. They seemed irresponsible."

"Mr. Springer, do you have access to Kevin's account information—deposits and withdrawals?"

Springer nodded warily.

"Can you access that information now—to let me know about deposits Kevin has made to certain accounts?"

Springer cleared his throat, then looked at him . "That would require a search warrant to let you have that information, Detective Ruiz."

"That's correct, Mr. Springer." Ruiz nodded. "But the reason I'm asking you about account information is that Kevin Dredger is being blackmailed. He's been paying large amounts of money to someone for the past year. I want to find out who or what he's been giving money to."

Donald Springer looked alarmed. He swiveled in his chair to the mouse and keyboard on his desk. His eyebrows pulled together as he moved his mouse to open a spreadsheet.

"Now that I understand the situation, what he's been doing makes more sense." Springer said distractedly as he pulled up another window on his screen. "And from my conversations with Angie Dredger, I'm sure she doesn't know this has been going on."

Ruiz waited, while Springer highlighted a column of numbers on the screen.

Springer looked up from the screen as if he were considering what to do. Then he pulled off a post-it note and wrote down some lines of information.

He handed it to Ruiz.

GALADRIEL INC
CAYMAN ISLANDS
08/31
10/24
12/29
01/20
3/29
05/13

"I'll have to go back and check, but from what I remember, these transactions correspond pretty closely to when Kevin called to make changes to his investments."

"I'll verify this with Angie Dredger. She may be giving you a call."

Springer frowned. "I can't imagine why anyone would blackmail Kevin. He's been a good client. This worries me. He's been with me for almost twenty years, and everything's been straightforward. At least until the summer of last year."

"Thank you, Mr. Springer."

They had an account name. Now they just needed to find a connection.

TWENTY-THREE

THAT NIGHT, Ruiz had the house to himself.

There had been a few more arguments between him and Reyna on the subject, but he finally agreed to let Jacky go to the sleepover.

Jacky had written him a letter, in which he explained why he wanted to go.

Jacky's handwriting was nearly impossible to read. But he'd illustrated the letter with two drawings—one of Jacky and Colin lying in sleeping bags, with ZZZs over their heads. Then a picture of friends, with giant golf clubs in their hands dancing around a mini-golf windmill with smiles on their faces.

Ruiz gave in.

Jacky could go to the birthday party and sleepover. The night before, the boy packed his duffle bag with pajamas and clothes and placed his sleeping bag near the door. The excitement in his eyes was so intense, Ruiz got teary-eyed. He should have known how important this was to the kid.

Reyna told him that morning that she was going out with a friend that night. Ruiz knew she didn't want to be alone with him. He knew from the phone call he overheard, this was a woman. Someone in the school PTA.

He'd be on his own, and he felt okay with that.

He'd taken some notes on the case and had gotten an update from Grasso at the end of the day. He wanted to do some research on his own into Rosalind Mabrey and the beginnings of Infinitas twenty years ago. And on Galadriel Inc.

Ruiz sat down in front of the computer at the kitchen desk, with a bowl of popcorn and a beer.

At least he didn't have to fight anyone for the computer tonight. With Reyna's approval, Ruiz had kept the family access to one basic desktop computer, which sat on a desk in the kitchen. Jacky could use it for 120 minutes per week, as long as his homework was done.

Reyna also wanted to use it, and after what had happened back in January, Ruiz was glad the computer was in the kitchen, and anyone passing by could see the screen.

Though Reyna still had her phone. If she wanted to talk to Mario Flores or anyone else, he couldn't do a damn thing about it. He'd drive himself crazy if he monitored everything she did and everyone she talked to. He didn't need that kind of hell.

He wondered what would happen—him worrying less and less about whether she would leave until he didn't care anymore. Or her actually moving out. It was wishful thinking on his part that the first of those would happen.

He finished the bowl of popcorn, then downed most of his beer.

Ten years ago, Reyna had been his brother Mateo's girlfriend—barely eighteen and living with Mateo in a trash heap of a house in south San Jose that they shared with eight other people. The cops came to arrest Mateo for selling meth. Reyna still had one of Mateo's phones.

She'd found his number in Mateo's contacts and called, asking if he could help her.

Ruiz brought her back to his place and let her have his bed while he slept on the couch. He helped her find an affordable studio apartment, and she started a job as a receptionist, thanks to one of the MVPD dispatchers who put in a good word with her sister's company. Later Ruiz helped her to get into a dental hygienist program. She'd excelled at it.

Within a year, they were married. Maybe she'd said yes because he was the clean, responsible version of Mateo. But she'd made the choice herself. He hadn't put a gun to her head.

But he knew—he'd always loved her. He'd seen her grow and take on the finances, saving and even investing. She took to it naturally. Eventually they were able to buy a house.

Five years ago, they'd been able to put money down on the two-bedroom fixer-upper in Santa Clara. That first year, he'd spent weekends re-tiling and installing new plumbing in the bathroom, replacing windows and drywall, clearing weeds and debris out of the backyard, and pouring a patio. Reyna had scrubbed the house mercilessly. She painted and decorated, hunted at garage sales for furnishings. Their home was made of parts of both of them. Just like Jacky.

He wondered how you separated the home from the marriage.

The affair had devastated him. Her words, spoken so calmly, ricocheted in his head for months: *I've never loved you.*

He could let it destroy him, let it fill him with anger and bitterness. But that would hurt him more than it did Reyna.

Or Mario Flores.

Ruiz couldn't say he didn't want to hurt the man. As a detective, he saw the worst in people. He saw the greed, lust and desperation that caused people to commit serious crimes.

In the past four months he'd seen that was wasn't much different than the people he arrested.

If he was alone in a room with Flores and knew he wouldn't get caught, what would he do? Would he get revenge?

He could relate to what he'd seen in the past two days with the Infinitas gang. People were assholes and hurt each other. Yet they were chained together, tied to each other like he remembered having his leg tied to his brother's in church picnic three-legged races as a kid.

What someone else did affected you. One person could bring you down quickly.

Ruiz had an advantage over Reyna—he knew what he wanted. She was still looking, strolling through the aisles of life, picking through the merchandise for anything that would make her happy. Thinking that the answer was something or someone new.

Maybe it was years of police work, but he'd developed a cynical side.

That new thing or person in your life was never going to fix things.

Tonight he'd look up background on Infinitas and its four founders if only to have straight in his mind the different people, their backgrounds, and what they'd been up to since the company's founding.

The Infinitas website was clearly set up for selling productivity software. From his first click to enter the site, he saw slim, good-looking men and women in office settings with lots of white, shiny surfaces and glowy lighting. They had smiles on their faces as they used the software to manage their workflow.

Hip, funky music with a bass groove played as these people entered info on their spreadsheets. Potential customers could see that the software was so much fun to use, it made you want to dance through your workday.

Under the heading, OUR STORY, Ruiz read that three engineering students—Rosalind, Kevin, and Tom--had worked on the software as a project before graduating from Stanford.

Once they graduated, they joined up with a business major, Philip Langdon, who wrote up a marketing plan. The plan and the product were so well received, the company received funding, even in a year when venture capitalists were starting to sour on tech companies as investments.

There was a photo of them--The Fantastic Four--standing together on a stage, hands linked, their arms raised high. It must have been early in the company's history because the four of them glowed with youth and optimistic smiles.

The website gave him the positive spin that Infinitas put on its story. He wondered if there was a darker side. So he googled *Infinitas bad reviews.*

There wasn't much to draw on. The main complaint was the price of the system. Most reviewers said the software was easy to use and did improve productivity--whatever the hell *that* meant—but it was too expensive for what you got. Some reviewers recommended less expensive options or separate systems that could be pieced together to do the same thing.

Ruiz couldn't imagine doing his job without the help of computers, databases, and digital forms, but he had zero interest in how it all worked.

Didn't know.

Didn't care.

He skipped the details about å Infinitas's software and moved on.

He did a search on each one of the four founders. A search for Rosalind Mabrey produced a list of her accomplishments and the website for Laurelwood, the foundation she'd started for her nature education and retreat center. There was a short article in the Monte Verde Patch about a city council meeting where Rosalind Mabrey presented her plan for the center. It was met with "vocal protests" from neighbors. One of the city councilmen wrote an editorial about Laurelwood's stubborn disregard for its neighbors in the Monte Verde hills.

Tom Weber's search turned up his purchase of fifteen acres in the Monte Verde hills. He'd also written a few articles for an organic farming magazine. He was married for five years to a woman named Sonia Forrester, who worked for Apple in Cupertino. They'd divorced ten years ago.

Kevin Dredger was featured in a recent article about software engineering management. Three years ago, he won an industry award for software innovation, and he stood holding a plaque, Angie pressed in next to him with a proud smile. Ruiz wasn't going to read the details of the award because they'd put him to sleep for sure. But the Kevin Dredger in the photo looked younger and more content than the man they'd interviewed and arrested two days ago. Kevin's face was now doughier, the ruts in it deeper, his eyes glassy.

He looked at the photo of Dredger and wondered what had happened. What had this guy done, that somebody could extort so much money from him? And after Rosalind fired him from Infinitas and his wife kicked him out—did keeping somebody quiet really matter?

Dredger should stop with the payments. Let the blackmailer do his worst. The life the man was leading now was killing him.

Unless Kevin Dredger had done something really, really bad. Or illegal.

Something his wife and children, his mother could never know about.

PTA president Mia Gerson was stylish and confident, the wife of a tech vice president.

Her clothes were simply cut and hung loosely on her thin frame; Reyna recognized them from a boutique at Valley Fair

Mall. When Mia moved or spoke, it was with an relaxed assurance, never hurried. The more time she spent with Mia at PTA events, the more Reyna Ruiz wanted to be just like her.

At the school landscaping subcommittee meeting Reyna led last week, Mia had mentioned she'd like to get together to chat about projects for the next school year.

Mia loved what Reyna had done with the school's landscaping and was impressed she'd managed to get donations from local nurseries.

Once she knew Jacky was going to Colin's sleepover, Reyna texted Mia and asked if Friday night would work.

Reyna felt a little flutter in her stomach when she saw her response:

I'm free that night. Thank you for initiating!

Reyna Ruiz didn't want to be at home.

She didn't want to see the hurt in Jimmy's eyes. He could put on a smile when he came in the door, and she could still see it. It hung heavy in the air between them when they were together. She could smell it on him like the residue of cigarette smoke.

She'd go out with Mia and leave it behind.

She justified it. *Maybe Jimmy will feel relieved, too.*

She and Mia met at a Spanish restaurant in downtown San Jose that served tapas. Reyna loved being able to have a little bit of everything rather than choosing one item on the menu. She added the prices up in her head, careful not to go over the budget she'd set for herself.

Mia was in charge of event planning for a tech company and spent most of the meal talking about the creative conferences and dinners she'd planned. She arranged celebrity appearances and came up with ideas for holiday events: costume parties at museums in San Francisco; a date night at the opera for executives, a daylong event with huge tents erected on the beach in Santa Cruz, so employees and their families could play at the beach, stay out of the sun, and enjoy a buffet of Hawaiian food.

By the end of dinner, Reyna wanted to live Mia's life. She didn't mind the dental office and enjoyed the work she did. But Mia's job was an endless series of parties.

The waitress brought the bill once they'd decided they couldn't eat any more. Mia laid down her card on the tray.

"My treat, Reyna."

Reyna scrambled to find her purse and pull out her wallet. "No, Mia—"

Before Reyna could pull out her card, the waiter swooped by and took the tray with Mia's card. Mia waved a hand dismissively.

"Don't worry about it. I had fun tonight. My husband took the kids to a Sharks game, which is *so* not my thing. I'm glad you texted."

Reyna loved going to Sharks games with Jimmy and Jacky. She made a note never to mention it.

Mia took a sip from her water glass. "Hey, I was wondering, Reyna—"

Reyna looked up suddenly.

"I'm looking to hire an assistant in the next few months." Mia smiled warmly. "You seem like a natural for this kind of work. I think we'd work well together. Would you be interested?"

Reyna took in her breath. She didn't want to gush, but she was excited at the idea of doing this kind of work. How did she tell Mia that without sounding too eager?

"I might be interested," she said, taking a careful sip of her wine. "Can you tell me a little bit about the job? I'd like to know more about your company."

Reyna surprised herself with how calm and businesslike she sounded.

Mia answered her questions, and Reyna finished the last

of her wine and thought about this possibility. She'd asked about the salary; it was lower than what she was making now. She would have to negotiate if she were to accept the job. After all, she'd need a good salary for when she left Jimmy.

After the last four months at the dental office with her gossiping coworkers, Reyna was ready for a fresh start. Working with Mia, she could start a new job where no one knew her. Her past erased.

"I'll start interviewing in the next two weeks. Get me your resume, and I'll get back to you with a time." Mia touched her arm, her eyes bright with excitement.

"I'm getting excited about this possibility, Reyna. I know it's a career change for you, but you've done fantastic work with the PTA. You'd be a great addition to the team."

They left the restaurant after a hug and Reyna's promise that she'd send a resume, which she'd have to figure out how to put together in the next couple of days. She had the one she wrote for her dental hygienist interviews on the kitchen computer. She'd revise it. Make it show she was qualified for this new job.

Reyna walked the two blocks to her car, down the narrow downtown side street, feeling light on her feet—from the big glass of Spanish tempranillo and the excitement of a new opportunity. She imagined what it would be like, working at a corporate headquarters. Dressing up every day instead of wearing scrubs. Should she tell Jimmy? She decided against it. Not for a while. She needed to put some things in place first.

She unlocked the Range Rover and sat for a moment in the driver's seat, her head against the headrest. She checked her phone for any messages from Jacky, and there were none. Just as she thought. He was getting along fine at Colin's.

It was 10 p.m. She turned the key to start the car. No response.

At first, she wasn't worried. She'd been through this many times.

She waited the usual 30 seconds and tried again. Nothing. She gave it two more unsuccessful tries.

She looked up to see that the people walking down the street past her car were changing—from couples walking side by side, coming back from restaurants to men on their own. Some stopped to poke through trashcans.

A big man stood on the sidewalk, watching her with glazed eyes.

Panic gnawed at her. She turned the key again. A click, then nothing. Dead. Frantically she kept turning it, though she knew it wouldn't do any good. Her luck with the Range Rover had run out.

Jimmy hated that she'd bought the car. He warned her it would be a lemon. The mechanic he'd taken it to had told him the same thing. Since then, it had gone through quite a few repairs. Jimmy said they needed to hold off on any more until they could afford it.

Who to call.

Mia would be almost home by now. She couldn't call her and make her come back.

Jimmy—no. The thought made her feel sick to her stomach. Pride, maybe. Not wanting to admit that yet again she needed his help. For a car he'd warned her not to buy.

Her parents? They'd ask why she hadn't called Jimmy, who was closer.

Reyna sat in the car, at a stalemate with herself, as she felt the night's chill through her jacket. A man stumbled by, his face pocked with meth scabs. His features reminded her of Mateo, whom she hadn't seen in ten years. Since the day he was arrested.

She went back to her phone, and on impulse, punched in the number. She'd erased the contact from her phone, but it had only been four months.
She knew the number by heart.

TWENTY-FOUR

Saturday
10:30 p.m.

DOWNTOWN GREW EVEN DARKER as Reyna waited in the car.

The street was noisier now, with the sounds that started up after visitors left for the quiet streets in the suburbs.

A big, fat sedan cruised slowly past, its bass turned up so high the music shook her seat. A group of young guys walked by, saw her in the window, and hooted at her. One of them pushed down on the Range Rover's hood and made the car rock.

She checked her phone again, wanting to text *Are you on your way?* She stopped herself. She would not show fear.

When she looked up from her phone, she saw the big man still standing on the sidewalk. His skin was wrinkled and mottled. Slowly his mouth turned up into a smile. Then he approached her window.

Without thinking, she reacted. She couldn't roll down her window without power. She shoved open the driver's side door with such force it hit him and knocked him back. She shrieked with a warrior-like fury she didn't know she was capable of.

"GET THE FUCK AWAY FROM MY CAR!"

The man's eyes widened in fear and he raised his hands, which were shaking. He turned around and stumbled down the street.

Soon after, she heard a door slam behind her car. Mario Flores approached the passenger side of the Range Rover and tapped the window. She unlocked the door and let him in.

"Jesus." He shook his head, his eyes wide. There was a faint smile on his face. "I just witnessed *that*. I don't know why you're scared. They should be afraid of *you*."

Mario Flores looked tired. She wondered if she'd woken him up.

"Here's how this is going to go, Reyna. You're going to call Triple A right now. You've got a card with you?"

She pulled it out of her wallet and punched in the 800 number on her phone. Once she got past the hold and explained her situation, she was told the wait would be 30 minutes.

"I'll stay here only until they come." There was no emotion. No kindness or interest in those warm brown eyes. Nothing like before. The loss wore away her thrill at seeing him again.

He went back to his phone, texting someone.

She almost whispered it. "Thank you, Mario."

"You should not be in this area alone at night."

He spoke clearly and unemotionally as if he were dealing with her in a police capacity. She'd missed him. Maybe she'd wanted something from him tonight. He was tired and angry, but she looked at his chest, his arms, and remembered how they felt when she was lying on him. She remembered the smell of his cologne and his warm breath on her face.

"You shouldn't have called me." He was angry. "Why the hell didn't you call Jimmy?"

Her face turned pink, and she turned away from him. "I didn't feel comfortable with that."

"Why didn't you let him know? Were you out with some guy?"

Her defenses kicked in. "I was with Mia, our school PTA president. Jacky's at a sleepover."

"Reyna. I don't know why you felt you had to call me—" His eyes weren't warm and kind now. They were burning into her face.

"You live close by."

"You are not supposed to be with me. I am not supposed to be with you." He gave her a glare. "This never happened."

The evening had been wonderful. A night out with Mia. The promise of a new job. Now, this.

Mario looked at his Apple watch. "We have 20 more minutes till the truck gets here. I'm going to tell you some hard things. Things you don't want to hear. I've done a lot of thinking in the past four months.

"I hit rock bottom when I got together with you. Lost my standing in the department because I wasn't doing my job. Because for a while, I was obsessed with you. I let down my team. It was with Jimmy's help that I solved the Karl Schuler case."

Reyna took her hands off the wheel and looked over at Flores. "I cared a lot about you, Mario."

"I know some things about you, Reyna. You have a history of hooking up with douchebags. There was Mateo. There was me—because that's what I was. Maybe still am."

She hoped and prayed AAA would come soon. Mario was right; she didn't want to hear any of this. She wanted to go— well, she wasn't sure where she wanted to go. But she didn't want to be here, in the car with this man, hearing this. She didn't want to be home with Jimmy either. For the past four months, she'd felt bad about herself. She wasn't happy staying with him, yet she felt she couldn't leave.

Mia's encouragement to apply for the job had lifted her spirits—for the first time in months. Maybe this was her way out.

"Jacky is a great kid, I'm sure." Flores continued, as he looked out of the car window. "But the best thing in your life right now is Jimmy. For some reason, he cares about you. Quit treating him like shit."

The words hit her like he'd just slapped her across the face.

"Don't tell me what to do!" She screamed it. He would not make her decisions for her.

"You were in this with me, Mario. *You* treated Jimmy badly yourself—and seemed to have a really good time doing it. You think you've got your life all figured out now, and you feel like you can lecture me? I don't want to hear it."

He rubbed his face and looked out the passenger window at a guy picking aluminum cans out of the trash and throwing them into a battered shopping cart.

He turned his head back to her, a weary look on his face. "He rescued you when Mateo was arrested, and you've never forgiven him. Jimmy could never be someone you actually cared about, just because of your fucking pride."

"Get out!" Her face burned. "Get out of my car, you motherfucker!"

"Yeah. Fine, Reyna. But if you ever felt anything for me, do me a favor. Make a decision. Tell Jimmy it's over and call a divorce attorney. Or get some counseling together and decide if what you've got is worth saving. But don't avoid him—he's worth more than that. You're both going to be miserable, and Jacky will pick it up. I know because that happened to me. I was that kid."

He got out of the car and slammed the door. He paced on the sidewalk, picking up his phone to text someone.

Within minutes, Reyna saw the flash of yellow lights in the rearview mirror. The tow truck was here. Tears stung her eyes, but she willed them to stop. Mario went to talk to the mechanic.

The truck backed into the space in front of her, beeping as it slowly moved into place. She stepped out of the car and went to stand on the sidewalk. Shivering, she folded her arms tightly against her chest. She felt colder and sadder than when she'd sat in the car by herself.

Mario talked with the mechanic, even laughed as they chatted back and forth. Then he ran his hand along the front hood to find the latch. He flipped it open, and the mechanic moved in to work under the hood for a few minutes. Then he called out for Mario to start the car.

Mario slid into the seat of the Range Rover, and soon the motor was revving.

Reyna texted Jimmy and told him she'd stayed out later than she thought, and that the car had a hard time starting, but she was fine. She'd be home in fifteen minutes.

As she got back into the car, Mario was on the sidewalk, talking on his phone with someone named Dawn. He assured her he'd call back soon. As a low rumble of jealousy passed through her, she wondered who Dawn was.

With a wave to the mechanic and no goodbye to her, Mario Flores walked back to his car and drove off.

TWENTY-FIVE

Sunday

EARLY SUNDAY MORNING, Ruiz left the house as Reyna slept in.

He got onto 280, which was nearly traffic-free, and headed south. He ended up in an area of San Jose he'd become familiar with back in January.

He turned onto the expressway where the aviation pioneer Karl Schuler had been shot on New Year's.

He'd watched Karl Schuler die. He'd looked into the 92-year-old's twisted car, wrapped around a eucalyptus tree on the shoulder, and heard his strange last words. That week he'd met 76-year-old Duke Sorenson, a retired aviation engineer. Duke was someone worth keeping in his life.

The sweet, greasy smell of donuts hit Ruiz in the face as soon as he parked in front of Donut Haven. The smell promised amazing things, and he wished he had more of an appetite this morning.

Kang, the owner, was busy behind the counter, boxing up donut dozens in pink boxes and shouting out greetings to his regulars. His daughter, Eliana Kang, poured coffee and rang people up at the register. Eliana flashed him a smile when she saw him and turned to pour coffee into a large Styrofoam cup. She passed it to him at the end of the counter. After these meetups with Duke, he was now part of the club.

Ruiz spotted Duke—white hair, pale face—sitting by himself at the back of the shop.

Duke Sorenson looked the same as when he'd seen him last. He sat in his faded, 1960s-era windbreaker, his Styrofoam cup, and the usual old-fashioned donut on a napkin in front of him. There was no gang of retired aviation engineers sitting around the table with him today. Duke and the donut gang that met here weekly had all been good friends with Schuler.

When Ruiz approached the table, Duke's face crinkled into a grin.

"You're getting skinny, son," Duke said when Ruiz sat down in a bright orange chair across from him. "You okay?"

"Must be the exercise. Jacky and I've been biking." Ruiz nodded as he sat down and began telling Duke about their rides.

"I've been busy." Duke's pale blue eyes were magnified behind his aviator glasses. "I got tired of sitting around at home by myself. I'm volunteering with the kids at East Point, where Karl used to tutor. The kids say I'm not as much fun as Karl. But they like me okay."

"Karl would be hard to beat," Ruiz smiled at the white-haired man. Even though he'd only met Karl Schuler in the last few minutes of his life, he came to know him through his friends and family. The scientist had had the curiosity and heart of a child.

Duke leaned forward in the circus-orange-colored chair, a mysterious look in his eyes. He had news to tell.

"You're not going to believe this, Jimmy. Randall Mulvaney and I are thinking of starting a business."

Ruiz laughed in disbelief. "You're kidding me."

Randall Mulvaney, Schuler's grandson, was a young hipster with an attitude. Back in January, Duke couldn't stand him. The two had made their peace when they planned the flight to disperse Karl Schuler's ashes over the Pacific Ocean.

"C'mon, Duke. You've been keeping this to yourself? Give me the details."

"We scatter ashes. We've done it twice since we did Karl's. I got a couple of pilots to help us." Duke smiled proudly. "I arrange the flight and do a kind of service for the departed. Randall makes the fabric slings for the ashes, so we can release them into the air, with no blowback into the plane."

"Randall." Ruiz grunted in disbelief. "The guy with the man bun. Full of himself."

Duke cracked a smile. "He's okay once you get to know him. He and Shayante had me over for dinner. They're good kids. We're not making a lot of money with this. But people seem happy with how we're doing it. And I get to fly."

It made him happy to see Duke so excited. Ruiz leaned back in the uncomfortable, low-backed fiberglass chair and took a sip of coffee.

He hoped he had the energy and enthusiasm to be out doing things like Duke in thirty-plus years. He hoped this tense time in his life would a distant memory by then.

"How's Reyna? And Jacky?" Duke smiled, his large blue eyes focused on him.

Ruiz shrugged. He didn't want to talk about it. Thinking about it was painful enough; saying it out loud made it real. He was going to lose his home. And there was nothing he could do about it.

But Duke Sorenson was here, sitting in front of him, listening. He wanted to hear about his life because he cared about him.

If he had anyone dad-like in his life, it was this pale white man, looking at him with kind, curious eyes. Duke was nothing like his own abusive father. For all he knew, his father was dead. Or living somewhere in Southern California. Maybe on the streets. Maybe with a new family. He'd never been curious enough to find out.

"Reyna had an affair." Ruiz tossed it off casually as if he were talking about the Giants losing a game. "I guess you could say I'm in a holding pattern. And I want to make sure it doesn't affect Jacky."

"Well, *shoot*." Duke looked down at his hands and frowned for some time, dumbfounded. "I'm sorry to hear it, Jimmy. I can't say I was any prize of a husband to Joanne. But I wouldn't think Reyna would have anything to complain about."

Ruiz regretted he'd said anything. Telling Grasso was one thing and even that was hard. He never talked this way with guys. Duke looked sad now, troubled by what he'd just heard. Ruiz was willing to bet that men of Duke's generation talked even less about these things.

"Reyna has a lot of complaints." Ruiz rubbed his face and turned to focus on the cold remains of his coffee. He took a sip and gave up on it.

"What are you going to do, Jimmy?" Duke looked at him, wide-eyed.

Ruiz shook his head and stared out at a family a few tables away. A man, woman, and their two kids sat eating donuts and laughing. The daughter's stuffed pony sat on the table next to her. The father was offering a pink, sprinkled donut to it.

"I'm not sure what to do. If she leaves, it'll be worse." Ruiz hated hearing his own voice. It wavered, sounded weak. It scared him.

"I guess it's all how you look at it." Duke had a soft smile on his face. "Maybe when it's over, you'll feel relief. There won't be anything else to be afraid of."

For a moment, Ruiz let himself imagine that. Not feeling anxious anymore. Feeling free, as if disaster wasn't stalking him like a hitman. Then something in his mind slid down like a steel plate door, and he couldn't see beyond his life right now.

Duke must have seen that. He paused for a moment, then changed the subject and began talking about a physics experiment he was planning for the students at CenterPoint. About blowing something up.

Ruiz's phone buzzed. He looked down to see a text from Grasso about something she wanted him to ask Angie Dredger about.

Duke stood up to give him a hug.

"Hey, if you and Jacky want to ride bikes someplace new, my apartment's right off the Guadalupe Trail. My complex has a path that goes out to Lake Almaden. You could ride around the lake. I walk there a few times during the week."

A new place for he and Jacky to explore. The outdoors had been his go-to for stress relief lately. Jacky was always the one asking to go, but Ruiz was the one who benefitted from it most. He came back feeling better. Lighter.

"Thank you." Ruiz smiled and clapped Duke on the shoulder. "We might take you up on that."

On his way back from the visit with Duke, Ruiz went north on Highway 85 for a visit to Angie Dredger.

She'd confirmed for him that there had been a series of transactions on the statements for Galadriel Inc. When she'd asked him the significance, Ruiz had told her about the blackmail. Angie offered to turn over any information she could find around the house on the transactions or the blackmailer.

Excited, he called Grasso as soon as he got back to his truck and asked if she could meet him at the station.

Grasso was sitting in the interview room when Ruiz got back.

He laid the copy of the statement on the table. She ran her finger over the transfers to the Caymans account.

"Galadriel Inc." Grasso repeated it quietly to herself.

"What's wrong?" Ruiz looked at his partner. She had an odd look on her face. He couldn't interpret it.

"It's a nickname Tom had for Rosalind Mabrey."

"I don't get it." Ruiz shook his head. "Does it mean something?"

"Galadriel is the elf queen of Lothlorien in *Lord of the Rings*." Grasso explained it like it was something everybody knew. "Tom thought Rosalind looked like Galadriel. I've seen the movies. Yeah, she did."

Could the blackmailer be Tom? Why would he give the fake company that name if it would incriminate him? Maybe he didn't think anyone would bother to track down the info for Dredger's transfers.

Did Tom have a thing for Rosalind? Maybe he'd been obsessed with her for years while they worked together at Infinitas. He'd finally made a move on her, and she'd refused him.

"We need to find the connection." Ruiz said, as Grasso stood next to him, lost in thought. "It's got to mean something. We have a name now. I'm going to see what I can find out."

TWENTY-SIX

Monday

"ARE YOU DOING OKAY, TOM?"

Amber Kennedy carried a thick hanging folder into his office and set it on his desk. The young woman looked drained, her lightly freckled skin even paler and her eyes red rimmed. He didn't expect her to stay at Infinitas once Rosalind's office was organized and her projects handed off to a new CEO.

"I thought you should have this. Rosalind's file on projects, ideas, and customer correspondence. She called it her 'Thinking' file. When she had some time, she'd sit down with these and see if there was a way she could implement something."

Tom had gotten calls from Rosalind, which he'd suspected were prompted by this file. She usually called when she had downtime, and he was busy. He'd add the work into his schedule and try to fit in what he could. He felt touched that he was now the recipient of the file. He also suspected that Amber was passing it on to him because she hoped he'd be the next CEO.

Rosalind had a quality that he suspected many CEOs didn't: she thought deeply about things. She listened to customer feedback and mulled it over. Even when things were running smoothly, she looked for ways to make things better—which, he remembered, was one of the goals she'd written in that desert charter twenty years ago.

Even though Roz's ideas made more work for him, they were usually good ideas.

"The management committee is meeting tomorrow. We'll talk to the board next week and make some recommendations. We've got a lot to consider with the loss of Roz and Kevin. Thanks, Amber."

He nodded at her. She'd been through a lot this week.

Amber gave him a sideways look. "Would you be interested in the CEO job? It makes sense, Tom. You're one of the founding members."

Oh, hell no.

He was so close to saying it, but he pulled back and gave a polite response. "I appreciate that, Amber. We'll probably look outside of the company."

"But Tom, you've been here since the beginning. You know the culture. I can't imagine Rosalind being happy with a hack and slash CEO."

Tom pictured Roz sitting in an executive chair in the Great Beyond, watching the selection of a new CEO with a slight, judgmental frown.

In this vision, she was her glowing Galadriel self, and was holding a list of comments in hand. Because, of course, she had opinions on this. She raised her finger and expressed them calmly and eloquently. She'd told him once that she'd done Model United Nations as a teenager. He could see sixteen-year-old Rosalind, beautiful and brilliant, expressing her strongly held ideals calmly and with insistence.

His throat tightened. When he responded, his voice was hoarse and strained.

"She wouldn't want that, Amber."

As he watched her leave, Tom felt despair and guilt come over him. His head pounded and acid reflux ripped at his gut. He dug through his desk for antacid tablets. He'd been popping them like candy.

He'd turned out to be the survivor.

Kevin was in his own hell. Maybe there would be a day when Kevin could come back. But there were many things Kevin needed to think through and work out, and he would need a lot of help.

And Langdon. He hadn't worked for Infinitas for fifteen years but he was still one of them. Their past tied them together. They understood each other from those intense five years together. He needed to talk to him about Kevin.

It wouldn't be appropriate to call Langdon from Infinitas.

He'd call when he got home.

As he drove to his home back in the hills in the fading light, Tom saw signs of the cool, wet spring giving way to a dry summer. Fields of deep, rich green had faded to a dull yellow.

He pulled the Corvette up in front of the garage, slung his messenger bag over his shoulder and got out of his car.

After a warm day, he smelled the grass, golden and dry. It was 7 p.m., but the sun was still up. After today's grief and uncertainty, he was relieved to be home.

Bart and Jennie Angwin sat watching their little girl out on a quilt in front of their house. The girl toddled around the perimeter of the quilt, clutching a big fat strawberry in her hand. She let out a squeal of glee. Her face was smeared with red juice. Bart picked up his daughter, who kissed him, planting a red splotch on his face. Jennie laughed and wiped his cheek with a napkin.

As Tom watched the scene, an overwhelming sense of loss filled him. It sucked the air from his chest. If it hadn't been for

Infinitas—could he have had something like this? He thought of all those hours at work spent fixing things, fighting fires, responding to Rosalind's requests. His face felt hot, as anger surged through him.

As he made his way up his front steps, Bart Angwin ran up and handed him a basket of plump, red strawberries.

"Tom, you gotta try these," Bart said, excitement in his voice. "Our best yet."

Bart and his wife had been experimenting through the winter and spring with a greenhouse outside their house. They'd produced a nice crop of vegetables and were now working on strawberries and some flower varieties Jennie was hoping to sell at a farmer's market.

"These look fantastic, Bart." The berries were deep red and smelled sweet.

Once inside his front door, Tom took a bit of one of the larger ones. The berry was ripe and succulent, with a rich, full flavor. A completely different fruit than the ones in the plastic clamshell containers he'd picked up at the grocery store last week. The flavor took him to a place far away, a humid summer night in Iowa when he was a child. His mom set out a bowl of fresh strawberries on the picnic table in the back-yard with a tray of homemade shortcakes, and that was dinner.

It would be strawberries for dinner tonight, courtesy of the tenants. With crème fraiche. The nice thing about living alone is, you can do whatever the hell you want.

He sank down into his recliner in the living room. Thinking about Infinitas and what would become of it. Thinking of Kevin now under arrest, his future uncertain.

He picked up his phone.

When he answered, Langdon sounded startled, his voice disjointed as if he'd been caught in the middle of something.

"Tom? Tom Weber? Is this you? This is out of the blue."

"Yeah. It's been a hell of a week for us. And I figured

you're still one of us. Infinitas forever, right?" By Langdon's reaction, Tom didn't feel it wasn't true anymore, even as he said it. "I thought I'd touch base."

"You'll have to excuse me. The love of my life was killed last week. It's going to take me a while. I'm having a hard time, Tom."

Langdon had just the right choke in his voice. Back when they'd worked together, Tom wondered whether Langdon felt things like a normal human being. Maybe Langdon was an android, a perfectly programmed marketing robot.

He remembered he and Roz watching Langdon talk to tech journalists at a show in those early years. She laughed as she watched Langdon, mesmerized.

"See how completely authentic he looks as he lies. That face. Those eyes. He's winning everyone over with the future he's writing for us. He schmoozes like no one else. We can use these powers for good, right?"

Tom needed Langdon to understand where Infinitas was right now.

"We're struggling, Phil. We've lost both Roz and Kevin. Kev's gone crazy in the past few months, plotting a mutiny against Roz. The other night, he told me he's being blackmailed."

Tom heard silence, then a laugh.

"You're not serious, are you? Now that I think about it, I'm not surprised. Kevin was so buttoned down. I always got the feeling he was hiding something."

"You wouldn't know anything about it, would you?" Tom asked. There was a mocking quality in Langdon's voice that bothered Tom. Langdon seemed like he was actually enjoying this.

"Kevin can't help himself right now," Tom said, hearing his own voice shake. "In the beginning, all four of us were friends. We helped each other out."

Silence on the line.

"Tom, I have enough going on right now, trying to wrap my mind around my grief. If Kev's got problems, he's brought them on himself. Maybe he even killed Roz. Have you thought of that? The man's been on edge. You know he has these sudden rages. And he doesn't even remember them. Like his meeting with Roz. And that time in Vegas with the girl."

The *girl.*

It was like Tom had been sitting in a dark room, and a bolt of lightning had struck right outside his window. Something came back to him. A story. Words he'd overheard in a hallway. Many years ago.

But what was it?

A chill came over him. Kevin was having a conversation with someone outside his hotel room early that Thursday morning before they went over to work the booth. He'd been upset. Tom had just rushed back that morning from his night with the blue-haired girl at the MGM.

In the stable quarters, he'd asked Kevin why he was being blackmailed. Kevin had mumbled something about "the girl" and "the drive."

Tom needed to find some things out before he talked any more to Langdon. Jog his own memory.

"Kev does have his issues." Tom made it sound like he was starting to see things Langdon's way. "I want to help him, but you could be right. He's gotten himself into this situation. I can't fix things for him."

"We've known about his issues for years, Tom." Langdon's voice took on a patronizing tone. "Glad I could help you out. I know you've got a lot on your plate at Infinitas. So take care of yourself, will you? My heart goes out to you guys."

After Tom hung up, he sank back into the chair. Uneasiness made his chest tighten, as scenes from the past came back to him.

If he had time in his crazy schedule tomorrow.

If--He'd make some calls.

TWENTY-SEVEN

KEVIN DREDGER WAS HUMILIATED.

One day, he was a corporate vice president. Three days later, he was being bailed out of jail by his mother.

Gail Dredger stood in the doorway of his old bedroom, watching him cautiously as if she thought he might attack her.

"I made the bed up again and the bathroom is clean and ready for you. I've washed and folded your clothes. They're in the chest of drawers."

Her lips were tight, her expression wary. She'd probably keep the Giants baseball bat by her bedside tonight.

Jesus, how had this happened?

He hadn't wanted to hurt Detective Grasso. The impulse came over him so fast, he couldn't stop himself. He'd been cornered like an animal. He saw no way out. That feeling had come over him more and more this past year.

The first message had come last August.

The last contact from the blackmailer was a message at 7:20 a.m. on the day Rosalind Mabrey had been murdered.

Spoken by that voice he'd come to dread. The woman's voice was soft and girlish, but her words were harsh. And taunting.

25K in the Cayman account or I tell what you did. How you left the girl there. Dead. What a great father figure you are to your two boys.

He curled up on the newly made bed, his arms wrapped around his legs. He rocked back and forth, side to side, like his son, Samuel, rocked to comfort himself when he was having a meltdown.

It worked better than the alcohol, which had left him dehydrated, sick, and unable to sleep through the night this week. He rocked now until tears came out and rolled back into his ears.

He wanted out. He wondered how bad it would get if he said no. If he blocked the messages on his phone. He would stop the payments. And see what happened.

After all, what did he have left? Angie wanted nothing to do with him. His mother seemed to be losing her remaining patience with him. She gave him a place to stay, but she looked at him as if he'd done something horrible and she was waiting patiently, stoically, for all the details to come out. Or for him to lash out at her just like he did to Detective Grasso. Maybe she was right.

As he lay on the bed, he closed his eyes.

He relived the drive in the desert one more time.

He had his own memories of that night in Nevada. The woman's messages filled in parts he couldn't seem to remember.

That night the moon cast an eerie silver light over the mountains. He and the guys from GuardWare had driven back from the brothels in Pahrump in their rental cars and pulled off the road on the way back, stumbling out into the night to take a piss and look at the stars, clear bursts of white-hot light in the sky.

He'd hooked up with a girl at a bar in Pahrump and she'd agreed to come with them. He was drunk and the country music was loud at the bar, but he thought he'd heard her name was Annalisa. She had long, blonde hair, almost white.

While they were pulled over, he and Annalisa took a bottle of whiskey and sat out under the stars. He was pretty sure he'd fallen asleep because when he woke up, the sky was pink. Annalisa was leaning into him. She looked like she was asleep, but when he moved, her whole weight fell against him.

He put a hand on her chest. It did not rise. Jesus, she was dead. *Dead.*

A few of the GuardWare guys sat on a rock, passing a joint. He called to them that the girl who'd come with them was dead. They had to get help. They couldn't just leave her.

He tried to stand up, but he stumbled as he ran back toward the cars parked by the side of the road. The guys leaning against the cars laughed as he pulled himself up, his face scraped from landing facedown.

He screamed and fought off the guys, but they picked him up and set him down in the back seat. They took off in the faint, pre-dawn light, headed for Vegas.

Leaving behind a shock of white that shone like moonlight. He could still see it, from where they'd parked.

By the time they'd gotten back to the hotel, he was fully sober. He splashed his face with water. He scrubbed his face and hands. He thought about calling the police and telling them what had happened.

He'd be arrested. The architect of the newly released Infinitas product line, a murderer. After the big, successful launch, the company would be in the news for all the wrong reasons.

Had he hurt her? He got that way sometimes. Violent. He didn't always remember how it happened. It was some impulse in him he couldn't control. Maybe he'd gotten drunk and had hurt Annalisa.

Jesus, maybe he'd killed her.

Last summer he received the first call. A woman's voice telling him she knew what he'd done in the desert twenty years ago.

So it began.

TWENTY-EIGHT

Tuesday
6 p.m.

ROSALIND MABREY'S murder had put life at Infinitas on pause.

As the one in charge of keeping the day-to-day machine running, Tom Weber was relieved that the pace of meetings, training, and special projects had slowed.

He and the remaining executive team met daily to take up the slack without Kevin and Rosalind.

As a team, they took a pragmatic approach to continuing to operate through the loss of their CEO and head of software engineering. Maybe it was because of her experience with Langdon, but Rosalind had tried to build one value into the company culture: leave your ego at the door. The small group that met, even the blustery Blake Hennessey, seemed so far to be working together for the best interests of the company.

Things would change. There would be a new CEO eventually.

Infinitas, the company that he and his friends had formed

twenty years ago, would go on. Hell, maybe it would live up to its name and survive them all.

Tom left early, after checking off his list of items for the day.

He'd been driving the Corvette to work this week instead of the Prius. It made him feel good.

It had been a stupid purchase. He'd bought it to impress Sonia years ago after he'd accumulated a good amount in the bank. Not his style. He'd wanted something fancy to pick her up in. He got it in red since one of her favorite songs was "Little Red Corvette" by Prince.

Sonia hadn't been impressed, but she liked going for drives with him in it. He'd kept it covered in the wooden shed on his property until this week.

Tonight, as the sun sank down behind the coastal hills, he wanted to drive up Interstate 280 to San Francisco. He wanted to follow the curves of one of the most beautiful drives in the Bay Area and feel the car's response. He wanted to look out at the lights on the peninsula, gems scattered across the landscape.

This week had been a personal hell for him. Rosalind, then Dredger, a drunken mess, with his story of being blackmailed. Then Langdon, acting amused at all of this when he told him.

Tom wanted to see, not feel.

The gate on the Infinitas parking garage opened for him with a lurching creak and he pulled out of the lot. When he came to the street, he hit the gas with a vengeance.

That's how you make an exit out of work.

He made his way down Arastradero and pulled onto 280 North. Most of the traffic was heading south. He moved into the left lane, feeling power surge through his body as the car accelerated.

He loved this land. Everything about the Bay Area—the hills, the bridges, the tiny local lakes, the massive redwoods, and the bay opening its mouth to French kiss the Pacific Ocean. The menthol smell of the eucalyptus trees, everywhere, from Stanford and up the peninsula.

He'd adopted this place as his home as soon as he'd moved here from Iowa to go to college. This place won him over. He stayed through the summers, and once he'd become part of Infinitas, there was no reason to go home.

He opened the window and smelled the fresh, damp air. As he wound along 280, following the earthquake fault that brought down a city in 1906, this land was his consolation.

Consolation for the regrets. For chaining himself to work for twenty years. For believing the lie that a product was more important than the people in his life and then making that choice every day.

Tom had realized something about working in the valley.

No matter how hard you work. No matter your brilliance. They will never put a little plaque on the desk commemorating you when you leave or die. They will just find someone else to sit at your desk.

Tonight he felt the heavy weight of the losses—Sonia, Rosalind, and the fellowship of the Fantastic Four, whatever that dream had meant. It had seemed so important to them all at the time when it was ideas shared over beers.

Tom followed the freeway as it wound north.

As he went into a curve, he touched the brake to ease into it. Was he that tired? It didn't slow him down, so he pushed harder.

Holy shit.

He struggled to control the car as he barreled out of the curve too fast. He downshifted then found an opening in traffic and careened into the slow lane.

He needed to get off the freeway soon or pull over to the shoulder. He wasn't an automotive expert, but he knew something was wrong. He'd taken the Corvette in just a few months ago. They'd checked his brakes, and they were fine.

When the highway sloped down into another curve, he knew he had to brake or he'd ram the car in front of him. He jammed his foot down onto the brake as hard as he could. Put both feet on it. It barely went down, and there was no change in speed.

His heart pounded as he looked at the line of cars in front of him. He saw red taillights. He had a split second to decide what to do.

He swerved to the shoulder quickly, but the car wasn't slowing.

The Corvette hit the guardrail, but the speed it had picked up shoved the car up over the rail. He plunged toward the hillside, feeling his stomach drop.

Then all went black.

TWENTY-NINE

WHEN RUIZ BROUGHT JACKY home that night, the boy brightened as soon as he sniffed the air.

The scent detective was on the case. He looked at his dad with big, solemn eyes. "Hey, that's pizza."

Pizza wasn't on Reyna's approved list—especially not takeout pizza. But there was a pizza box on the kitchen table and the smell of pepperoni in the air.

Reyna was at the kitchen computer, working on something. Ruiz couldn't see what it was. She immediately turned off her screen and rubbed her eyes.

"They just delivered it. I found a coupon." She stood up and pulled a stack of plates from the cupboard. "I need to finish something tonight."

Ruiz wanted badly to know what it was. The fact that she'd turned off the monitor as soon as he'd walked into the kitchen filled him with that same fear that had risen and fallen in him over the past four months.

A divorce filing. Maybe a rental application for a new place to live.

Ruiz and Jacky dutifully washed their hands and sat down at the table. Jacky was just about to take matters into his own hands and grab a slice when Reyna distributed napkins and opened the box.

"This is the best night ever." Jacky picked the pepperoni off first, then ate his piece of pizza in what looked like three bites. "Can we watch something?"

"Homework done?"

The usual response. A roll of the eyes.

"I finished it at afterschool care." As he grabbed another slice of pizza, he blurted out. "Can we watch a Thor movie?"

"Sure, *mijo.*"

Reyna looked relieved. She finished the last of her pizza slice and gathered her plate and napkin. "Go ahead and watch it without me."

Jacky picked the funny Thor movie, which made Ruiz laugh out loud. Hearing Jacky giggle at the movie's slapstick humor made him laugh harder. He realized how badly he needed this tonight. He paused the movie to make the two of them some microwave popcorn, and he looked away while Reyna worked on her project a few feet away.

They continued watching the movie, finishing only a few minutes later than Jacky's 8:30 bedtime. Ruiz made sure the boy brushed and flossed, then sat on his bed with him, as they repeated the funny parts from the movie.

"G'night, Papa." The boy used the name he called him when he was a toddler.

Something in Ruiz melted.

"Good night, *mijo.*"

Reyna was in the bathroom, getting ready for bed. Ruiz poured a drink of water at the sink and passed the computer desk, where Reyna had left her phone. The phone lit up with a text from someone named Mia. He tried to avoid looking. He tried to make himself turn away, but he couldn't do it.

As soon as he read it, he felt sick.

Leaving a marriage is tough, girl! Thanks for the resume. I'll put in your new salary requirement XOXO

THIRTY

Wednesday
7 a.m.

GRASSO WAS GETTING ready for her run when her cell phone rang.

She stopped tying her shoes and scowled. Interruptions to her morning routine annoyed her.

She leaned across the bed to her nightstand to pick up her phone.

"Detective Grasso?" The voice was shaky but familiar. "This is Amber Kennedy. I wanted to make sure you heard. Tom Weber was in a bad accident last night near Redwood City. He's at a hospital on the peninsula. Critical condition. He may not make it."

"What happened? Was he hit?"

"Looks like his brakes failed."

"Is he conscious?" Her not-yet-awake mind was trying to make sense of this. She felt like she'd just received a punch in the stomach.

"Not yet. He's just had emergency surgery to stop the internal bleeding."

"Thanks, Amber."

Realizing she wouldn't get her run today, Grasso called Redwood City PD to get more info on the crash.

She was on hold, till Officer Darius Green came on the line to help. Apparently at 6:40 p.m., on a curve on 280 near Edgewood Road, Tom had been unable to stop his car. The car had continued over the guardrail, landing on its side on the ground fifteen feet below.

Grasso swallowed. *Jesus.*

"Mr. Weber is involved in a current murder case down here in Monte Verde. I'm concerned there could be foul play involved. Will a mechanic be checking over the car?"

"I'm glad you called, Detective. We'll have a forensics mechanic check out the car in the next day or two. I'll keep you posted as soon as we know something."

Grasso was now fully awake. She mobilized for action. She made herself an espresso and paced her kitchen while drinking it.

Oh, God. Tom.

She called Ruiz. No answer. Maybe he was taking Jacky to school.

Could this just be an accident?

Monday Ruiz had been suspicious of Tom, thinking he'd been the blackmailer. If the brake failure was foul play, he was likely not the blackmailer.

Unless, of course, he was, and Kevin Dredger had found out and gone after him, tampering with his brakes.

She had to be honest with herself. She did not want this to be the case.

She had energy to burn right now, as she thought about how this development affected the case. She went into her second bedroom, her improvised gym, to do some time on the elliptical machine.

As her feet raced, her thoughts started to calm down.

Settle into a more logical pattern. The same thing that happened when she ran.

She reviewed what she knew.

Rosalind. Kevin. Tom. Philip Langdon.

The Fantastic Four. Friends and schoolmates at first.

After twenty years, not so much.

Kevin, put in a corner by the blackmailer, started undermining Rosalind's leadership. Impatient to push an acquisition that would make him some money, since he was paying off a blackmailer. Did he have a motive for killing Rosalind? Yes.

Tom was Kevin's confidante. Kevin had admitted to Tom he was being blackmailed. Possibly, Kevin didn't know the identity of the blackmailer, but Ruiz was right. It seemed odd that Tom would rush to the police station to tell her and Ruiz that Kevin was being blackmailed.

Did Tom have a motive for killing Rosalind? Maybe. The name Galadriel Inc., if Tom had been the one getting money out of Kevin, implied that he had some kind of a stalky crush on Rosalind. Maybe Tom had wanted a relationship with her, and she'd shut him down.

It was an off chance, but Tom did live in the Monte Verde hills, like so many of the opponents of the Laurelwood nature center. She'd never asked how he'd felt about the project.

Philip Langdon. He was the question mark. He was convincing as a grieving ex-husband in his interview at the station. But Rosalind ended her meeting with him abruptly and kicked him out of her office. His company, from what she understood, did something related to what Infinitas did. Could that be important?

Did Langdon have a motive for killing Rosalind? Maybe, but she needed to find out more. She had some questions to ask. And a little research to do.

When she got off the elliptical, she showered, then called Ruiz.

Still no answer.

Then she called the hospital, to check on Tom's condition. He was in surgery now.

Without Ruiz to bounce ideas off of, she bounced them off herself as she exercised. And did an okay good job of it.

She knew what needed to be done.

She was ready to go to the station and do it.

THIRTY-ONE

Wednesday
3 p.m.

LAUREL CONFERENCE ROOM at Infinitas was nearing capacity.

The management team made up of heads and interim heads of marketing, sales, manufacturing, and operations, squeezed chairs in on all sides of the long table. The security man could be seen visibly counting and recounting.

By now everyone had heard about Tom Weber's accident. Everyone was curious. Rumors had been going around the company in the past twenty-four hours that it hadn't been an accident.

Some blamed Kevin Dredger, convinced that he'd also had something to do with Rosalind's death. Everyone wanted to know where the company was going to go, after the loss of its remaining founding members.

There was a younger contingent at the company that felt it was time for the old guard to step aside. That Infinitas needed new leadership during this time. They'd gotten used to Rosalind as a stable, restrained CEO, the founder who kept the company on an even keel but didn't take advantage of new technologies and opportunities they knew were out there.

Some of these people had supported Kevin Dredger in his push for the acquisition because it meant at least some kind of change would happen.

But the group today, Infinitas's top management, was older, made up of those who had joined Infinitas in the first ten years and knew the four founders well.

Hennessey, current VP of marketing and the most senior member of the management group, stood and addressed the group. "It's only been four days since her death, but we know Rosalind would want the company in good hands. She'd want us to take action to ensure the company is resilient enough to handle these setbacks and survive. We need leadership. The board needs recommendations for our new CEO."

Hennessey cleared his throat and continued. "We need someone who can keep us stable through this hard time while exploring new technologies. Someone not afraid to devote resources to R&D. What we have is fine for now, but we need to be thinking about where we'll be in five years. We need someone with a strong technology background."

Murmurs and conversation erupted throughout the room.

"Wait a minute. Are you saying Roz didn't have that? I can't think of anyone better suited for the position." Cheryl Rakestraw, a product marketing manager, faced Hennessey and took him to task. "The woman had degrees in computer engineering *and* business. She knew the market and had the technical background. She went out in the field to meet with customers and tried to figure how we could better meet their needs."

"Seriously, Cheryl?" Hassan Marwan from engineering slapped his hand down on the table. "We're barely keeping up with our closest competitor, Caslonic. Rosalind was great with customers, but we need more. A better product. We need new talent for R&D. I agree with Hennessey."

Gordon Lo, who worked in operations under Tom Weber, stood up.

"If we're going to talk about this, let's be civil. As soon as we lose our ability to hear each other, we're not working together as a company. Please say what you have to say, then sit back and listen to your colleagues."

"Thank you, Gordon." Hennessey nodded. "This is a tough time for Infinitas, but if we can stay calm and work together, we can get through this. Now I'd like to have some initial recommendations. I don't want to waste time debating the names during this meeting. So please, take the paper in front of you and write down anyone you would consider a legitimate prospect for Infinitas CEO."

Conversation subsided. The group sat, squeezed in next to each other for about ten minutes, writing on the sheets in front of them.

After twenty minutes, Hennessey and Lo collected the folded-over sheets.

"Thank you for your participation today." Hennessey stood up and surveyed the group. "I do have some good news to share with you. Tom Weber has made it through his first surgery. His condition has been upgraded from critical to stable."

A sigh of relief rippled through the attendees.

"Once he stabilizes, doctors are hoping to operate on his shattered leg. It's hard to say what his recovery curve will look like."

"Any news on the murder investigation?" An engineering manager asked.

"It's continuing. We'll update you as we know more."

"Do the police think it's someone who knew Rosalind?"

Hennessey shook his head. "I'm afraid I have no information on that."

Dismissed, the group headed back to their departments, sailors continuing to swab the decks on a captainless ship.

The male nurse ushered Grasso through a sliding glass door into the ICU room. Tom Weber lay in a bed surrounded by a curtain.

Machines monitored his heartbeat and probably half a dozen other things, while Tom lay asleep, his bruised head immobile against the pillow.

"He's come a long way since he was brought in." The nurse raised a muscular arm to pull the curtain aside. Grasso hadn't seen a nurse looking this buff before. "The surgery stopped the internal bleeding into his abdomen, and they removed his lacerated spleen. He'll have surgery on his leg soon—to stabilize the fractured upper thigh with metal plates and screws. He'll have a long road to recovery, unfortunately."

Grasso watched Tom, who was almost unrecognizable with his swollen face and an IV tube taped onto his arm. It made her wince. But the faint movement of his rising chest was reassuring.

"Is he in pain?"

"Probably not." The nurse checked one of the monitors as he passed it. "Not with the pain meds we're giving him. He'll have some pain as he starts to recover, but we'll try to keep it under control so he can move around and do physical therapy. He's probably feeling pretty good right now, considering his injuries."

The nurse checked the IV inserted into Tom's arm, and the pump giving him fluid.

Grasso noticed a man in a suit, leaning forward in a chair as he watched a show on fly fishing on the wall-mounted television.

"And that is---" She looked inquiringly at the nurse.

"He's from Redwood City PD. Officer Hansen. Twenty-four-hour guard started last night. Mr. Weber's been made a "Do Not Announce" patient for his own safety. Nobody should know he's here."

Grasso must have looked relieved. She nodded at the officer, who pulled his eyes from the television long enough for her to introduce herself.

"He's in good hands." The nurse smiled at Grasso, with a look of curiosity. "So you're a detective. The patient's involved in one of your cases?"

"His boss was murdered. I interviewed him in the case."

"Nice of you to make a personal visit like this."

Grasso's cheeks felt hot. Flustered, she wondered why she felt she needed to come here.

When the nurse left, Grasso said a prayer of healing for Tom under her breath. Then she went back out through the sliding doors and headed toward the elevators.

She was tired of waiting for the local police to pass on the information. She needed to figure out what had happened to Tom's car that night.

She'd go directly to the source.

The mechanic at the shop off Woodside Road gave Grasso an annoyed look when she came into the garage.

As if she was a customer demanding her car before it was ready. Or another Karen coming in with a complaint.

"I'm Detective Grasso from the Monte Verde Police Department. Officer Green told me you're working on a car involved in one of our cases."

He nodded. "The Corvette. Yeah. We're going to pass the report on to him later today."

"Can you give it to me now?" She pulled herself up to her full 5 foot 2 inches. "I'll wait."

The man cursed under his breath. "Give me 15 minutes. Come back then."

Grasso went back to her car and popped open a diet Mountain Dew and started downing the caffeine. She wondered what would happen if the mechanic found nothing. Maybe no one had tampered with the car. Tom had just been negligent or distracted that night. Things were tough at Infinitas. He could have been worn out and stressed after Rosalind's death.

If the car had been tampered with, could it have been Kevin, mad at Tom for telling her and Ruiz about the blackmailer?

Thoughts swirled through her mind. The facts she knew and some theories that were a stretch.

She'd come home exhausted the past couple of nights and hadn't even played games.

She needed downtime.

A winnable game. Against game bosses with predictable moves. And someone who could help her finish the fight.

In a few minutes, she'd found a game on her phone from the app store. She played around with it, did the tutorial, but it was cartoonish and silly. Not satisfying. It looked like another "pay to win" game, where she'd have to pay money in the app to have any chance of winning.

After finishing up her soda, she got out of her car and headed back to the mechanic's office.

He was pulling pages off his printer. He put the compiled pages together and hammered a stapler down on the corner with his fist.

"What you got for me?" Grasso's voice sounded to her like she was channeling a tough cop in a noir movie.

"It was a simple trick. Musta took whoever did it less than five minutes. Guy pulled the vacuum line out of the brake booster. There'd be no pressure for the brakes, so he'd have to pound 'em to get any response at all. How is the guy, by the way?"

"Not dead."

"I'm surprised." The man grimaced as he handed the report to her. "I heard about the accident. You don't see many of those beauties. The Grand Sport. That was a gorgeous car, and it kills me to see it in such shape."

Grasso wondered why she'd had to wait fifteen minutes for a report on what sounded like a quick and straightforward tampering job.

She also thought it was interesting that he valued the car over the human being driving it, who was probably in worse shape. She thanked him and headed back to her car. But now she knew.

Tom's accident was attempted murder.

This had become a much bigger case than the murder of Rosalind Mabrey.

THIRTY-TWO

Thursday
morning

RUIZ WOKE up at 5 a.m., agitated.

When Reyna left at 5:30 to go to the gym, he still didn't know where she was going afterward. But he knew she wouldn't be back before he took Jacky to school. He got up, got dressed, and considered his options.

Before Jacky woke up, he took out a pencil and a pad of paper and spent some time drawing out the case of Rosalind Mabrey's death, and the interconnections between her and the other three founders.

He did a little more research on Kevin Dredger and Philip Langdon. After Tom Weber's accident, assuming there was foul play involved, it looked like Infinitas's VP of operations might be off the list of suspects.

When Jacky woke up, Ruiz asked if he'd like to walk to school. They'd walk through Central Park to get there.

Jacky got out of bed, washed, and got dressed in record time. They took their time walking through the park, since it was still early.

As they passed the pond, they named the ducks. Jacky said one of the ducks was a police duck since it kept trying to round up the other ducks. Ruiz said it was probably a mother duck, gathering up her chicks, and that sometimes the two jobs had the same responsibilities.

Jacky arrived at school and excitedly told everyone that they'd walked to school—as if it was a form of transportation technology that had just been invented. Ruiz said goodbye and walked back home to his truck, his throat thick with emotion he couldn't express.

When Ruiz got to the station, he saw Grasso was out. She'd left him a message saying she was up in Redwood City, checking out the mechanic's report on Tom Weber's Corvette.

When he'd read the text message on Reyna's phone last night, he'd felt he had been hit by a train. If he'd thought that finding out Reyna's plans would make him feel better, he'd thought wrong. Seeing her decision in words cut him to the core.

There was no fantasizing now. No hoping for the best.

Reyna was leaving. Apparently, she was getting a new job, too.

Everything would change. There would be negotiations about Jacky–who got to have him and when. As if he were the child in the story of King Solomon's judgment between the two mothers: Cut the boy in half.

Yet he needed to focus on the case this morning. He shot a quick text to Grasso.

How's it going?

Mechanic verified car was tampered with.
Saw Tom W. Looks bad but he's improving.

Ruiz sent back a thumbs-up emoji, then went to fill up his coffee cup. He ran into Frank Ladera at the coffee station. Normally, he tried to steer clear of the officer, who'd been dealing with his divorce, just finalized.

Lonely in his new apartment and only able to see his kids on Wednesdays and every other weekend, Frank had been inviting everyone he knew over to hang out and watch Giants and Sharks games.

Ruiz knew he'd been avoiding Frank, but he hadn't wanted to be part of the awkward gatherings at his bare, cold apartment.

Though he hated to admit it, he now had something in common with Frank. It depressed the shit out of him, but it made sense to talk to the man. He could be helpful. Maybe he'd been avoiding Frank because he was afraid Frank's lonely life was his future. He'd been trying to tell himself it wouldn't happen to him.

"See the Sharks game last night?" Ruiz asked as he filled his mug.

Frank groaned. "That last call was shit."

"Sorry I couldn't make it to your place for the game." Ruiz looked around then pulled Frank aside, his voice low. "Got a minute to chat?"

Frank, who was used to being ignored by Ruiz, opened his eyes wide, the beginnings of a smile on his face.

"Yeah. Come by my desk."

Ruiz looked at the crowded space by Frank's desk, wedged up next to another detective's desk and a few steps from the break room.

"Let's do the interview room."

Frank did a double-take. This was *big*. "Sure thing, Jimmy. You wanna do this right now?"

Ruiz nodded wearily.

The two men headed into the room with their coffee, and Ruiz shut the door.

THIRTY-THREE

Thursday
7 p.m.

IN THE LAUREL CONFERENCE ROOM, Hennessey and the managers presented their recommendations to the Infinitas board of directors.

"One name came up repeatedly on the lists from our management meeting. This person satisfied the need for continuity. Yet the team felt this candidate could also bring fresh ideas to the company."

Hennessey looked around at the directors. "And that is Philip Langdon."

"We've been talking about acquisitions for the past few months. As a way to expand our offerings. Give our customers more."

Most board members nodded.

Hennessey wished he had a slicker presentation to accompany this. He wanted the group to see that Langdon was their best possible move right now.

Langdon knew exactly what was going on with Infinitas.

After all, Hennessey had made sure to stay in close touch with Langdon after he'd left the company.

"One possibility would be to acquire Langdon Software Solutions, then bring on Langdon as our CEO." Hennessey was seeing his moment right now, and it felt good. The board was listening to him, as he proposed that this solution was exactly what the company needed in order to move forward after Rosalind's death.

"Langdon founded this company, so he's familiar with what we do—with our processes and with our company culture. LSS has its own database management technology, which could be a complement to our product line."

The chairman and the board members looked around at each other. Chairman of the board Virginia Marsden cleared her throat.

"You've done quite a bit of research into Langdon and his company. But we haven't seen the financial reports. We know you worked under Langdon when he was here, Blake. You are somewhat biased."

"People seem to be making a big deal of the fact that Langdon worked here before," Mary Landauer said, a quizzical look on her face. "But the guy worked for Infinitas *fifteen* years ago. That doesn't make him a shoo-in. It's like you're holding the door open for him just because he was a founder."

Hennessey listened to the completely different trains of thought emerging in the room. They were coalescing into two camps: those who felt Langdon was the obvious choice for CEO, and those who had serious doubts about him. Each side looked at the other as if they were deluded, obstinately refusing to see the facts. Hennessey had to admit, he couldn't see where the two women were coming from. This would be a tough position to fill, and it was hard to see a better match than Langdon.

Board member Aashish Viswanathan looked impatient

with the naysayers. "Personally, I agree with Blake." Viswanathan looked at those around him as if hoping to pull hesitant board members over to his side. "Langdon's marketing expertise got this company launched twenty years ago. He's got a good eye for new technologies, and he's proven he can run his own company."

"Langdon's a perfect fit," said Roger Demarest, CEO of an older electronics company. "But we could be wasting our time here. Does anyone know if he even *wants* the job?"

Grasso had taken *Unnon* up on his offer of dinner.

Grasso hadn't been to her grandfather's house in almost two years.

Childhood memories came back to her as she pulled into the curving driveway at the front of his Saratoga home. The house was huge and looked like a California adobe crossed with a Tuscan villa.

She remembered visits with her brothers, punching and pinching each other in the back seat of the car on the way, then spilling out onto the large, landscaped front yard. They explored the backyard, played hide-and-seek among large clay planters and a scary, modernist statue of St. Francis. They hiked up the hill and pushed each other down it. They drank cherry Italian sodas until their tongues and teeth were bright red.

Grasso parked her Mini Cooper at the side of the drive, pulled the sun visor down, and checked herself in the mirror, not something she typically did. She'd applied a little makeup before she'd left her condo, and so far it seemed to be staying on.

She'd brought a bottle of wine, which she'd gotten at Grasso's Fine Foods. An aged Nebbiolo from Italy, earthy and almost orange. She remembered it was one of his favorites.

He answered the door himself, wearing a fisherman's

sweater. His cheeks were ruddy and his moustache and hair looked jet black as usual. When he gave her a big hug, she picked up the smells of the store—cheese, smoked meat, herbs, and fruit.

"*Unnon!*"

"Daniela, it is wonderful to see you. Come in. I'm having Milvia set out dinner on the terrace, since it's been warm today. We've got the heaters set up if it gets cold."

She followed him through the house to the back. Milvia, his chef, was busy in the kitchen, where steam billowed out of pots on the big stove. A helper was assembling tasty-looking meats, olives, and crackers on a rustic wooden board.

She and her grandfather took seats on the terrace, lit by strings of bulbs strung across the surrounding trees. It felt just like she'd remembered it on summer evenings growing up. Magical.

"I was reliving my memories of this place as I drove up. I haven't been here in almost two years."

"You were very busy with the academy and training." He handed her an *aperitivo*. It was bubbly and pink. "You are glad to be done with school, I take it."

"I'd rather be out *doing* something than just reading about it." She took a sip of the aperitivo.

Giovanni Grasso laughed. "I am the same way. I want to live it. What good is it just picturing it in my head?"

"Exactly." She smiled over her drink. "Investigating this murder case is nothing like I expected. It's had some really strange twists. I don't think I could have prepared for it. I'm learning every day as I do the job. I'm sure I'm making lots of mistakes."

"The big secret is, everyone makes mistakes, Daniela. It is ridiculous that no one wants to admit they make them. Each one comes with a prize."

Milvia brought out the charcuterie and set it on the small table in front of them.

Giovanni Grasso picked some olives from the board. "I got very angry when you told me you weren't going to work for me. It took me a while to calm down. I never expected that you would say no. Nobody, of all my children and grandchildren, has ever said no."

She took another sip from her glass. "You're not mad anymore. What changed things?"

He held out the wooden board to her, and she took some prosciutto and a handful of crisp, buttery cerignola olives, her favorite.

"I was shocked when you said no. I was very hurt. And then I realized I would rather have a grandchild who was happy doing a job somewhere else, than a grandchild who was very unhappy working for me."

She ate the prosciutto, and the paper-thin, succulent slice was the most amazing piece of meat she'd ever tasted.

"I have a young man working for me. His name is Jamal. He isn't related to me, but he is loyal and good at what he does. He's managing the meat counter now. Someday he will run one of my stores. Because he loves the work. And he's very good at it."

She smiled faintly. "Jamal took the hit for me."

He didn't smile. "He's where he should be. You're where you should be."

"*Unnon*, can you please tell my parents and brothers this?" Her eyes teared up. "They're not speaking to me. They're doing this because they're afraid of you, and they think I've offended you by not accepting a job at the store. My dad hardly calls me anymore. My brother told me I disrespected the family. I miss my niece and nephew."

While Giovanni Grasso had come around in his thinking about her working for him, she wondered if he didn't want to spoil a good thing. He was now employing her father, her aunt, and her brothers. Would he give them a pass, too? This new attitude could change things.

Giovanni Grasso looked down into his glass at the last of his pink *aperitivo*. Maybe wrestling with a choice that would shake up the family. And his stores.

"Okay. I will talk with your father, Daniela."

Grasso returned to her condo, with a light buzz from the prosecco *aperitivo* and Nebbiolo.

She was so full of Osso Bucco, pasta, and bread, she was pretty sure she'd never need to eat again. With the quality of the food served tonight, she didn't turn anything down, though it meant she'd be sluggish as hell on the trail the next morning.

It was probably a good thing, but she could not even try to figure out where the Rosalind Mabrey case was right now. Her mind was mush. Or maybe polenta.

With the news that Tom Weber's car had been tampered with, the case had grown more complicated and layered.

She needed an easy fight.

That night, Grasso settled in for a quick quest in *Scrolls of Arendor*. It was supposed to be one of the easier quests and wouldn't take her long.

In this quest, she had to find a magic healing book, The Herbarium, which she knew she'd need to revive a dead king in a later quest.

She had an idea it would be under the mountain, so she headed for it. She had to fight a pack of wolves, but the magic staff she'd acquired enabled her to kill them easily.

Maybe too easily. It wasn't a big thrill. But it was a win, and she'd been looking for one. She headed for bed feeling good.

Pleasantly full and with a victory under her belt, she slid under the covers.

Soon, with her grandfather's help, her family troubles would pass. And in the next day or two, Tom Weber would be conscious.

And hopefully able to tell her and Ruiz who tried to kill him.

THIRTY-FOUR

Friday
8 a.m.

THIS MORNING REYNA left a note behind, saying she had an appointment after the gym.

Ruiz tried not to think of what that appointment was, though a few thoughts ran through his mind. Job interview. Checking out an apartment. Maybe breakfast with her new lover.

Ruiz would walk Jacky to school again.

The walks were so enjoyable to them both, Ruiz wondered why they hadn't thought of doing it before this week. The park was huge and beautiful and right near Jacky's school.

He'd never let Jacky walk on his own through the park, but walking instead of driving was a much better way to start the day. It calmed him down, which he needed.

The two of them watched the birds and the ducks. They talked about everything Jacky was thinking about. Which was usually video games, basketball, and his friends.

Sometimes he made up his own jokes, and then he repeated jokes his friends made up. They didn't make any sense but watching Jacky laughing at them made Ruiz crack up.

"Knock knock," Jacky started in, so excited he was already giggling.

"Who's there?"

"Atch."

"Atch who?"

"Bless you!" Jacky laughed so hard he almost fell over.

"You made that up yourself, *mijo*?" Of all Jacky's jokes, this one kind of made sense.

"Because *atchoo* is like a sneeze. So I said *bless you*. Get it?" Jacky ran a few feet ahead, very happy with himself.

Ruiz had been thinking about his talk in the interview room with Frank yesterday. A lot of what Frank had said was bullshit, him trying to justify why he was right and his wife was wrong in how they'd handled the divorce.

But Ruiz took one thing from his talk with Frank that made sense to him. Don't spring the divorce on the kid. Prepare him. Give him a way to talk about how he feels.

"Hey, Jacky. What do you think of your life with me and your mom? What do you like best about living with us?"

Jacky turned and looked up at him like he was crazy.

"You're my mom and dad. You guys are nice, I guess. I like that we got pizza the other night."

Ruiz should have expected that response.

"Do you have friends whose parents don't live together?"

"Yeah. Gabriel's parents are divorced. So he goes to visit his dad on weekends sometimes."

"Does he like it?"

"That's just how it is. He gets cool things at both places. Like his dad has this big box of Legos and a skateboard ramp in his backyard. And at his mom's he gets really good food."

"Do you think he feels bad that his parents don't live together?"

"He wouldn't get as much stuff if they lived in the same house," Jacky said matter-of-factly.

"Uh-huh. I get that."

They approached the school, and Jacky started walking faster, excited about seeing his friends. After they crossed the street to the entrance, in sight of Jacky's classroom, the boy looked up at him suspiciously, studying him. But he didn't say anything.

Then Ruiz saw Colin waving from the classroom line.

"Goodbye, Papa!" Jacky called back and ran toward his class.

It was a start. A rough one.

Ruiz wasn't sure how the hell he was going to do this.

Tom Weber opened his eyes.

He'd floated in and out of a haze.

He heard a beep coming from somewhere. At first, he thought it was a low-battery warning from one of his smoke detectors. He'd have to get up and figure out which of the damn detectors needed batteries.

He was tired, and his body felt heavy and immovable. If he got up, he didn't think he'd be able to stand up for very long. Then there was that tubing connected to his arm, nasty little tubes inserted into his nostrils that he didn't want to think too much about. On the end of one of the fingers, there was a wire connected to what looked like a bandage, with a bright, red light glowing on it.

His eyes moved around the room, noticing the TV mounted to the wall and big bouquets of flowers on the table beside him. A man sat in a chair, calmly watching him. It was a little creepy. He wore a blue suit and had a mustache so big that it looked like a small brown bird was perching under his nose.

"Good afternoon, Mr. Weber."

Tom eyed the man suspiciously. "I don't know who you are."

"I'm Officer Ted Hansen from the Redwood City Police Department."

Shit. Fear crept into the haziness in Tom's mind. *I'm under arrest. I killed somebody.*

"I'm in custody." Tom said soberly, as his thoughts raced. He'd need to call a lawyer. Maybe Infinitas's corporate counsel could recommend one.

The officer's mustache turned up at the corners.

"You're not under arrest, Mr. Weber. I'm here to protect you."

Protection from what?

"What day is it? How long have I been here?" Tom had a sudden fear that he needed to be at Infinitas. That he'd missed meetings. Appointments. Hadn't returned messages. He'd have to call Rosalind—

Then he remembered and it drained him.

"It's Friday, Mr. Weber. You've been here since Tuesday night."

Friday. He remembered now. Wednesday, Rosalind had been killed. But wait--not *this* week. Last week. He remembered that much. It was good to have a marker of time.

But how had he gotten here?

"What's the last thing you remember?" The man asked.

"The last thing I remember is backing my Corvette out of the garage in the morning, getting ready to drive it to work. And strawberries. I remember Bart, the tenant on my land, giving me a box of strawberries from his greenhouse."

The sweet taste came back to Tom, exploding like fireworks in his head. His senses seemed intensified now. All he could think about was those strawberries.

"It happened on 280 near Edgewood Road." Officer Hansen seemed distracted by something happening on the TV but quickly pulled himself back. "You went over the guard rail and down the embankment. They brought you here with a head injury, internal bleeding, and a shattered leg. From what the nurses said, you've had a couple of surgeries."

Tom was starting to remember the general outlines of his life, but there seemed to be big chunks missing in the middle.

He remembered going to see Kevin, at his mother's. He remembered the horrible smell at the stable, and he started to feel sick. The memory played large and vivid like a movie with Dolby sound in his head. Kevin was drunk. Why was Kevin drunk? He'd been upset, worried. What about?

The slow release of information in his brain bothered him. What the hell had happened to him that he couldn't remember the everyday details of his week? People he'd talked to. What he was doing at work. He'd be lost if he had to go back to work. How could he do his job if he didn't remember what it was? Or who worked for him?

The car didn't matter to him, but it made him sad that he'd wrecked it. What stupid move had he made, that he'd crashed? He wondered if he'd hurt someone else.

"Do you know if there were people here visiting me? Looks like a lot of flowers."

"You want me to look?" The officer got up and moved over to the table next to the bed. He pulled out a card stuck on a plastic prong on one of the flower arrangements.

"This is from somebody named Angie Dredger. *Please rest and come back to us, Tom.*" The officer moved to another bouquet.

"*From Bart and Jennie Angwin. We miss you. Come home soon.*"

Also, there was a detective here. A young woman. Tiny thing."

"That's Grasso. Dani Grasso, from Monte Verde PD."

"There you go. Your memory's kicking in just fine."

The officer looked pleased with himself, as if he'd been instrumental in returning it to him.

Tom was still confused. What had happened that he needed to be protected? He didn't remember anyone threatening him. If someone was out to kill him—which sounded unlikely for someone like him—he had a right to know.

"Officer Hansen, can you tell me who you're protecting me from?"

"I can't, Mr. Weber." Hansen shook his head, his lips tight. "But the nurse told me Detective Grasso is stopping by later. Maybe you should ask her."

In the early morning quiet, Reyna Ruiz sat in the dental office break room, setting up her budget.

She felt good today. Doing the planning and budgeting for her new life made it seem real. The new life she'd been waiting for would be hers in just a few months.

Based on the salary she asked for at the events job—plus child support from Jimmy—she could afford a decent apartment in the same school attendance area.

She let out a sigh of relief.

Jacky could continue in his school. He'd be with the same friends and would have no big change to his life.

She and Jimmy would split the proceeds from the sale of the house. She wouldn't be able to afford to buy a new place for a while, but she'd get by on the higher salary she'd be making.

She knew how to save; she'd set a budget and shopped frugally for years, until they were able to put a down payment on their small house near the park. She could do it again.

From down the hall, Reyna heard the click of the key in the lock. Rocio, the receptionist, was here to listen to phone messages, start the coffee and get the front desk ready for the day.

Reyna heard her stop in the hall, probably puzzled that

the alarm wasn't set. She could hear the footsteps down the hall, coming closer.

"Rocio, it's just me, Reyna." She called out to the woman.

The small, birdlike woman appeared in the doorway, her brown eyes wide behind her wire-rimmed glasses. None of them knew her age. She could be in her thirties. She could be in her fifties. Or somewhere in between.

Of all the women in the office, Rocio was kindest to her. She didn't like gossip, and she was quiet and kept to herself. Reyna knew the woman had heard the rumors in the office. But she always treated her professionally.

Today Reyna was giddy, filled with thoughts about her future. She felt like being nice to everyone. After all, she would not be at the dental office much longer.

"Good morning, Rocio. You're here earlier than usual." Reyna smiled. The woman seemed to calm down at seeing a co-worker's face.

"Oh. It's you." Rocio put a hand to her chest and took in a deep breath. "I was worried we had a break-in."

Reyna closed the spreadsheet on the computer and began to put her things away. "I came in to work on my budgeting. Easier to do it here than at home."

"It's good to see you so happy today, Reyna." Rocio smiled, then went over to the coffee machine and began dumping coffee into the filter basket from a Costco bag of French Roast.

"I've been doing some planning for the rest of the year. It feels good to have things figured out."

Reyna felt so excited, so light and free right now, she almost wanted to tell Rocio her plans. It would feel good to share with quiet, accepting Rocio. But she kept her mouth shut.

You never knew who could make an offhand remark. Let something slip. She hadn't told Jimmy about the new job or even hinted that she would be leaving him. She certainly hadn't told Dr. Hansford that she was planning a career change.

Reyna put her things away in her cubby, tied her hair back, and went to the restroom to wash up.

She looked at herself in the mirror and liked what she saw. A woman on her way to what she wanted. Maybe the problem with The Plan was that she'd been relying on a man to come into her life and make it happen for her.

From the other night in the Range Rover, she heard Flores's voice repeating in her head, talking about Jimmy. *He rescued you … And you've never forgiven him. He could never be someone you actually loved, just because of your own fucking pride.*

She hated him now. Flores had no right to say these things. He knew nothing about her. He knew nothing about her marriage or what she thought or dreamed about.

Or where she'd come from.

Things would change. She knew it. This job had come her way, a gift from the universe. It would be hers.

Mia had said it herself—she was perfect for it.

It could not come soon enough.

THIRTY-FIVE

GRASSO WALKED into her cubicle and found messages waiting for her.

And no Ruiz.

Charlotte Baldwin had called and said she wanted to come in and talk to her about an anonymous threat the Laurelwood Foundation received this morning.

Darius Green left a message demanding to know why she'd bypassed him on the mechanic's report.

Ruiz passed by with a fresh cup of coffee, his eyes puffy and tired.

"Hey, you. Wanna touch base in a few minutes?"

"Sure." His face was expressionless. "Your cubicle. Five minutes."

Grasso laid out on her desk a pack of macarons she'd picked up at a bakery on her way back from Redwood City. Ruiz pulled up a chair to her desk but didn't even touch the pink box. Something was wrong.

"Here's what happened with Tom's car, according to the

mechanic." She put a report on the desk. "The vacuum line in the Corvette was removed from the brake booster. When that happens, braking's a *lot* harder. You hit the brake pedal, and it's hard to even push down. Looks like Tom was speeding down 280. Somebody might have slowed or changed lanes in front of him. He hit the brakes and couldn't stop, so he swerved to avoid hitting the car in front of him and went over the guardrail. I drove that stretch of road to check. The guardrail is low there."

"The car was in the parking garage at Infinitas before this?"

"That's probably where the tampering happened," Grasso said, grabbing one of the macarons. "The mechanic said if someone knew what they were doing, it would be quick."

Ruiz leaned back in the seat and rubbed his face. "Someone on the inside at Infinitas? Depending on the system, it could be easy to get in the garage. It could have been anybody."

"Any news on the Galadriel Inc. account?" Grasso asked as she took a gulp of coffee to wash down the macaron, her early lunch.

"No names yet. I guess that's why it's in the Caymans—they keep their mouths shut. Dredger deposited a total of $240,000. That's a lot of money in about nine months."

"Holy crap. I want to know what the secret is."

"No kidding." Ruiz grimaced.

She studied Ruiz's tired, puffy face. What was it? It had to be something with Reyna.

"You okay?" She asked.

"Not great."

"Wanna talk about it?"

"Nope." He swallowed and looked around the desk. "I need something to do. Keep my mind off it."

She reached behind her to her messages. With the trip to see Tom and the mechanic, she'd forgotten.

"Can you meet with Charlotte Baldwin? Laurelwood Foundation received a threat this morning. She wants to come in and talk about it."

He nodded, his expression still unenthusiastic. He took the message slip.

"This will do."

Charlotte Baldwin must have grown up in a family with money.

She sat in the reception area wearing a white jacket, white pants, and silver shoes with sparkly things on them that looked like diamonds.

Ruiz escorted her into the interview room and made sure she had a decent chair to sit in.

"Thank you, Detective Ruiz." Baldwin pulled out the chair and sat down. "I am tired of this battle with the neighbors. The latest threat is the worst yet."

"Can you show me what you received, Ms. Baldwin?"

"I'll play it for you." She took out her phone and tapped on it. She came to a voicemail message, hit play, and put it on speaker.

You're still not getting the message. We don't want you here. If you continue with your plans, the center will be destroyed. You have been warned.

Ruiz raised his eyebrows, startled. This was a whole new level of NIMBY for Monte Verde.

"When did you receive this?"

"This morning at 8:30. I don't recognize the number. I've gotten used to messages or complaints from the neighbors I've talked to. I recognize most of the callers."

She wrote down the number and passed it to him.

The area code wasn't 650, the usual code for the area. He'd have to look it up.

"You haven't received any other threats up to now?"

"They weren't threats like this. There was the town council meeting, where people showed up just to heckle Roz and complain. Then the foundation line has gotten messages from neighbors telling us we can't do this, even though we've gotten the necessary permits. That it was never sanctioned by the city and shouldn't be built. That the traffic will be a hazard. Roads would be blocked."

"What else are they complaining about?"

"They say we'll be bringing people in from other areas that don't belong here.'"

"Can you tell me, Ms. Baldwin, what Rosalind Mabrey was trying to do with Laurelwood?" Ruiz had read something about it a couple of months ago—an interview with Mabrey--but couldn't remember what the purpose of the place was.

Baldwin took in a deep breath. "Rosalind wanted to have an education center, where children and adults from all over the Bay Area could learn about nature. And retreat cabins for tech workers and families to have an escape from Silicon Valley." Baldwin wiped her eyes with a tissue. Her voice came out, a combination of anger and sadness. "Can you tell me what is so horrible about that? Why are people such selfish assholes?"

Ruiz raised his eyebrows. There was a lot of that going around.

"Ms. Baldwin, I'll make sure we have a car patrolling the roads around Laurelwood. How much of the construction is done now?"

"The slabs have been poured, and the wood frames have been erected for the center and the cabins."

"I'd like to go up and see it some time. Would you show me?"

Charlotte Baldwin smiled for the first time.

"I'd be happy to show you around, Detective Ruiz."

Ruiz looked down at the strip of paper in his hands.

"Meanwhile, I'll track down the number and see what we can find."

Baldwin wiped her eyes with a tissue. "Thank you, James."

He looked up at her suddenly, surprised by her use of his first name. It felt familiar and respectful in a way that touched him.

Ruiz led Baldwin out to reception.

He realized his mood had improved.

THIRTY-SIX

Friday
11 a.m.

THE BOARD CONTINUED WORKING its way through the list of possibilities for the job of Infinitas CEO.

"We're in an extraordinary situation." Chairman Marsden looked over the names. They had narrowed their list down to five. She addressed the group.

"Kevin Dredger and Tom Weber would normally be recommended to step into the position for the interim. We obviously can't call on either of them. We'll start with this list and contact each person to gauge interest. Then proceed with interviews, based on what we hear. You all have the names."

The board members were scanning the list.

"I'm interested in Dr. Swati Sandhu. She's got the academic background for our technology," said Infinitas Operations manager Gordon Lo, the newest member of the board. "She's young. She'd bring in some new ideas."

"We talked about Langdon at our last meeting," Aashish Viswanathan said, insistently. "He could unite the team. Long-timers and newcomers."

There was a stirring in the room, as members talked with each other as they went through the list.

Another board member spoke up.

"Langdon's products would complement ours if we did an acquisition. At least we need to talk to him. He's in Vegas. Why can't we fly him in for the day?"

"Didn't he come in to meet with Rosalind to discuss an acquisition?" Gordon Lo shook his head. "I heard she told him no—ten minutes after the meeting started."

The chairman frowned and sat back, waiting for more feedback.

Roger Demarest had a smirk on his face. "You know there could have been other issues at play there. The two were married for three years."

A few of the board members laughed. Chairman Marsden did not.

Mary Landauer, CEO of a financial software company, threw up her hands in frustration.

"Does that matter? Rosalind Mabrey was a smart, capable woman. If she decided an acquisition with Langdon Software Solutions wasn't a good idea, I trust her judgment. I'd vote against it."

After a round of discussion, a vote was taken to proceed with exploring interest among the five candidates—with more than half the board in favor of pursuing Philip Langdon as top choice.

If Langdon was interested, he would be flying in to meet with them less than two weeks after he'd met with Rosalind Mabrey--the day before she was killed.

By mid-morning, Grasso had made her way through the backlog of things on her list.

She called Officer Green and apologized, sorry but not

sorry, for getting the mechanic's report straight from the source and not waiting for him.

Then she called Kevin Dredger and asked him to come in and explain, for the record, where he was between 6:45 and 8:15 a.m. on the day Rosalind was killed.

Grasso was a little nervous about the confrontation since his stay in jail was because of his attack on her.

She and Ruiz would interview Dredger again this morning. Grasso wanted to bring up the blackmail, but in a way that encouraged him to talk about it freely—and to break free from the situation he'd been in for the past nine months.

When Ruiz brought Kevin Dredger into the interview room, the man looked in better shape than when she'd seen him last. He was clean-shaven, and he'd had a haircut.

He was wearing a clean, neatly pressed button-down shirt and nice blue jeans. He wore a pair of horn-rimmed glasses, which was new. They made him look kindly and intellectual. She wondered if Kevin was trying to upgrade his image on the advice of his attorney in case he ended up in court on trial for Rosalind's murder.

"Hello, Mr. Dredger." Grasso smiled as Ruiz came in with Kevin.

Kevin looked blankly in her direction but didn't respond. Ruiz sat next to Dredger on the side of the table opposite her.

Grasso had her notebook out. "We wanted to discuss a few things with you and ask you some questions."

"Okay." Dredger's eyes darted nervously between her and Ruiz.

"I need you to tell me the truth about where you were a week ago Wednesday-- between when you left Infinitas and when you arrived at your financial advisor's in downtown San Jose."

Kevin flexed his hands on the table.

"I was on a call, on my cell phone. I pulled over to take it."

"Who were you speaking to—that you would need to pull to the side of the road?"

Kevin's face grew dark. He lowered his eyes.

"Mr. Dredger, can you tell us who were you talking to?" Ruiz turned to Kevin and asked in a gentle voice.

Kevin swallowed hard and looked down at the table. "Somebody called me. I had to answer it."

Grasso shot a look at Ruiz, who asked.

"It was someone you didn't want to talk to?"

"Yeah." Circles of sweat formed on Dredger's neatly pressed blue shirt.

Ruiz continued. "What would they do if you didn't answer?"

Dredger's face twisted. "They would tell my wife. My boys. My mother. They would tell them everything. And it would kill me."

"Who was it that was calling?"

Dredger shook his head. He was getting more and more agitated.

"I-I don't know. But they know everything. What happened that night. All the details. They'll ruin my life if I don't pay."

Ruiz changed his stance, turned so he was facing Kevin, in a way that he appeared to be listening with interest to a good friend tell a story. Grasso had seen Ruiz do this before, and she was always in awe. She wanted to model her interrogation methods after his.

It worked, without him having to say a word.

"It was in Vegas. That first show the four of us went to. Our debut. It was the night before our second to last day of the conference. I drove with some guys from another booth, out to the brothels. An hour away. On our way back, we went to a bar. And I met this cute girl. We drank till we could barely stand up. I asked the girl to go with us back to Vegas. For some reason, she said yes, and got in our car."

Ruiz and Grasso listened. Grasso hardly took notes, she was so transfixed by the story.

"We pulled off the side of the road on the way back. The stars were bright. Some of the guys had to pee. So Annalisa and I took a bottle of whisky with us and sat down and watched the stars. We made out for a while. Then we fell asleep, I guess.

When I woke up, she was leaning against me. But when I tried to get up, she fell over. She was—she was dead."

The room was silent except for Dredger's hoarse voice. Ruiz and Grasso could not help but watch this man as the story was wrenched from him.

"The guys screamed for me to get back to the car. I told them, she's dead. They screamed for me to get in the car. I tried to pick up Annalisa, but she wouldn't move. We left her there."

Now tears were rolling down his face. He wiped them with his shirt sleeve.

"The thing is, I don't know if I did something to her. Sometimes I do things—it happens so fast, and I can't control it. I was drunk that night. Whatever happened that night, I don't remember it."

"What did you do when you got back to Vegas?" Ruiz asked quietly. "Did you call the police?"

Kevin shook his head. "I was so scared. I thought I killed her. This would wreck Infinitas, the success we'd had at the show. I couldn't do it—"

Ruiz showed great restraint, she thought. How the hell could the guy not have called the police? He was okay leaving a dead woman out in the desert. Or at least keeping his job and making the company look good had been more important to him.

"Kevin, let's go back to the phone caller." Grasso sat ready to take notes. "Can you tell me—when was the first time you received a phone call from this person?"

"Last August. It's a woman. I hate her voice. Hate the sound of it. She told me she knew about the girl. She knew lots of details from that night. Even stuff I didn't remember that well. She told me she would tell the police if I didn't transfer $25,000 to an account."

"So you did it. Did she give you a name or any other identifying information?"

Kevin shook his head. "She said she was a friend of a friend. The number on my cell phone said UNKNOWN."

"How often did she call to ask for money?"

"She called about four times. The rest were messages. So I transferred money six times. Including the day Rosalind was killed." Tears flooded his eyes.

"Did you ever try to stop making the transfers?"

"How could I?"

This is where Ruiz leaned in, pressing in a little closer to Dredger. He reminded Grasso of a priest in a confessional.

"Kevin. What do you really have left?"

The man sat slumped in his chair, wiping his eyes with his sleeve. The tidy look he'd had when he came in was gone.

He nodded. "What can I do to stop it?"

"Say no. Say that you've thought about it, and you don't want to pay any more money. When you do that, this person will get angry or threaten you more. But they may also reveal more information that will help us find out who they are."

"Help me." Kevin pleaded, his eyes bloodshot, his sweat circles taking up more and more of his shirt.

"We can help you. We can tell you what to say. But you have to decide to do it."

Kevin looked at Ruiz with terror in his eyes. "I want to do this."

"Good." Ruiz nodded reassuringly at Kevin.

Ruiz's personal life might be breaking down, but right now he was in the zone.

THIRTY-SEVEN

Friday
1 p.m.

AFTER THE INTERVIEW WITH KEVIN, Ruiz called
Las Vegas PD.

He asked for any record of a woman's body being found
on State Road 160 the week of November 11, twenty years
ago. He gave the description of Annalisa that Dredger had
given them.

He was transferred to records, where they could do a
search.

"Now that's interesting, Detective Ruiz." A woman's voice
came on the line. He heard clicks on a keyboard.

After being on hold, Ruiz woke up from his thoughts.

"Why? What did you find?"

"No record of a body found that week, in that area.
Nobody missing, according to reports. But--."

"What?"

"Somebody called us last July and asked the same
question."

After he hung up from talking to LVPD, Ruiz pinged Grasso and told her to come to the interview room.

"No record of a body being found that week twenty years ago. Nowhere along the stretch of 160 between Pahrump and Las Vegas."

"Okay." Grasso's stomach was making weird noises as it continued to process last night's huge Italian dinner. "Animals could have taken care of the remains?"

"Also no reports of a missing woman meeting that description."

"She could be a runaway."

"I asked them to do a search, according to the location Kevin gave. They're going to get back to us. But it's a well-traveled road, because of the brothels, which are only allowed in rural counties, not in Las Vegas itself. They expect there wouldn't be anything left of a body after 20 years, even if one had been out there."

But who else would have called, interested in finding this same information?

"Listen to this, Dani. Somebody else called LVPD records to ask about a woman's body in that area for that same week." Ruiz widened his eyes. *"Nine months ago."*

"So the blackmailer knew there was no body." Grasso sat up, excited. "This woman was messing with Kevin. She played on his fears and fed him a story over the past nine months."

"Yeah. I was thinking that. Maybe Dredger did have some memories of that night, but they were hazy. The caller could have put ideas in his head. Said they knew what really happened."

"Dredger wouldn't be able to deny it. He's the perfect mark for this since he has an impulse problem. He's not sure if he killed this girl or not."

Ruiz frowned. "That's a hard thing to live with for twenty years. I feel bad for the guy."

Grasso rubbed her forehead and took a sip of the stale diet Pepsi she'd been nursing all day.

"Jimmy, think about this. If the caller could convince Dredger that he killed this girl, how long would it take for the caller to convince him that he killed Rosalind Mabrey?"

Reyna's interview for the events assistant job had gone well. Very well.

She sat in the Range Rover, sipping her *ube* bubble tea, after the morning interviews at Mia's company.

There was something satisfying about sucking the tapioca balls up through the straw and popping them in her mouth. It was an expensive habit, but today she deserved a reward.

Since dressing for corporate work was a new thing to Reyna, Mia had given her some tips. She'd worn a stylish yet professional red and black dress with a soft, textured jacket she borrowed from Mia. She saw heads turning her way from the moment she'd walked into the building.

Mia had coached her with questions to ask and some company goals and buzz words to use in her conversations.

"Mention improvement. We're big on goal-setting this year." Mia said, as she prepped Reyna on the phone the night before. "Also, teamwork is huge here. Give examples of times you've had success working with other people. Doesn't matter that you're in a different field if you explain how you worked with your team at the dental office."

Reyna felt confident. This was the kind of job she'd be good at. She loved the idea of planning fun events for employees and customers. And there was creativity involved with this job that she didn't have at the dental office. She could do this. She could excel at it.

After an interview with a manager in Human Resources, Rebecca Wade, the woman who handled trade shows for the company, came in to talk with her. Rebecca was less friendly than the HR person but seemed satisfied with Reyna's answers. She told Reyna that she'd need to travel a few times a year to trade shows for the company. Reyna hadn't heard this from Mia, but she was excited by the idea of traveling for work. Jimmy could take Jacky on those days. They'd work it out.

Reyna had told the dental office that she had an appointment that morning.

After lunch, Reyna came in to work, stripped off the interview clothes, and quickly changed into blue scrubs in the bathroom. She was nervous, but excitement fluttered in her stomach. She couldn't remember the last time she'd felt this much hope about her future.

As she was applying polish to her last patient's teeth, Reyna heard her phone buzz.

It wasn't till she finished with the patient and cleaned up her work area that she had a chance to check it. It was from Mia.

> Girl, you KILLED it. They love you. Should know more by the end of the week. xoxo

Reyna sat down in the swivel chair and almost cried.

"Blake, Langdon's on the video call."

"Give me three minutes," he called to his assistant Martelle Jones in the adjoining office.

Blake Hennessey prepared the notes for his second talk with Philip Langdon.

The first virtual meeting, prompted by questions from the board, had been exploratory. Was Langdon interested in returning to Infinitas? Langdon said he was very interested in Infinitas acquiring his company. And would consider the possibility of taking on the job of Infinitas CEO.

Of course, Hennessey had heard the rumors about Langdon. Mostly stories of his altercations with Rosalind Mabrey. Having worked with Rosalind, he could see how the two would clash. Rosalind was literal, with an engineer's resistance to hype or partial truths. Langdon was a big-picture guy. Brilliant conceptual marketer, with less of an interest in the details. Of course, they'd clash.

Hennessey had worked for Langdon for a year before the Infinitas founder had left. Langdon had been a good boss, in that he was fine with however the job was done, as long as it was done in accordance with the long-term plan.

Hennessey got on the video call. Langdon was sitting in his office, wearing a light blue sports coat and orange and white buttoned shirt underneath. Desert chic. He looked like the kind of guy who used fashion like a chameleon's skin, so he blended in wherever he went.

"Hey, boss. You're looking good, Phil. How's life in Vegas?"

"Scorching hot by your NorCal standards. I think it's supposed to be 85 today."

"Sounds fucking perfect to me." Hennessey laughed. "Sure you want to trade that for our foggy, overcast mornings? What I wanted to do today was go over our plan for the next week. You're flying in on Wednesday. I thought we'd have a catered lunch on the terrace with the board and the execs. Then drinks with top management that night, as we kick around plans for the future."

"Works for me, Blake. It'll be great to be back."

"The board will want to meet with you, but I'll leave that for Virginia Marsden to set up." Hennessey said. "Sorry, you'll miss your fellow founders. You probably heard about Kevin. And then Tom Weber--"

"Dear God. Horrible accident. I read about it in the news." Langdon sighed. "Tom always loved his fast cars. I guess it finally got him."

Hennessey hadn't heard that about Tom, who'd struck him as a quiet, laidback guy. He'd been surprised at the accident. But then Langdon had known Tom since college days.

"Be ready with some reports. The board wants to see LSS's financial results—which we still haven't gotten. And the execs will want to hear your ideas for Infinitas's future. There's a lot of different opinions on that, so it should be a lively discussion."

"I'm sure there are. The old and the new, right?"

Hennessey ended the call, feeling like he'd done his job. The boxes were ticked. The right questions asked. They had gone through the necessary steps in a very short time. Infinitas could have a CEO again soon. Someone many in the company were already familiar with.

Things would go back to normal.

Though he suspected it would be a very different normal.

THIRTY-EIGHT

Friday
2 p.m.

THE 280 FREEWAY was getting busy as Grasso drove her Mini Cooper north to Infinitas in Palo Alto.

The freeway curved along the green, wooded western hills, through the wealthy communities of Palo Alto, Woodside and Hillsborough. For good reason, Ruiz called it Rich Man's Freeway. It curved through Stanford University property, past the big radar dishes, then crossed over the Stanford Linear Accelerator, a two-mile building for doing particle physics research that looked like an elongated garden shed.

Grasso had left a message for Ruiz saying she'd be back around 4 p.m. She'd arranged to talk to Infinitas Security about the parking garage gate. It turned out there was a security camera mounted near the gate. She'd be able to go through footage from the day of Tom's accident.

This was not the beautiful visitor lobby with its walls of living plants and tasteful earth tone décor. This was a dingy beige workhorse of a lobby with a long counter, for the purpose of screening vendors and contractors and employees who had misplaced their badges and couldn't use the card readers on the building entrances.

A grizzled, solemn man at the security desk, whose badge read IVAN, printed her an adhesive badge with the Infinitas logo and made her sign in. A guy named JASON waited for her to finish the process, then took her through the door to the side of the desk. Jason looked about her age, and he seemed immediately comfortable with her.

"This is where you get to see everything that goes on here." Then he shrugged. "But usually, nothing really happens."

"At least you're prepared if it does." Grasso smiled.

They were in an alcove with a bank of eight screens, displaying feeds from cameras throughout the headquarters.

Jason pulled a chair out for her, and they both sat down in front of the screens. Jason had a remote control, which he seemed to enjoy pointing and clicking, as he brought up different sites throughout the Infinitas campus on the screens. It must make a young guy like Jason feel pretty powerful.

"Here's the feed from the parking garage gate." Jason clicked on a display in the bank of monitors. "This is what it looks like right now."

The video camera was mounted on the side of the building, to the left above the garage entrance. She'd seen the parking garage at the end of the building on the times she'd visited Infinitas.

As they watched the screen, Grasso saw a car approach the gate and pause at the card reader which was mounted on a metal post. A hand reached out to tap the reader with a card, which triggered the gate opening.

"So you have a record of everyone entering the garage from their card," Grasso said, as she watched the car enter the garage. "That would be employees, people who come in regularly."

Jason nodded. "And vendors and contractors. Anyone who's coming in regularly is issued a card for the garage. We have a record of everyone, for every given day, with their time of entry. Visitors have a special parking lot, near the front lobby. You must have parked there. We monitor that, too."

They continued watching. Two more cars came up to the gate.

The driver of the first car tapped his card on the reader. The gate opened and he drove in. Quickly the car behind it slid in quickly just as the gate was starting to close.

"Wait a minute." Grasso frowned. "Someone can just drive in after another car, without authorization? That's not a great system."

"Well, yeah. But the license plates are all recorded. It's all on the video."

"Still, just anybody could come into the garage, whether they should be there or not. And it would be a while before you knew it."

"Well, shit." Jason looked confused and maybe a little embarrassed.

Grasso wanted to see the recordings for the day of the accident, up until Tom Weber left work.

"I need you to show me Tuesday—from 7 a.m. to 6 p.m."

"You sure?" Jason turned to her with a skeptical look. "That's a lot of footage. It's going to take us a while."

"Jason, do you know most of the regular cars in the garage? If you saw one that didn't belong, would you recognize it?"

"I patrol the garage every day I'm on duty." He radiated pride. "I'm kind of into cars. So, yeah. I know all the regulars."

For the next hour and a half, Grasso and Jason watched the feed for the day of the accident. She was trying hard to stay alert and focused, since she'd come in feeling sluggish.

She had gotten up late and missed her run. She'd need more coffee soon. A lot of it.

They were a half hour into the video.

"Stop it." She commanded Jason, as she saw another vehicle slip into the garage behind another car, as the gate started to come down. "That car behind the BMW. The old one."

Jason looked at her and started laughing. "The old Mercury Sable? A grandpa car. That's Ivan's at the security desk."

They continued, until the time stamp read 2:30 p.m. Fewer cars were going in and out. At 2:36, a Prius came to the gate. A white pickup truck pulled up quickly behind it. Both cars went in through the open gate.

"What the fuck—" Jason stopped the feed. "I've never seen that truck before." He rolled back a few frames.

"Can you get the license plate for me?"

Jason clicked to stop on the best view of the back of the truck, and Grasso copied down the number. The truck had a lockbox strapped to its bed.

"An old Toyota Tacoma. A 2008." Jason looked confident.

They continued to watch the feed from the truck's entry. About ten minutes later, the truck came back out the gate. Jason started to get excited.

"That doesn't belong to an employee. Let's go look at the logs to see the contractors checking in that day."

More time while she watched Jason going through the online log for that day in the security lobby. He looked up from the log, his eyes wide.

His world had been shaken.

"It's not here."

Grasso texted herself the license plate number of the pickup.

. . .

After leaving Infinitas, she decided to visit Tom.

When she showed her badge at the nurse's station, Grasso learned that Tom Weber had been moved to an acute care room. He no longer needed the ICU. Her prayer had been answered. She sent up a mental thank you note right there.

When she entered the room, she nodded at Officer Hansen, the man she'd talked to earlier that day.

Tom was awake. His eyes had more life in them, but there were still tubes in his nose and his face was still swollen.

"Welcome, Detective Grasso," His voice rose, thin and weak, from the bed. "To my *evil lair*."

Grasso gave him a wry smile. "You aren't very believable with that voice."

"I wasn't awake yesterday. I heard you came by."

Grasso blushed. "We were worried about you." *Make it sound like it was the team, Ruiz, whoever. Not just you.*

"Detective Grasso, I need to know." Tom's eyes looked pained as he shot a glance at Hansen, who was binge-watching a bowling tournament on TV. "Why am I being protected?"

Grasso took the seat next to the bed.

"Your car was tampered with, Tom. Somebody hired a mechanic to detach your vacuum line from the brake booster."

"What would that do? I don't know a lot about cars."

"It would make it very hard for you to brake. If you got in a situation where you had to brake quickly, you'd be in trouble."

"I'm starting to remember the drive. I remember hitting the brakes. It didn't do anything. There were cars in front of me. No one else was hurt?"

"Just you, Tom. Whoever paid the mechanic was trying to kill you. They know you're not dead. It's possible they'll come back and try to finish the job."

"Fuck." He moaned and closed his eyes.

"Can you think of anyone who might want to kill you, Tom?"

Tom opened his eyes again. "I'm still not completely clear on all that happened this week. Who I talked to, what I did. I've got a lot of gaps."

That was what Grasso was afraid of. Tom could have heard something, figured something out. With his head injury, that knowledge might be gone. Forever.

"What about the day of the accident. Do you remember what you were doing that day? What you were thinking?"

"I was feeling down about Roz, so I wanted to go for a drive after work. That day I'd talked with managers about recommendations for a new CEO."

"Let's take it a step back from that." Grasso said, hoping to get a little more out of him. "What about the day before?"

"The tenants living on my land gave me a box of strawberries they'd grown in their greenhouse. They were one of the first things I thought of when I woke up."

"Okay, agreed." Grasso snorted with amusement. "Strawberries are amazing. Anything else you remember?

"I called somebody. About Kevin."

"Maybe Angie Dredger?"

"Can't remember. The way Kevin was acting scared me."

"Was it somebody at Infinitas?"

Tom seemed to be tiring himself out with the effort to remember.

"It was somebody who knew Kevin. I think--I wanted help. What to do about Kevin. The most I can remember is that I felt uneasy after the conversation. Everything seems off to me right now, but that phone call felt weird."

Had Tom picked up a red flag from whoever he'd talked to? It would be easy to get phone records.

She wondered if it made sense to grill him at this point. His memory might come back soon, and all of this could be a waste. Tom's eyelids were drooping, as if talking with her had depleted whatever reserves he had left.

As if on cue, a nurse came in and told them it was time to change the dressing on Tom's leg.

"Bye, Tom. Do me a favor and listen to your nurses."

He smiled and raised his hand slightly, in a pathetic thumbs up.

Before she left, Dani touched base with Officer Hansen.

"Quiet up here, huh?"

The man watched a bowler throw a strike on the TV screen, then turned his attention to Grasso.

"Pretty much. Another hour, I'm relieved."

"You haven't seen anyone wandering around?"

"Nah," the officer shook his head. "No one knows he's here. I don't think they'd get past the nurse's station. They're a tough crew."

"Good to know, Hansen."

THIRTY-NINE

Friday
4 p.m.

TRAFFIC WAS GETTING bad as Grasso headed back to the station on 280 then exited at Foothill Expressway. The clouds were moving east, and it almost felt hot out. A preview of the summer that was only a few weeks away.

She opened the sunroof for the short time on Foothill, just to feel the sun on her. It was warm, but it had the effect of waking her up, not putting her to sleep.

From her marathon viewing session with Jason, she now had the license plate number of a vehicle whose driver could have tampered with Tom Weber's car.

With the hospital safety procedures and the officer posted outside his door, Tom should be safe. She'd call tonight to check in, to see if he was alert and able to communicate.

Ruiz was on the phone when she got into the station. Sounded like he was trying to understand someone on the other end who didn't speak English well.

"That's right. The last name. The *surname*."

He popped his head over the cubicle wall.

"Cayman Islands English is not what we speak here. After twenty minutes, I got them to understand my question. Now they have to get back to me."

Grasso was excited to share her news.

"I just got a license plate number for a truck that entered the Infinitas parking garage on the day of Tom's accident. I suspect the driver tampered with Tom Weber's Corvette. I'll look it up."

"Do it *now*." Which she'd learned over the past year, was Ruiz's favorite response to almost anything.

She gave him a glowering look, then spun around to her computer to look the plate up through the database. While she waited, she grabbed one of the macarons from the box still on her desk. It already tasted stale.

"Here we go," she said, scanning the screen. "The truck is registered to Horacio Perez. On the east side in Menlo Park."

"Any reason we can't check this guy out now?"

"Yes. *Traffic*." Grasso frowned at him. "Seriously, Jimmy. I just got back." But she grabbed her handbag and went to pour herself a very large cup of coffee.

Ruiz drove the investigations car as they cut across Mountain View, heading for Highway 101. At least she'd see a different freeway this time.

She was happy to see that Ruiz seemed less down. She could only speculate on what Reyna had done now. Maybe she finally said she was leaving. Or that she was going back to the guy she'd had an affair with.

Grasso had seen Ruiz come out of the interview room with Frank Ladera yesterday. It had seemed odd to her, since Ruiz avoided the guy. Of course, it could have been about a case. She also wondered if he'd been talking to Frank Ladera about the only thing they could possibly have had in common. Divorce.

"Everything okay?" She asked, as casually as she could.

"Fine." Ruiz grunted.

"You know you can always talk to me if—"

"Yeah, I know." He gripped the wheel and stared straight ahead at the road. "You wanna talk to me about Tom Weber?"

Grasso's face burned hot, and she looked out the side window at passing cars.

They got off on the Marsh Road exit and followed the GPS down a series of narrow, cracked asphalt streets, badly in need of resurfacing.

They finally reached the address, a small house with a lawn of dead grass. There was a beater of a Honda Civic in the driveway, but no Toyota pickup truck to be seen.

They got out, checking the property around the side of the house and the front carefully, because you had to know what you were walking into. As they approached the front door, they saw a notice posted on the door. Ruiz recognized it before Grasso.

NOTICE TO VACATE
By May 15th

Ruiz rapped on the door. They waited. He knocked again. Soon a woman came to the door with a toddler on her hip.

"Ma'am, is Horacio Perez here?"

"He's out doing a job."

Ruiz waved at the toddler, who stuck his thumb in his mouth and buried his face in the woman's shirt.

Grasso smiled at the woman. "Is Horacio your husband? What is his job?"

The woman nodded, but her eyes gave each of them the once-over, suspicious. "He fixes cars for cheap."

"Did somebody pay him to do a job? On Wednesday. A very quick job. In Palo Alto."

"He got a lot of money. We need money." Her eyes strayed to the notice on the door.

Grasso's eyes met Ruiz's. What Horacio did was illegal

and almost killed a man. But she was sure they both were thinking the same thing. Who paid him to do it? How much was that information worth?

As a mechanic, the man knew what he was doing when he disconnected the hose.

They needed to find Horacio.

"We'd like to talk to your husband." Ruiz lowered his voice, and it made him sound like a *mafioso.* "Tell him it will be worth a lot for him to call me."

The woman's eyes narrowed as she studied him, probably trying to calculate how much that meant and what her husband would have to do to get it. Maybe she already knew what Horatio had been paid to do. When your living situation is at stake, morality is a luxury.

Instead of handing her his MVPD detective card, Ruiz took out a pen and wrote his cell number on a slip of paper. He handed it to the woman and smiled warmly.

"Have Horacio call me. I would like to talk to him."

Grasso gave Ruiz a look with a question in it. *Are you allowed to do this? This guy almost killed Tom Weber.*

"Thanks for your time, Mrs. Perez." Ruiz smiled at the toddler, who was looking at him with a mixture of terror and fascination. "I am sorry for your situation. I will be praying for your family."

For the first time, Mrs. Perez's skeptical facade melted. Tears filled her eyes. "Thank you so much."

As they walked back to the car, Grasso turned to Ruiz and shook her head.

"Holy shit, Jimmy. What are you thinking here?"

"We need to find out who paid Horacio to tamper with Tom Weber's car. The man is desperate to get money. He and his family are getting evicted. They probably have no place to go. If he calls, I'm going to talk to him and get any information I can get. And I'll make sure he gets rewarded for it."

"You're really going to pray for them—or was that just something to say so she'd have her husband call you?"

"I'm praying a lot more these days. These people are way worse off than me. Plus, I could see a giant Jesus painting on the wall inside. And I *really* want the guy to call me back."

When Grasso looked raised an eyebrow at him, he shrugged. "It worked."

Reyna couldn't stand it for much longer. The waiting was horrible.

She forced herself to focus on her patients throughout the day, but her mind kept racing. She tidied and re-tidied after each patient left, wiping down everything. Washing her hands multiple times.

Mia said the company would make a decision this afternoon.

It was almost 5 p.m. Why hadn't she heard anything?

Reyna passed Tiffany on her way to the restroom as she headed to brush her teeth after eating a snack. The other hygienist looked away, as if she didn't see her.

My God, Tiff. Really?

Reyna sighed to herself. Her last few weeks at the dental office were going to be hard. She'd have to dig in and deal with it. She looked forward to the day when she could submit her resignation and move on to a place where she was liked, appreciated. It would be the beginning of a whole new life.

She'd been looking at apartment listings online. There were decent places in Santa Clara. It would be a rental, but she could decorate. Those bright white walls were not so bad —they gave the place a clean look and were easy to dress up.

Their house would sell quickly. A starter house, something hard to find in the valley. She'd been checking realtor sites to see what houses sold, how quickly, and for how much. The market was doing well, and supply was low. They could expect overbidding.

The past week she'd walked through the house before Jimmy and Jacky got home. She tried to look at everything as a prospective buyer would look at it. They—well, Jimmy--had done a lot of work on it. Painting, installing all new plumbing fixtures, re-tiling the bathroom walls and shower. It had come a long way in the five years they'd owned it.

She stood in a doorway and, just for a minute or two, felt like crying. She walked into Jacky's room and sat on his bed. She remembered when he'd been in a converted crib, bouncing on his mattress early in the morning, until Jimmy would bring him back into their bed. She remembered back in January when Jacky had almost been taken from them by a sharpshooter's bullet, not far from their house.

She walked into their bedroom, the place where they slept next to each other, and now *only* slept, every night.

She tried to remember what she'd felt that first year. She remembered feeling good for the first time. Good about life. She'd been in awe of him. His kindness. He'd listened to her, asked her opinion on things, unlike Mateo. She didn't know how to take it all in. It had been so new. She had not known anything like it before.

When did her feelings change? She smoothed her hand over the comforter on their bed. She could hear Flores's words in the car now, that she resented Jimmy because he'd rescued her. But she'd loved that once. She had been in love with the feeling of being treated well. Of being listened to.

Now, it wasn't enough. She woke up next to this man she wasn't attracted to anymore. Someone who didn't want what she wanted in life. When she was with him, she could only think of what she was missing out on. What she didn't have.

She could hear Jacky talking and laughing loudly as he and Jimmy approached the front door. An overwhelming sadness filled her.

She wiped her eyes and got ready to serve dinner.

FORTY

Saturday
morning

HORACIO PEREZ LOOKED like the kind of man who'd be the life of the party at any other time in his life.

But right now, circumstances had turned him into a wiry little man with circles under his eyes, who felt his doom was just around the corner. And it probably was.

Ruiz sat on a bench next to him in a park in Redwood City. The man scratched his arm and looked around the other tables nervously. The young man's hands were grey, and he had oil under his fingernails.

"Miranda says you got a job for me."

"You fix cars for a lot of people?"

"Yeah." Horacio scratched his arm and looked down. "I used to have a job at a garage in San Mateo. Guy said I was stealing parts and fired my ass. So now I'm on my own. It's all word of mouth. People call me, I come and fix their cars. At their house. At their work."

"Hard to make enough money that way? You got a kid now."

For a split second, Horacio's eyes went soft. "Yeah, it's tough. You always gotta buy stuff for 'em. Miranda's mom died last year, so now Miranda can't work. Nobody to take care of the kid. We missed rent for three months."

"Kids are expensive." Ruiz nodded. "So you can't be picky about the jobs you take."

Horacio shook his head. "Like a guy earlier this week. He paid me so much. I had to do it."

"You didn't feel good about doing it."

Horacio slunk down onto the bench. He looked at Ruiz suspiciously. "So what's the job?"

"The job is, I want you to tell me who hired you to detach the vacuum line from the brake booster on the Corvette."

For a moment it looked like Horacio was going to get up and run away. But he continued sitting on the bench.

"The guy went through a guardrail on 280, Horacio. He's been in the hospital since Tuesday."

"Shit. He told me it was a prank. That the guy would figure it out right away. It took me like five minutes to do." He pulled his hoodie up around his head.

"I need you to tell me who hired you to do it. I'll pay you."

"You're a cop." The man swallowed. "What will happen to me?"

"We'll talk about that. But we need to find this person. Do you have his number on your phone? You got a name?"

Horacio showed him the number, then sent it to Ruiz's phone.

"Guy said his name was Hank. Hank Adams."

Ruiz handed Horacio some money, along with his card. The man looked down at it, a hint of a smile on his face. "Yeah. I thought so. Thanks."

"We'll be talking to you again. No leaving town."

•   •   •

With just a short gaming session the night before, Grasso got out of bed that morning, ready and rested.

She looked out the window and saw the beginnings of a clear day, as dawn crept up on her part of the valley. It covered Cupertino's condos, the huge Mediterranean-style McMansions, and the sprawling flat business parks with a tinge of pink.

Seeing Tom awake and recovering yesterday had made her feel good. And from what she and Ruiz had accomplished in the past two days, they were closing in on whoever had tried to kill him and whoever had been blackmailing Kevin Dredger.

It was easy, in her current sunny-day mood, to conveniently imagine that whoever had done these things had also killed Rosalind Mabrey.

She rooted through the fridge for something for breakfast and saw a container of polenta and Bolognese sauce from her dinner with *Unnon*. It sounded like a good breakfast to her.

Rancho felt clear and crisp this morning as she headed up the trail. There was a warm scent in the air.

As she came down the trail, she neared the spot where she'd seen Rosalind's body. There were more balloons and ribbons tied to the tree above the gully where her body had been found. It was becoming easier for Grasso to pass the spot. She didn't feel that catch in her breath, that tension winding up in her as she approached.

She seemed to be losing many of the fears she'd had, even two weeks ago. Fears of what her family thought of her. Fears that she was weird, too different, because she'd never been in a relationship and was probably asexual. And her fears that, while she'd always wanted this job, maybe she couldn't handle it.

Grasso ran down the final path and finished her run with stretches at the bars.

She hadn't solved Rosalind Mabrey's murder yet. But she

and Ruiz had successfully traced some of the leads in this complicated case.

After an invigorating run on a beautiful day, she felt optimistic.

They had to be close.

FORTY-ONE

Monday
morning

THE HOUSE WAS empty when Ruiz got back from walking Jacky to school.

He'd gotten used to it. He wasn't sure where Reyna went in the mornings after the gym since she didn't have to be at work till 9. Maybe she went in early. She didn't feel comfortable being around him, but he was getting used to that.

And caring less.

He rinsed his dishes and put them in the dishwasher. When he passed the computer desk, he was tempted to check to see if she'd been working on a resume. But even if he could find it, it wouldn't make him feel better or satisfy him. It would just fuck up the rest of his day.

Frank Ladera came in through the back entrance of the station at the same time as he did.

"You're looking good these days, Jimmy." He patted him on the back and gave him a knowing look. "Tell me. How're you doing?"

Ruiz didn't feel like telling him. He smiled and returned

the pat on the back, maybe with a little more force than the original, then headed for his desk, by way of the coffee station.

Yesterday he'd called the number Horacio had given him. No answer. No voicemail recording.

It was 9 a.m. Normal business hours. He'd try again.

He hit redial and waited. Two rings. Three rings. Then a woman's friendly voice.

"Galadriel Industries. How may I direct your call?"

A little explosion went off in Ruiz's head.

"Philip Langdon, please."

"Mr. Langdon's not available at the moment. Would you like to leave a message?"

"No, that's fine," Ruiz said casually. "I'll touch base with him later today."

When Grasso came in a few minutes later, Ruiz gave her the look.

"What happened?" She tossed her handbag under her desk.

"I know who's behind Galadriel Industries." Ruiz told her about what had happened when he called the number from Horacio.

"If Philip Langdon was behind Galadriel, then he was blackmailing Dredger." Grasso's black eyes snapped with excitement. "And he arranged for Horacio to tamper with Tom's car."

"But we don't know why he did any of this. Or if he killed Rosalind." Ruiz took a swig from his water bottle. "And that was our job."

"Look at The Fantastic Four, as Tom called them. One's dead. One was almost killed, and one's been pushed over the edge by the blackmailer. And the last one sounds like he's doing fine. That sounds suspicious to me. How can these things not be connected?"

"It's all in the proof. You have to put together a case that ties these things to Langdon. We don't have that case yet, Dani."

Ruiz watched Grasso's optimistic expression start to fade. "Garcia's to strategize. 12:30."

Grasso nodded. "Back booth. I'll reserve it in advance."

Garcia's was noisier and a lot more crowded than they'd expected it to be.

People lingered at tables talking, taking their time over beer and the remains of food on their plates.

David Garcia spotted Ruiz and Grasso when they came in and ushered them to the back booth. He brought them a large bowl of chips and some salsa.

"The usual?" He asked, and they nodded.

"So what's next?" Grasso asked Ruiz as they sat down.

"Tell me what *you* think is next." Ruiz raised an eyebrow and gave her a mocking grin.

"The trail leads from Horacio back to Langdon. We've got him on attempted murder with the tampering with Tom's car. Also, we've got him on blackmail—we've got a case for that with information from Dredger's financial advisor."

"There's a problem here, though." Ruiz frowned as he took a drink from his water bottle. "The only one of the crimes we're investigating that took place in Monte Verde is the murder of Rosalind Mabrey. These other crimes are probably related to Rosalind's death. We know that. But we don't have proof."

"We've got to find it." She felt frustration growing in her. "There's got to be a way to connect these events." Grasso dipped a chip into the salsa. "Tom told me yesterday that he remembered having a conversation with someone before the accident—it was about Kevin. He said it left him feeling uneasy. He doesn't remember who it was he was talking to. He's still getting his memory back."

Ruiz cleared his throat and looked across the table at her. He had the same look on his face when she'd made a stupid mistake during her field training. When he spoke, it wasn't in the tone of a partner; it was in the tone of a commanding officer who'd brought her into his office for one of those talks.

"Dani, you need to check your motives. We may be close to proving that Langdon blackmailed Dredger and set up Tom's accident. But we still don't know who killed Rosalind Mabrey. We haven't ruled anyone out, not even Tom Weber. You seem to have decided that for yourself. Right now, you're wrong. And your personal feelings need to stay out of this."

The reprimand hit her hard. She felt her throat tighten.

As she felt the sting of Ruiz's words, chatter at the tables around them got louder. Sirens wailed as they looked out the window to see two fire trucks careen onto quiet Main Street, heading west up the road into the hills. Since this wasn't a common occurrence, customers spilled out of Garcia's onto the sidewalks to see what was going on.

Grasso sniffed the air. She'd been smelling something burning but assumed it was meat charring on the grill. Now it hit her. It was the smell of burning wood.

Ruiz's phone buzzed and he checked the text. He stood up.

"That was Charlotte Baldwin. The Laurelwood Foundation construction site is on fire."

FORTY-TWO

"DAVID, we need our food to go." Ruiz approached the counter and called to the owner.

"No problem, Jimmy. We're on it."

In five minutes, she and Ruiz were on their way back toward the station, bags in hand.

By now, black clouds billowed up from the wooded hills. The smoke looked uncomfortably close. A thin orange line flickered on the hill just a mile or two up from the street they were walking on.

When they approached the station, Ruiz went around to the back lot.

"I'm taking a car up to Laurelwood. Sounds like they may need some help."

"Please be careful up there, Jimmy."

"I probably won't be up there long." He looked back toward the hills. "I'm hoping it's contained quickly."

Grasso went back into the station to finish a report and

continue to work with the different strands of the Infinitas case and its players.

If Tom's conversation had been with someone significant to the case, he might have remembered something by now. Who he'd talked to and what had made him feel uneasy.

Still, she felt hesitant now to drive up to see Tom again. Ruiz was right.

The smell of smoke was making its way into the station. She remembered the crisp dry air this morning when she ran. Just four months ago, they'd been drowning in rain, an atmospheric river. Now there was overgrowth everywhere. And the dry weather made the overgrowth ripe for wildfires.

Had the fire been set intentionally? Grasso wouldn't be surprised, having heard Charlotte Baldwin talk about how much the neighbors hated the idea of the Laurelwood center. The man she'd talked to earlier had been so sure that the children and adults coming into the nature center would wreck his quality of life.

But now, with the weather conditions dry and primed for fire, the neighbors' homes and even downtown Monte Verde itself could be in danger.

Today there would be no *us* and *them*. They'd all be at risk.

Grasso was finding it hard to focus, so she turned her thoughts back to the case and wrote out everything they knew so far:

1. Rosalind M killed on trail, kicked down the hill. Weapon: serrated knife, not found. Time 7-7:30 a.m. Assailant approached from behind.

2. Kevin D – now possible alibi between 7-8 (on a call with black-mailer) but need to pin down with phone records. Tall enough to approach Rosalind M from behind. KD angry at Roz for stopping acquisition and at Tom for telling us – has anger issues.

3. Tom W -- Alibi till 9 a.m. Resented being Infinitas clean-up guy. Maybe too short to approach Roz from behind. Called Roz "Galadriel." Probably not blackmailer but was in Vegas during "the drive with the girl."

4.Philip Langdon – Could have alibi for Roz murder but tall enough to approach RM from behind. Runs Galadriel Inc and very likely the blackmailer or working with her; hired Horacio to tamper with brake hose. Was in Vegas during "the drive with the girl."

Once she'd written her notes, she felt a growing sense of dread. It had been almost two hours and she hadn't heard from Ruiz. The smell of smoke in the station was getting worse.

She walked to the back door of the station and stepped outside. The edge of flickering orange on the hill had grown wider. The grey haze over the hills was spilling into down-town, and she couldn't see businesses on the other side of the street. The smoke in the air scratched the back of her throat and made her want to cough.

Ryan Dawson got out of a patrol car and ran up the steps toward her. His face was smudged and sweaty.

"They're evacuating the area to the west of Laurelwood Road. The winds are kicking up, so the fire's spreading fast."

West of Laurelwood would be Rosalind's house and Tom's, from what she knew.

"Did you see Ruiz?"

"I heard he was going door to door, helping with the evac-uation. That's hard in that neighborhood, with the houses spread out. It's getting harder to see."

"Did they think the fire was set?"

"Not sure. Ruiz will handle the investigation once things calm down. Hopefully, that's soon." Ryan pushed past her, as he headed inside.

It was then that she got the call. Angie Dredger's number.

"Dani Grasso here. Mrs. Dredger?"

"Kevin's missing." Angie's voice was tight and pinched. "Gail Dredger hasn't seen him since yesterday morning. He didn't show up for his time with the boys this weekend. That's not like him. I wanted to let you know. I'm worried."

When she hung up from talking to Angie Dredger, Grasso saw she had a call from her father.

She listened to the voicemail her father left. Grasso's heart pounded as she returned his call.

"A possible stroke. What does that mean, Dad? Does *Unnon* have any paralysis?" The words tumbled out of her mouth as her mind filled with questions.

The last she'd seen or talked to Giovanni Grasso had been their dinner at his house. He'd been lively, full of jokes, and eager to hear about detective work.

"He's resting at the hospital. They're keeping him overnight for observation."

"Can I visit him?"

"Your mother and I don't think it's appropriate, given the situation," her father said, hesitantly. "We'll keep you posted on his health. I thought you should know."

Grasso was tired, stressed and completely out of patience.

"I had dinner with him last week. We had a great time. He isn't angry with me, dad. This is between me and *Unonn*. It has nothing to do with you and the rest of the family."

There was a long silence. Finally, her father spoke, in a cold tone. "He's never said anything about this, Dani."

Big shocker. Her grandfather hadn't kept his promise. He had too much to lose.

She'd taken her close-knit family for granted all her life. Friends told her they envied her for it. There was always someone to hang out with, to talk, or text with. To share something funny that happened. Now she saw it was conditional. Knowing that didn't take away her grief. She missed them. She couldn't write them off.

This was how it worked. Families had used this since the beginning of time to control their offspring. Cut off communication. Withdraw love. Until the wayward child sees the error of their ways and comes crawling back.

Giovanni Grasso wasn't going out of his way to explain his acceptance of her decision to the family.

She'd enjoyed the relationship she had with him over the past few weeks. She'd loved having his encouragement as she handled her first murder case. But Giovanni Grasso held her relationship with the family in his hands.

Until he explained his change of heart, there was nothing she could do.

FORTY-THREE

A THICK BROWN haze hung over the Laurelwood Road area as Ruiz trudged from house to house, notifying residents of the evacuation order.

From his conversations with firefighters, Ruiz learned that the fire had started at the southwestern corner of the Laurelwood Foundation property.

If the wind hadn't changed, the fire would have stayed near the construction site, burning through the wood frames that had just been erected. It could have been stopped at the clearing.

But as the winds shifted, the fire was pushed toward more fuel—the forest and the surrounding houses. The wind whipped against his face and felt hot.

He approached a sprawling two-story house and knocked on the door. An elderly couple stood at the door, ready to go, bags in hand and a whimpering dog on a leash.

"You'll need to be out of here within the next ten minutes. The fire is heading in this direction. Take Old Mill Way down the hill, and you'll stay out of danger."

They thanked him as they made their way to their car, and Ruiz moved on to the next three houses on the road.

From their search two weeks ago, Ruiz remembered Rosalind Mabrey's home was at the end of the road. He wondered if Charlotte Baldwin had been up here today working on the Laurelwood Foundation's files. He hoped she'd had the sense to get out early.

After he found no one home at the next two houses, he continued for a quarter mile to Rosalind's house. The white two-story looked old-fashioned, something you'd see on a farm, with a long, pillared porch and a porch swing.

It looked deserted at first, but then Ruiz noticed a car parked along the side of the house. He ran up to the door and knocked hard.

Charlotte Baldwin answered, her face stark white. She was coughing into a handkerchief.

"It's gone." She said quietly, a blank look in her eyes. "All of it. I ran down to look at the site. It only took a few minutes. Everything we worked so hard to build for three years."

"Ms. Baldwin, you need to leave now," Ruiz pleaded. He could feel the heat from down the road. "The wind's moving the fire in this direction. Show me what you need to save."

Charlotte opened the door, and he followed her into the house.

"We need to take all of this. We'll need the info and documentation to rebuild."

Two big stacks of filing boxes were piled not far from the door.

"Let's get these in your car, Ms. Baldwin. "Pull your car around front."

She brought her car around, and Ruiz loaded the boxes in her trunk and backseat.

By the time they'd loaded up, the fire was visibly closer. The lights of a firetruck shone dimly through the smoke, as it moved their way.

Charlotte stood next to her car, looking back at Rosalind Mabrey's house. Her eyes were red rimmed and watery.

She looked at Ruiz, paralyzed.

"Looks like they won," she said weakly.

Ruiz didn't have the emotion of Grasso the rookie, who was angry at Rosalind Mabrey's killer and wanted to bring justice for her. But it was hard to watch Charlotte Baldwin cry at the loss of the Laurelwood Foundation center, a project she'd worked hard on with Rosalind Mabrey. If this fire was set, he wanted to see the arsonist caught—and locked up for a long, long time.

"Ms. Baldwin, you need to get out now. You okay to drive?" She still looked in a daze, and Ruiz was worried about her.

"I will leave. I can do that." She swallowed, her face contorted with grief. She went around to the driver's side to open the door, then ran back to Ruiz impulsively and held him in a hug.

"Thank you." She breathed into his chest. He felt the warmth through his jacket.

Ruiz didn't know what to do but hug her back. She had no idea what this felt like for him. To be held and touched, after years without much physical contact from Reyna. He sunk into it, wanted to soak it up. It lit up every part of him. He didn't want it to end.

Finally, Charlotte Baldwin broke away.

"You've been a great help, Jimmy Ruiz."

She got in her car and merged into the line with the other evacuees heading for Old Mill Way.

Ruiz watched till he saw her round the corner. Then he began the long walk back to his car, through the heat of the fire.

FORTY-FOUR

Monday
4 p.m.

REYNA HAD HEARD NOTHING.

It had been two days since Mia told her they'd make a decision on the position.

Of course, the person up for the job always cares more than the ones trying to fill it. Reyna realized this, but it didn't make the wait any easier.

Tonight was the PTA meeting. Jimmy would be home with Jacky. She looked forward to getting out and having something else to think about.

The office was busy this afternoon. One patient after another, with a small break in between. A chance to sit in the breakroom and drink some tea and look up rental listings.

As she sat, she heard the conversation in the next room—Tiffany and her patient, an older man who had a hearing loss and talked very loudly.

"If you look over at the western hills, you can see the black smoke. The town looks like it's going up in smoke."

"Oh, yeah? Reyna, one of our hygienists, is married to a Monte Verde cop."

Monte Verde. Reyna suddenly felt sick. She'd never worried about something happening to Jimmy at work. Nothing ever happened in Monte Verde. The crime rate was low. The streets were safe. Fires happened in the Santa Cruz mountains. Not in Monte Verde.

She picked up her phone and texted Jimmy.

> U ok? I heard about the fire

Jimmy was good about getting back to her. She waited. Maybe he was doing some patrol work, helping out. Like Jimmy did all the time.

Maybe the fires had reached downtown.

On her break, she called the station. No response.

After her break, she went in to greet her next patient, a knot in her stomach. Her phone was in her purse in the drawer of the sink cabinet. She waited for the buzz. The company with news of the job. Jimmy's response to her text.

No buzz for the next two hours. Her chest felt tight as she scraped and polished.

She kept going, carefully picking at teeth. Scraping. Rinsing. Polishing. Advising patients either to up their flossing routine or congratulating them on their good dental hygiene. Handing off goody bags of toothbrushes, floss, and toothpaste.

When her last patient left, she washed up then went to look at her phone.

She called the station number.

"This is Reyna Ruiz. Is Jimmy there?"

"He's up at the fire, helping with the evacuation."

"Has anyone heard from him?"

"I think he called in a couple hours ago. You want to talk to his partner, Grasso?"

"Yes. Please."

Reyna waited, checking the time. If Jimmy couldn't get home, she'd have to pick Jacky up from childcare herself.

She heard Grasso's voice, sounding like a teenaged babysitter.

"This is Dani Grasso. Hi, Reyna."

Reyna tried to keep her voice steady.

"I heard about the fire. I texted Jimmy and haven't heard back. Is—everything okay?"

"I was worried, too. But he just called that he's on his way back down to the station. There's a backup with the evacuation but he said he should be home by 5:30. He's fine."

"I've been hearing the reports. It's scary."

"Yeah—it looks like an apocalypse when you look up at the hills. They think they've built a wall. They're hoping to contain it as long as the winds don't change direction again."

Reyna thanked her and hung up. Apparently, she wasn't someone who could handle stress well.

Within 45 minutes, Jimmy came home with Jacky. She could hear him cough as they came in. He smelled of smoke and his eyes were red. His hair was dusted with ashes, and he looked like hell. He apologized that he hadn't been able to answer her text.

She shouldn't have worried about Jimmy.

But she did. It was all she could think about. And it wasn't just that she needed him home to watch Jacky.

Reyna left Jimmy and Jacky with pork tamales she'd bought from Rocio, who made them with her mother.

Reyna steamed them and left them on the table, along with a cooker full of rice and a salad.

Then she drove over to the school for the meeting in the cafeteria.

It was the general monthly meeting, so it was a large

group. Reyna took a seat next to Colin's mom, Sindhu, who'd been waving to her that she'd saved her a seat.

"I heard about the Monte Verde fire. Jimmy's okay?" She asked, her eyes wide with concern.

"He's home now, with Jacky. Safe." Reyna nodded.

The meeting was about the budget for the next school year, which normally would interest Reyna, since she loved numbers. But she couldn't focus on anything. Her thoughts bounced around.

Jimmy was safe, but she still hadn't heard anything about the job. No messages. No voicemails.

Mia was speaking now, going through the budget and the additions that had been made for the fall.

It seemed to Reyna that Mia was avoiding her eyes. Mia was a good speaker and did that thing where she tried to look across the room, making eye contact with every attendee. Making each person feel like she was speaking to them alone. It was another thing that Reyna admired about Mia.

But Mia seemed to be passing over her. Was it just her imagination?

After the meeting, Reyna talked with Colin's mom, then when Sindhu had to leave, Reyna approached Mia, who was packing up her materials in a messenger bag.

"I was curious," Reyna said tentatively. "Have you heard anything about the position?"

Mia looked at her differently than she had when they were out at the tapas restaurant, laughing and enjoying wine. She looked at her now as if she were an unpleasant interruption.

"I did, Reyna. I talked with the VP of marketing and HR today." Mia's eyes looked blue and cold now. "It was the salary. We couldn't pay you what you requested—not for this position, given your lack of experience. I hope you understand."

Reyna blinked at her. Something inside her crumbled. Fell hard into a dark hole. She was not Reyna Ruiz anymore. She was 18-year-old Reyna Habalo, who'd moved into a room in a filthy house with her loser boyfriend, after barely graduating from high school.

If she remembered what she'd said to Mia Gerson just then, it was probably what she had been taught as a child to say graciously with a smile when something did not work out.

"Thank you for the opportunity."

Reyna walked to her car, stumbling in the dark to the school parking lot. She sat in the Range Rover, not caring if it started or not.

The look in Mia Gerson's cold blue eyes tonight had gutted her like a knife. Sobs choked in her throat. In the quiet of the car, she let everything out.

All the things that made her less.

That made her nothing.

Wearing her cousin's badly fitting hand-me-downs at school, being the butt of everyone's jokes, her scrawny arms sticking out of drooping sleeves made for a bigger, heavier girl. Or when she hit puberty in fifth grade and was teased by the girls and groped by the boys who only seemed to focus on her breasts. Her mother didn't think she was old enough for a bra, so she wore her brother's undershirts under big baggy t-shirts. To hide herself. Protect herself.

Then that one night in the house in East San Jose, when Mateo had gone out to a concert with friends. The other people living in the house, all men, scared her. A big man, Ramon, who lived in the garage, stared at her whenever he passed her in the kitchen. Twice he pinched her ass while she was loading groceries into the fridge. Mateo had threatened him after she'd told him about it.

That night she hid in the bedroom all night with the door locked, talking on her phone with every friend she could call. Then she'd had to pee so badly, she left the room for the bathroom down the hall.

When she got back, the big man from the garage was waiting in her room. He pushed her down on the bed and tore off her sweatpants—she'd screamed and clawed at his face, leaving his face covered with bloody scratches.

There were other people in the house. Somebody must have heard her screaming.

But nobody came to help. No one.

She'd told Mateo. But at that point, he was dealing with his legal problems and had listened to her with a dull look of disinterest.

She never told Jimmy.

After Mateo's arrest, Reyna sat outside the front door of the house in south San Jose, waiting for Jimmy Ruiz. A man she'd never met.

She had her belongings in two black trash bags—makeup, clothes, flip flops, and a pair of fake leather boots from Walmart.

She wondered what Jimmy would be like. He was a cop. That didn't mean anything. Cops could be bad, too. As Reyna sat outside waiting, she felt in her purse for the small paring knife she'd taken from the kitchen two days ago. If Ramon, the big man from the garage, tried anything while she waited, she was prepared this time. If Jimmy Ruiz turned out to be a bad man like his brother, she was ready, too.

Jimmy pulled up in his truck, smiled, and loaded her trash bag luggage into the truck, with no judgy comments. When they reached his apartment, he made up his bed for her. He put blankets on the living room couch for himself. Then he made her dinner.

And her new life began.

FORTY-FIVE

GRASSO'S MINI COOPER in the back parking lot was covered with a layer of ash.

She started the car, ready to drive back to Cupertino to get takeout and bury herself in a game after a stressful day.

But before she put it in drive, she sat for a moment, thinking of the summary of the case she'd written up during the fire today.

Despite her conversation with Ruiz, she decided to drive up to the hospital to see Tom.

Once she'd gotten to Palo Alto, the smoke was behind her, and the darkening sky was clearer. The lights of the mid-peninsula began to glow in the semi-darkness. She opened the moon roof. It felt good to take in the cool fresh air.

A new officer was sitting in Tom's room. He looked older and more serious than the previous one. His name badge read GIRARD.

Girard spoke to her in a low voice.

"Heads up. We had a couple of guys wander through

today. They weren't on the list. They were asking to be let into his room." With his long, rutted face and beaklike nose, Girard reminded her of Sam the Eagle from the Muppet show. "The nurses handled it well. They pretended to look up Tom's name on the computer while alerting hospital security. They told the two guys there was no Tom Weber on the patient list."

"What did the men look like?"

"One was young, Hispanic. The other tall, Caucasian. They refused to show ID. They were escorted out by hospital security."

Horacio and Langdon. She'd talk to the nurses at the station.

"It's time for Mr. Weber to be moved."

Tom was awake and almost sitting up. He was eating what looked like orange paste from a blue plastic plate, with a plastic cup of juice as a chaser.

When Girard excused himself for a bathroom break, she took a seat in his chair, making sure it was a distance away from the bed. She'd approach this more professionally this time. "I heard the good news, Mr. Weber. Ruiz said your property was spared in the fire."

"A fence near the fire boundary burned down, but I was lucky. My tenants hosed down the roof and the gardens. They said it's still smoking, but we're good. Rosalind's house took a lot of damage. And Laurelwood is gone." A shadow passed across his face.

"This is your neighborhood." Grasso leaned forward, hoping to get anything that might help Ruiz's investigation of the fire. "Think one of the local residents could have done it?"

"It's possible. Not everyone in the neighborhood hated the idea of Laurelwood, but some were angry enough."

"You starting to remember more?" This was why she was here; she'd stick to business. This was a case of attempted murder, and she needed to know if Tom was beginning to fill in the events and conversations he'd had before his accident.

"More is coming back to me. I must be feeling better. I keep dreaming of ways to escape." She could tell from the look on his face that Tom was mulling over something. He had something on his mind, but she'd wait for him.

"I can understand that." Grasso nodded as she looked with disgust at the goo on his plate.

"The chicken wasn't great. So I told them I forgot I was vegan. They gave me squash. It's not the worst thing I've eaten."

Grasso got up to look at the new flower bouquets on the table. One was from the Infinitas security staff.

"Tom, did anyone tell you two men were trying to get into your room this afternoon? I'm requesting they move you."

Grasso described the men, based on details from Girard.

"I think the younger Latino is the man who detached the hose in your car. Can you think of who the taller white man could be?"

Tom bruised face looked somber. He set down his fork.

"There are some things I should tell you, Detective Grasso."

FORTY-SIX

Monday
7 p.m.

WHEN THE NURSE came in to give him his pain medication, Tom sat up against the pillow.

Grasso wondered how long he'd be coherent before the meds kicked in. Her chest tightened as she watched him swallow the meds.

Progress on this case depended on Tom's ability to think clearly right now.

"I called Langdon that night before the accident. I checked my phone. I wanted to tell him about Kevin, since he'd been losing it, with the blackmail. If I remember correctly, my reasoning was, he was one of the four of us. He should know."

"What did he say when you called?"

"He seemed startled. Wondered why I was calling. When I told him Kevin was getting worse, he laughed. He said he always knew Kevin had issues and it was a matter of time. Let the guy implode on his own. And he said, *remember he left that girl.*"

"Kevin came in and told Ruiz and I the story. He was a wreck by the end of it."

"That morning, our last day of the show, I overhead Kevin telling Langdon something about a drive back from Pahrump. Kevin was terrified. He mentioned a girl. Langdon knew what had happened. It didn't make any sense to me at the time."

And somebody had called Las Vegas PD nine months ago, before the blackmailing started—to ask if a woman's body had been found twenty years ago.

It hadn't been Kevin. Or Tom.

It had been Philip Langdon.

"Langdon taunted Kevin about that night, knowing he hadn't left a dead woman in the desert." Grasso shook her head.

"Langdon gets off on manipulating people. It makes him feel good about himself." Tom's eyelids drooped and he seemed to be running out of steam. "When we were young, I didn't see how bad Langdon was. He was so over the top, it was laughable. Entertaining. We didn't take it seriously."

There was no doubt in Grasso's mind that Langdon had blackmailed Kevin. Taken delight in destroying him.

Langdon knew that he'd let something slip that night he'd talked to Tom. And he wanted to make sure Tom wasn't able to share it with anyone.

But Grasso needed to find out—had he also killed his ex-wife?

FORTY-SEVEN

THAT NEXT MORNING, Grasso's cell phone startled her from sleep at 6 a.m.

Ruiz's number. *Can you let me sleep a few minutes longer?*

She'd already reconciled herself to the fact she wasn't getting a run this morning.

When she answered, she managed to sound professional. And awake.

"Just got a call from a hotel manager in Palo Alto," Ruiz said, his voice still thick with sleep. "The guy's name is John Cormac. Says they've found something we might be interested in. The maid was turning the mattress in one of the rooms last night and found it stashed along the inside of the mattress frame. The room hadn't been used in a week. The room was booked by Infinitas."

Her heart pounded.

"Wait, what did they find?" She wondered if she was so sleepy, she'd missed that part.

"A knife. The kind they use in their kitchen to slice bread. Covered in what looks like dried blood."

Grasso let out a stream of profanity and gratitude under her breath. Really hoping that in that moment, God was okay with both.

Holy shit. Thank you, Jesus.

"Did I just hear you swear?"

"I swore out of happiness," she said defensively. "That's different."

Ruiz let out a snort of laughter. "We're meeting the manager at 8:30. Get some coffee before then."

Grasso drove today. They took one of the investigations cars. Grasso pulled onto 280 north, heading for Palo Alto. She was getting a little too used to this drive.

"This better be our link." She pulled off 280 at the University exit. "I want so badly to nail this guy. You got my message about the two men trying to get into Tom's room?"

"I did. That worries me. I'm glad you had him moved." Ruiz moved his seat back to accommodate his legs. "We don't know if this knife had anything to do with the case. Or how long it's been there. It'll have to be tested for DNA."

"You take the excitement out of *everything*, Ruiz."

Grasso frowned as she glanced at the GPS on the screen.

"I want you to think in terms of what we can prove." Ruiz leaned back in his seat, as they headed down University. "Documentation we can present in a case. If we don't have that to back us up, the bad guy gets away with it."

The hotel was elegant and upscale, with a fountain in the middle of an outdoor plaza. It was close to downtown, Stanford and a score of tech companies in the area. The arches around the plaza reminded her of what she'd seen on the Stanford campus when she'd visited once. Grasso felt underdressed in her leggings and blazer. Ruiz, in his jeans and Giants polo shirt definitely was.

They walked through the heavy oak double doors into a cavernous lobby, with a smooth terra cotta tile floor.

John Cormac was an older man in a tidy navy suit. He invited them into his office, then unlocked a drawer and gingerly pulled out a zip lock bag.

"The maid didn't want to touch it. She used her gloves to pick it up and bag it." He looked at Grasso and Ruiz with a solemn face. "I understand it's important not to contaminate the evidence."

He laid the bag flat on his desk. Inside was a large bread knife with a scalloped edge. There was dried blood on the edges and broad streaks across the blade. Grasso winced, thinking of this knife being used on Rosalind Mabrey's neck.

"Mr. Cormac, you said the rooms were booked by Infinitas. Is there any record of who actually stayed in that room?"

"Guests check in and have to show ID. We'd have a record of that. Give me a few minutes and I should be able to get the information for you. You can take a seat in the lobby if you'd like."

Ruiz slid the bag into a chain of custody envelope. Then the two walked across the terra-cotta-tiled floor and found oversized wicker chairs with large, fluffy cushions and wraparound sides. Good for guests wanting privacy for taking phone calls. Ruiz sunk down into one and put his feet up on the cushy footstool.

Ruiz groaned with pleasure, stretching out his legs. "Feels good after all the rounds I made through the neighborhood during the fire."

Grasso's phone buzzed. She had her ringer turned off. She pulled the phone out of her bag and listened to the latest voicemail.

"Angie Dredger wants to talk to us."

"We'll stop there after we get the evidence to the station." Ruiz crossed his feet, obviously very comfortable in his chair. "How urgent?"

"She sounds upset in the message. Yesterday Kevin went AWOL and didn't show up to see the boys. Now she's saying he left her a message. He sounded angry and like he'd been drinking."

Grasso sat up in the depths of the large chair and leaned forward, so she could see Ruiz and have a conversation. She was still feeling ashamed that Ruiz had talked to her about her motivations for visiting Tom.

"I found out two things when I checked in on Tom Weber in the hospital. The two men who were trying to get into his room. And Tom's conversation with Langdon."

She told Ruiz the story of her visit to Tom.

"When Tom talked to him, Langdon mentioned the girl in the desert that Kevin talked about," Grasso said. "Tom thinks Langdon realized right away that he'd let that slip. That's why he had Horacio tamper with the Corvette."

"We know who we're dealing with now." Ruiz took a breath.

Grasso noticed John Cormac summoning them from the registration desk. Ruiz reluctantly pulled himself from his chair.

"I've got the name for that room," Cormac said, reading from the photocopy. "It's Katherine Stromberg. From Las Vegas, Nevada."

Reyna had a day to grieve the loss of the job.

And the new life she'd pictured for herself. The thought of seeing Mia Gerson and her cold blue eyes at the next PTA meeting made her tense up in anger.

She hadn't given up hope.

She could still make it work. As much as she wanted to leave the dental office, she made a decent salary there. It wasn't as high as the salary she'd asked for with the events job.

But she could stay at the dental office and make cuts to her budget. Between what she'd estimated with child support and her salary, there had to be a way.

At 7 a.m., Reyna sat in the back room at the dental office, the spreadsheet open on her screen. She added in the new numbers based on her current salary. She made sure she'd included all the expenses. Rent on a new place, water bill, estimated gas and electric, groceries, gas for her car, Jacky's soccer fees and uniforms, school materials, and field trip fees. School clothes for Jacky. Clothes for herself. Coffee and an occasional dinner out with friends.

She played with the numbers, made many small cuts. Then put things back in that she knew realistically she could not cut. She took out Jacky's soccer costs, which she could almost certainly get Jimmy to cover.

It did not work. The numbers would not cooperate with her. She had worked hard in her job, but she knew realistically that some things had come her way because of her looks. But numbers were assholes. They didn't care. They were immovable. They would not give in to what she wanted.

Reyna Ruiz had managed to save enough with her and Jimmy's salaries to put a down payment on a house in an expensive valley. She could not make this work.

She went into the bathroom, shut the door and locked it. She turned the water on in the sink. She sat on the toilet lid, covered her mouth with her hands, and screamed.

Outside she heard Rocio moving around in the office. She heard her listening to patient messages on the answering machine. The coffee machine gurgled as it started up. The easy listening radio station started flowing from the speakers.

It was another day. Hot silent tears trickled from Reyna's eyes as she thought about her future.

This was Silicon Valley.
Divorce was another expensive thing she couldn't afford.

Angie Dredger opened the door for Ruiz and Grasso as if she'd been watching for their arrival.

There were circles under her eyes. Ruiz heard video game noises coming from the living room.

"We can talk in the kitchen."

Ruiz and Grasso took their seats at the kitchen table.

"Kevin called this morning. I don't know where he is." She took a deep breath and sat down. "I asked, but he wouldn't tell me. He says he knows who the blackmailer is."

"Did he tell you who, Mrs. Dredger?" Grasso asked.

Angie Dredger shook her head. "He's drinking. And he's angry. Very angry. He said he wants to handle it himself. He told me he loves us and that he's figuring out a way for us to be taken care of in case anything happens to him. That scared the shit out of me. Pardon my language."

If they put a trace on his phone's signal, they'd know where Kevin Dredger was. If Langdon was the blackmailer, as they suspected, he might be on his way to Vegas.

Grasso's phone buzzed for a call. She drew it out quickly.

As soon as she realized who it was, she put it on speakerphone.

"Gail Dredger here. Kevin came by and took two of the shotguns from the gun cabinet while I was with the horses."

Ruiz called out. "Mrs. Dredger, this is Jimmy Ruiz. How long ago did he come by?"

"Somewhere between 1 and 2, when I was out there. I'm

always careful to check the cabinet. It was locked before I went out. When I came back, it was unlocked, and the guns were gone."

Grasso connected with Ruiz's eyes.

"Gail and Angie, if either of you hears anything from Kevin, call us."

FORTY-EIGHT

Wednesday

THE MORNING of Langdon's arrival, Blake Hennessey was up at dawn.

He hadn't slept well. He was too excited.

He got into the office before his assistant, coffee in hand.

He was preparing for what he hoped would be a healing moment in Infinitas's recent tragic history. One that he'd been instrumental in pulling together.

Philip Langdon was flying in from Vegas, set to appear before the Infinitas board of directors and management. With the exception of Chairman Marsden, who was still waiting to see LSS's financials, Langdon had most of their support—and the support of a majority of management.

It looked like Philip Langdon would be the next CEO of Infinitas.

Hennessey was a marketing man. Had been for all of his career. Working with an engineering-focused CEO and a volatile, opinionated VP of Software Engineering had been a challenge for him. Not that he didn't respect the technical superiority of the product that Infinitas had launched into the world twenty years ago.

Now he would work under the man he'd learned from when he'd first come to Infinitas. A man who'd taught him the power of the big picture.

The plan was for Langdon to come in at eleven for lunch with management on the terrace outside the cafeteria, where he'd say a few words. Express his sympathy at Rosalind's death. Talk about the great legacy of her leadership. He should share a personal anecdote about her. He must have a ton of them. Then talk about his plan for helping the company move forward.

Of course, Hennessey had been hit hard by Rosalind's murder. But this moment—Langdon's return—would be priceless. And it would be the company's first step into a new era.

His assistant had come in, looking stunning in the tight-fitting orange dress she'd worn to the winter cocktail party.

"Looking amazing, Martelle. Is the terrace set up?'

"It is, Blake." She ticked off the items on her fingers. "Table and decorations, sound system tested and ready. The buffet tables are set up, and the caterers are set to arrive by 10:15."

Hennessey paced the length of his office, energy surging through his legs. Everything needed to be in place for this. The day would be perfect.

"The limousine's picking Langdon up at San Jose International and bringing him here. I'd like you to consider riding over, so you can be there to greet him."

Martelle Jones didn't look excited about the idea. She frowned and shifted on her high heels.

"I guess I can do that."

"Excellent." He breathed out the word as his pacing stopped at his executive chair. "We're set."

Blake Hennessey turned to look out the window behind

his desk. The sun was working its way up into a clear blue sky, making the lush grounds of Infinitas with its waterfall and reflecting pond a thing of beauty.

Just as he was about to turn back to his desk, he was startled to see a large hawk rise up from the pond with something alive and wriggling in its beak.

A light film of ash coated car windshields in the MVPD backlot.

Two days after the fire in the Monte Verde hills, the smell of wood smoke still hung in the air.

As soon as he got in to work, Ruiz received a call from a neighbor off Laurelwood Road whose house had sustained damage in the fire. The man had seen his neighbor in the Laurelwood Foundation area the morning of the fire. He thought the police should check it out.

Ruiz knocked on the door of Rick McCabe's house. The man's name sounded familiar. He was sure he remembered Grasso talking to him about his Laurelwood complaints a week or so ago.

"Looks like you missed him. Rick just left," an older woman answered with a nervous laugh. Her eyes were red and puffy. "He's headed for the airport in Palo Alto to fly out. He has important business in Fresno today."

Ruiz grunted. *Yep. The important business of leaving town to avoid arrest.*

After questioning the woman about her husband's activities in the past week, Ruiz had a hunch and told the dispatcher to send patrol officers to the airport. He'd meet them there.

An hour later, Ruiz arrested McCabe as he prepared to board his plane. A resident near the foundation had security footage of Rick carrying a red plastic gas container over to the Laurelwood building site at 11:15 a.m. on Monday.

The man's business cell number was the number Charlotte Baldwin had given him—McCabe was the out-of-area caller who'd left the threat on the Laurelwood Foundation's phone line.

Rick McCabe had tried to keep Rosalind Mabrey's foundation from bringing outsiders to the neighborhood. But when the wind whipped the fire at the nature center out of control, his neighbors paid the price. Three homes along Laurelwood Road had been destroyed.

Along with Rosalind Mabrey's dream.

FORTY-NINE

Wednesday

LANGDON DIDN'T ARRIVE at Infinitas until 11:40 a.m.

Hennessey's pacing had hit fever pitch. He walked from his office to the terrace. Then back again. Where the hell was Langdon? He checked Google Maps to see if there was traffic coming up north on 280 from the airport. There wasn't.

He texted Martelle. She replied that the woman with Langdon had to freshen up in the bathroom and they were waiting for her. She ended the text with a frowny-face emoji.

Fifty managers and board members were waiting on the terrace for Langdon. As Hennessey thought about it, he realized that was probably exactly what Langdon wanted. He would sweep in, with everyone assembled, like a headliner at a rock concert.

There was an element of showmanship in Langdon's style. Hennessey had seen that even when he'd worked for him. But today the man had raised it to an annoyingly new level.

Hennessey got a call from security saying that the limousine had pulled up in front. He walked to the front lobby and waited.

Martelle got out of the limousine first, a vivid splash of orange, then an attractive woman in a pink suit—this must be Katherine Stromberg, whom Langdon had mentioned.

After a significant pause, Langdon followed in a black suit with a yellow rose boutonnière. It reminded Hennessey of a president-elect pulling up to his inauguration. It seemed excessive. Still, he couldn't help but admire the entrance.

As Langdon approached, Hennessey stepped forward and put out his hand. Langdon grasped it, then pulled him into a hug. Hennessey knew, as Langdon did, that everything they were doing was in full view of the terrace where the board and management attendees sat.

By the time they reached the terrace, the attendees seemed to have forgotten about their long wait. When Langdon came in with Katherine, the group applauded.

Hennessey walked to the podium with Langdon. He gave him a pat on the back and Langdon turned to the crowd.

"Philip Langdon, one of the original founders of Infinitas. Welcome back, Philip."

Hennessey looked out at the group. "It's been fifteen years since Langdon left Infinitas to start his own company, Langdon Software Solutions. His business plan helped launch this company twenty years ago."

Hennessey continued, as the crowd listened attentively.

"We have been through unthinkable tragedy in the past two weeks. Our CEO, Rosalind Mabrey—" Hennessey paused to wipe away a tear. "Was murdered down the road in Monte Verde. Then three days ago, Tom Weber was in a life-threatening car crash. It all seems..too much."

Hennessey turned toward Langdon. "But at this very hard time in our company's history, one of our original founders, Philip Langdon, has come back. He's offered to step into leadership, at the recommendation of the Infinitas board of directors and management team."

Applause broke out, though there were a few people who

did not clap, Hennessey noticed. There were several managers who disagreed with the move to bring Langdon back.

"Philip, would you like to say a few words?" He handed the microphone to the man.

Langdon cleared his throat and looked down at the podium soberly.

"I realize my new role as CEO comes in the wake of a great loss." He sniffed, then raised a handkerchief to his face. "It is your loss. And my personal loss. Rosalind, as many of you may know, was my wife for three years."

He looked down at his lapel, at the yellow rosebud. "I wear this rose today to remember Rosalind. Her favorite flower was the yellow rose. I used to send her a dozen every year on her birthday. Rosy, wherever you are, I'm thinking of you today."

Hennessey thought the sentiment was excessive, but that was Langdon. Langdon was right to mention and commemorate Rosalind in his speech. He could not pretend she hadn't died two weeks ago today.

He did notice that a few of the women, some who knew Rosalind well, were looking at Langdon with distaste.

Langdon continued. "Twenty years ago, Rosalind, Tom Weber, Kevin Dredger and I started a company. During one of the worst times possible—during the dot com bust. On top of that, it was Y2K."

There were knowing looks around the room. A few laughs.

"We thought our cars and refrigerators would stop working." Langdon was performing now. His sentences rang with perfectly timed pauses. His eyes gleamed with a gentle but wise sense of humor. He had a look about him that rang with authenticity—the young whiz kid made older, wiser, and softer after facing his mistakes of the past 20 years.

"But Infinitas rose to the top. We proved we were different. We would *last*—hence, the name." He smiled affably and a ripple of cheers moved through the group. "The next year we grew to a company of 100. By the next year, we were 500. Our software was helping companies all over the world manage their workflow, save money, and provide better services and products for their customers. We—all of *you*—did that."

Hennessey nodded his approval. This was good. Sharing the credit with the managers and the team that made it happen. Langdon was hitting the points he needed to hit today.

Hennessey began hearing noises in the background. Rising from the area near the visitor's lobby. Sounds of a struggle. Someone shouted. He heard the scratchy sounds of Infinitas security radios.

"We must allow ourselves to do two things, my fellow employees. First, we need to congratulate ourselves on the world-class company we've become. Secondly, we need to take time to grieve our losses. As human beings, we need to do this—but only for a time. Then we must move on. That is what Rosalind would have--"

The noise below the terrace escalated. Hennessey heard people arguing, then screams. A crash as if something metal had been upended. The pop of a gunshot. More screams.

Then Kevin Dredger, armed with a shotgun, walked out onto the terrace.

Langdon froze as he stared at Kevin, one hand on the podium. Like somebody had paused a movie with a remote.

"Langdon, you blackmailing, murdering piece of scum."

Dredger pulled the shotgun up with two hands, aiming it directly at Langdon. Surprisingly, Hennessey thought later, no one in the room made a sound.

In fact, no one seemed to be breathing. The only sounds now were birds, chirping in the trees below the terrace, oblivious.

"You blackmailed me for almost a year, Langdon. You made me think I left that girl in the desert, dead. You had me thinking I went crazy and killed her. There was no body found in the desert. And you *knew* that, you sadistic son of a bitch."

Kevin Dredger raised the shotgun and fired a shot above the podium, just over the roof of the cafeteria.

Langdon gasped and ducked down behind the podium.

"I trusted you. I was terrified that morning in Vegas. I told you what happened, and you saved that information for later. Used it against me when you needed to, so I'd drain my life savings to make sure you didn't tell my wife and kids I was a murderer."

Dredger kept the shotgun trained on Langdon, while he turned his head toward the tables of frightened attendees.

"Did any of you ever get a financial report from Langdon Software Solutions?" He turned to Virginia Marsden, chairman of the board, who was sitting at a table of fellow board members. "Did you, Virginia? I bet you didn't. Because it would show that for the last two years, Langdon Software Solutions was losing money. Phil was desperate. He got it wherever he could get it. Including from me. I have a feeling I wasn't the only one. He laundered it through a company he set up in the Caymans. Galadriel Inc."

Hennessey looked at Langdon, wondering if this could be true. Finally, Langdon stood up. He seemed to relax a bit. His voice returned to the cadence of the speech he'd been giving.

"You all know this man. Sadly, Kevin Dredger has a serious mental illness. You're seeing it now. He had a fit in Rosalind's office the evening before she was killed and was escorted out by security. He threatened her. He probably killed her, too. But he has these episodes."

Kevin Dredger fired the gun into the stone floor by Langdon's foot. The bullet chipped the stone and ricocheted under a table next to the podium. Langdon jumped back with a shriek.

His shriek seemed to free up the rest of the crowd. There were screams around the tables. Many people ducked under their tables. A few suited executives crouched down and made a run for the lobby across from the cafeteria.

"What does it feel like, Langdon?" Dredger took another shot, at a row of planters behind Langdon. "To have someone threaten *you*?"

The bullet pinged off a planter a foot to the left of Langdon. Langdon backed away from the podium and stood behind one of the supports for the cafeteria roof.

"There's no reason I shouldn't kill you now, Langdon." Dredger walked up between the tables until he was next to the support. He placed the end of the gun's long barrel up against Langdon's head.

"Don't hurt him." Katherine Stromberg cried out from her table near the front. She looked around at the crowd sitting at their tables on the terrace, petrified. "Oh, my God. Why isn't anyone stopping him?"

Kevin paused, staring at the woman in amazement. He lowered the gun.

"It's you. You're the voice." He turned to the woman, mesmerized. "You're the one who left the messages."

Then a voice came from the other end of the terrace, from the steps that led to the parking lot.

The calm voice broke the silence more profoundly than a gunshot.

"Put the gun down, Kevin. You'll only be hurting me and the boys. We know what Langdon's done. The police have proof."

Angie Dredger. She stood behind two detectives, both with guns drawn. Beyond them, Hennessey saw the parking lot, full of police cars and emergency vehicles.

Dredger lowered his gun and stood with his mouth open, in a daze.

"Angie. Oh, God."

"You didn't do anything to anybody in the desert. The girl, whoever she might have been, didn't die. Langdon put a story in your head. He made you believe a lie."

Could Langdon have done this? Hennessey looked at the man he'd called his mentor. Langdon now appeared shaken. Sweat trickled down his face. Then Hennessey's eyes swept over the crowd and found Katherine Stromberg.

Katherine Stromberg looked pale—and terrified. She slowly got up from her table, in an attempt to follow the exodus of managers toward the lobby. A couple of uniformed officers went after her, restraining her and quickly putting her in handcuffs.

The big detective—Ruiz, he remembered—moved to the front of the room, and Dredger handed him his shotgun. The detective put his hand on Dredger's shoulder and took him aside to talk.

Detective Grasso walked up to Langdon and placed him under arrest for the murder of Rosalind Mabrey. Then with another officer's help, she put restraints on him, and led him away.

Dredger left with Ruiz willingly, after a talk and a hug from his wife.

Blake Hennessey would never forget that day at Infinitas. Or those two weeks of his life. It would be a while before he understood exactly what had happened. It made him question what he'd admired in Philip Langdon.

He would later quit the corporate world to research and write a book about Langdon, based on his experience with him at Infinitas.

Though the book was about him, Langdon never got a cent.

FIFTY

Saturday

RUIZ SLEPT IN SATURDAY. Something he rarely got to do.

It wasn't like he was trying to stay in bed. His body wasn't giving him a choice.

He'd been moving all week. He'd worked with the firefighters up at Laurelwood, notifying neighbors of the evacuation orders and working crowd control for five hours up in the hills around the camp. His Fitbit said he'd walked twenty-two miles that day. Two days later, he'd tracked down and arrested Rick McCabe, then rushed to Infinitas with Grasso, after Angie Dredger told them she knew Kevin planned to confront his blackmailer.

After the arrest, he'd gone home a little early but remembered he'd promised Jacky a bike ride. So on that daylight-savings-time evening, they went out for a long bike ride around the park and the boy's school.

He and Grasso spent the rest of the week staying late to put together the paperwork. To get all documentation in place to increase the odds that Philip Langdon and Katherine Stromberg would be convicted for their crimes.

Today, his body told him *You're not going anywhere.* He fumbled for the nightstand and checked his phone. Grasso had called him with some follow-up questions about Wednesday for the paperwork. He'd call her back later.

Duke Sorenson left a message asking if Ruiz would like to go to an airshow at Moffett next weekend with the donut gang.

Around 10, Ruiz got up, put on his robe, and made the bed. Then he went out to see what he could find for breakfast.

There was a plate of pancakes on the table with a bottle of real maple syrup. Jacky was eating a stack soaked in syrup, while kicking his legs under the table and singing the Pokémon theme song. Reyna was drinking her coffee and reading a magazine. Sun was streaming in through the back window, casting shadows of leaves across the table.

He had woken up this morning, and it was a good day. He still had a home.

He poured himself a cup of coffee and piled two pancakes on a plate.

"This is a surprise." He smiled at Reyna.

Once he'd finished and was drinking his coffee, Reyna called to Jacky.

"You want some video game time?"

Jacky jumped off his seat and ran toward the computer desk. "Oh, yeah!"

"Then put on your headphones." She gave him a warning look. "You get one hour."

Jacky sat down in the computer desk chair and quickly put on his headphones. An elf king appeared on the screen, along with a party of goofy-looking dwarves on ponies.

Reyna put a hand through her hair and swept it back behind her ear. She glanced at Ruiz. No smile.

"Let's go in the bedroom and talk."

The weight of every fear he'd had in the past four months fell over him. It robbed him of the satisfaction he'd been feeling about Langdon's and Stromberg's arrests. The satisfaction of seeing justice done, and the joy of working with Grasso to close a big murder case.

The thing he'd feared, resigned himself to, was going to happen. It was going to happen now. It would hurt like hell.

The pancakes he'd eaten now churned in his stomach. He flexed his hands. They felt shaky.

They went into the bedroom, and Reyna closed the door. She sat on one side of the bed, and he sat on the other.

She swallowed and laid her neatly manicured hands on the bed.

Her round dark eyes met his, and they were full of something he couldn't read. Something unfamiliar.

So this was the end. After months of uncertainty. Closure. He'd been through a lot in the past few months, and it had changed him. It would be painful, but he could handle it now.

She took a deep breath.

"I want to do marriage counseling with you." Her lips trembled, and she drew her hands back.

He couldn't find his voice. Tears filled his eyes, and he couldn't stop them. *What the fuck.* If he had heart trouble, what she'd said would have finished him off.

When he finally opened his mouth to talk, his words sounded raspy. He felt, for a moment, Charlotte Baldwin's arms around him. How good and warm and right it had felt. But he wasn't with Charlotte Baldwin. He was with his wife.

"My life has been on hold for the past four months. I didn't know if I should get a lawyer. You wanted nothing to do with me, Reyna. Couldn't stand to be in the same house with me. I've been good to you. I'm not going to live in fear anymore."

Now her lips were twisted. Tears rolled out of her eyes. "I'm sorry."

"You're willing to do counseling." He looked at her, trying to figure out if this was real. He had seen her cry two times before this. When he'd picked her up after Mateo's arrest ten years ago and then when Jacky was born.

"I'm scared." She looked him in the eye, which she had not done in several months. "But I want to try it."

Ruiz's first instinct was to comfort her, but she was feeling things she needed to feel. There was something going on in her. He didn't know what it was, and he couldn't control it. And that was how it needed to be.

"Tell me why you're scared." He asked quietly.

"Because I don't know what I want."

They talked for the rest of the hour. They shared feelings they'd never told each other about. She told him about what had happened to her with Ramon in the house in South San Jose. He listened to her. He hadn't known any of this. He cried.

At one point, they shut down and stopped talking. They stayed there and waited. Then they talked a little more.

It wasn't long before Jacky was knocking on the bedroom door, asking if he could play for another hour.

"I wanted to thank you for all you've done on the case, Detective Grasso." Tom said after she answered the phone. "I was released today. I'm home."

Grasso felt her lips turn up in an involuntary smile. "That's great, Tom."

"I've got a lot of physical therapy ahead of me. Probably years of it. I'm not very mobile, and my old bones are going to take a long time to heal. I'll be working from home. I need a break from Infinitas, anyway, after all that's happened."

"I just want to make sure you know," she said with amusement. "That my first name isn't Detective."

She heard him clear his throat.

"*Daniela*, I would love it if you would come to my house sometime soon to eat strawberries."

"Let me get this. I come over, I eat the strawberries. And we're done."

"We could do that." He laughed. "What would you think of playing a game? Do you play board games? Maybe video games?"

"What gaming platform are we talking about?" She felt a flutter of excitement in her stomach, whether it was for game-playing, Tom, or both.

She didn't know who Tom would be to her. Maybe he would be a friend. She knew she felt in sync with him from that first interview. He was almost twenty years older than she was, but she liked him. He made her feel comfortable.

After the news of Langdon's arrest came out, she'd heard nothing from Giovanni Grasso. And it hurt.

When your family disappoints you, it's a relief to know you have other options.

You can pick your own family.

FIFTY-ONE

Six months later

THEY DECIDED to drive instead of fly.

As they neared Las Vegas, they took the Blue Diamond Road exit for 160, heading out into the desert hills. Tom and Kevin had looked at a map and figured out the location. It looked very different during the daytime.

They weren't drunk this time. Kevin started AA not long after his plea bargain release and wouldn't go near alcohol.

"I think this is it," Kevin said, as they neared a line of shrubs along the road. He pulled off to the side, stopping the car in a flurry of dust. "Near that rock. I think this is pretty close."

Kevin got out and stood in the mid-afternoon sun, his hand over his eyes.

Tom used his cane, the one with the carved raven head that Dani had given him, to make his way to the rock.

"I don't know where the hell to start." Kevin kicked around in the dust.

"I brought a metal detector—and a shovel. Bring out the

duffle bag in the back of the car." Tom leaned on his cane. "I'm sure as hell not walking back to get it."

"Why would a metal detector help?"

"Because I put an Infinitas keychain in the time capsule."

Kevin nodded and walked back to the van. In a few minutes, he came back with both tools. He paced a large circle in the dust with the detector, listening for the beeps.

Soon it was beeping steadily. While Tom leaned on his cane, Kevin dug in the dry soil with the shovel. It took him a good twenty minutes.

The first things he pulled out were shards of brittle plastic. The remains of the Big Gulp cup. He dug deeper and found the pack of condoms. Tom snickered.

The corroded Infinitas keychain was next. Kevin pulled out the cracked, rolled-up charter Rosalind had printed in her precise hand that night.

"Oh, god." Kevin's voice went hoarse. He closed his eyes and shook his head. "This is hard to read right now."

"What's that thing in the bottom?" Tom had spotted the card.

Kevin pulled out Bill Gates' business card. Langdon's proud acquisition from Microsoft's founder, the first day of the show.

He showed it to Tom, and they flipped it over. It read:

I AM CEO.
P. Langdon
11-16-2000

Tom felt the wind whip up dust around them. And he knew.

Rosalind never had a chance.

THANK YOU!

Thank you for reading this book!

If you enjoyed it, I hope you'll leave a review on Amazon, Goodreads or the review site of your choice. Your reviews are a gift to me. I'm truly grateful for the time you take to do this.

———

ALSO BY VL KAZARIAN

Silicon Valley Murder

(Detectives Ruiz, Grasso and Flores)

Swift Horses Racing - Silicon Valley Murder, Book 1

A Tree of Poison – Silicon Valley Murder Book 3

Writing as Victoria Kazarian

The Laughing Loaf Bakery Mysteries

Drop Dead Bread - Laughing Loaf Bakery Mystery #1

Bread to Rights - Laughing Loaf Bakery Mystery #2

Trouble You Don't Knead - Laughing Loaf Bakery Mystery #3

Sourdough and Cyanide - Laughing Loaf Bakery Mystery #4

Stop, Drop and Rolls: A Laughing Loaf Bakery Short Mystery
(prequel novella)

ACKNOWLEDGMENTS

Thank you to my family, for the incredible support in the past three years that I've been writing. Thanks, Armen, for reading this through with your sharp eyes.

Thanks to Sisters in Crime National, the Guppies, and my local chapter, SinC Coastal Cruisers, groups that have given me the kick in the pants and encouragement I needed.

Thank you to my writing groups—the Philz group: authors Patrick Andersen and Pam Milliken; and the Highway group: authors Rie Neal, Leira Lewis, Rosanna Griffin and Becky Cuadra George. And my fellow Cruiser turned Wisconsin resident, Alec Peche. Writers in their lonely caves need support, and I've been given a massive supply of it.

Thanks to Dr. Noel Kerr, for her medical expertise, unique writing mindset, and patience. Ken Sanders, for the automotive advice. To my husband Pete, my children Armen and Lisa, and friends at large for their viewpoints on gaming and for vetting my gaming passages, and to Duncan McDonald for the Minecraft TNT duplicator suggestion.

There have been so many supportive friends this year, it's hard to name each one, but thank you all. Special thanks to Chris Anderson, for reviewing my manuscript and spotting timing issues; Debbie Cunningham for good food and for promoting my books to everyone who walks through her door; and to my sisters Pam and Kerry for their love, friendship and support, and of course, all the wine.

ABOUT THE AUTHOR

Victoria Kazarian lives and writes in San Jose, California. A former Silicon Valley marketing professional and high school English teacher, she now writes full time. When she's not writing, she's baking artisanal breads and forcing her children and dog to go on road trips to the Pacific Northwest.

IN A BOOK CLUB?

Interested in reading any of *Silicon Valley Murder* or *Laughing Loaf Bakery* mysteries?
I'd love to appear at your book club virtually -
or possibly in person, if you're in the San Francisco Bay Area.
Contact me at thelaughingloaf@gmail.com